PENGUIN BOOKS

# THE MAGPIE SOCIETY

## TWO FOR JOY

# THE
# MAGPIE
# SOCIETY

## TWO FOR JOY

### ZOE SUGG
### AMY McCULLOCH

PENGUIN BOOKS

## PENGUIN BOOKS

UK | USA | Canada | Ireland | Australia
India | New Zealand | South Africa

Penguin Books is part of the Penguin Random House group of companies
whose addresses can be found at global.penguinrandomhouse.com.

www.penguin.co.uk
www.puffin.co.uk
www.ladybird.co.uk

Penguin
Random House
UK

First hardback edition published 2021
This edition published 2022

001

Typeset by Jouve (UK), Milton Keynes
Printed and bound in Great Britain by Clays Ltd, Elcograf S.p.A.

The authorized representative in the EEA is Penguin Random House Ireland,
Morrison Chambers, 32 Nassau Street, Dublin D02 YH68

A CIP catalogue record for this book is available from the British Library

PAPERBACK ISBN: 978–0–241–40238–2

All correspondence to:
Penguin Books
Penguin Random House Children's
One Embassy Gardens, 8 Viaduct Gardens, London SW11 7BW

MIX
Paper from
responsible sources
FSC
www.fsc.org  FSC® C018179

Penguin Random House is committed to a
sustainable future for our business, our readers
and our planet. This book is made from Forest
Stewardship Council® certified paper.

*For all our readers – always beware the magpies*

# PROLOGUE

## LAST SUMMER

The night Lola died, we were off on an adventure.

It was her favourite thing to do.

*Take me somewhere*, she'd say, and I'd be compelled to oblige, meticulously planning each step, making the most of every minute of our time together. We'd sneak off the school grounds, jump on a train and end up at the top of the Shard; we'd go out on to the water to chase dolphins through the white-capped waves; we'd scramble along the cliffs to look for caves to explore on a long summer afternoon.

Then we'd creep back to Illumen Hall and pretend we were barely more than strangers.

It killed me at first, the pretence. But she convinced me that it was our little secret. And now the finish line was so near; only one year left until we could be free. I could wait.

In the meantime, we had our adventures. It would have to be enough.

That night was always meant to be special. We'd started at the school, of course. It was the society, after all, that bound us. I thought she understood that, especially when she let me draw on her back, the tip of the pen following the sharp lines of her scapula, giving her wings. Everyone else was out, heading to the party. We had the place to ourselves.

It should have been perfect.

But something was wrong; the adventure wasn't going as I had planned. She said she loved the drawing – how much it looked like a real tattoo – but I sensed she was lying. In the car, she was too interested in her phone – scrolling through her social media, ignoring me. She wanted to go to the beach. She wanted to be surrounded by other people when she knew full well that I preferred it when we were alone.

When I wouldn't do what she asked, she turned surly, whining about being bored and how much she wished the adventure was over. We arrived at our destination but she was snappy and impatient, complaining about the wind, the water – things she normally loved. I tried to stay the course, knowing that what I had planned would be worth it, but it was as if the ground was moving, swaying beneath my feet; I couldn't keep her in focus.

She was slipping away from me like quicksilver.

She grabbed a jacket to cover the artwork on her back. I didn't like that. It was as though she was ashamed of it.

Ashamed of me.

'*Can we see the party from here?*'

She stepped closer to the edge and spread her arms wide. I thought of the wings on her back, a bird about to take flight.

'*Take a photo of me?*' She turned round and grinned at me. She patted the pockets of her jacket. '*Oh, I must have left my phone in the car. Use yours?*'

I couldn't refuse her (though I'd locked her phone in the car on purpose so there'd be no more distractions). She removed the jacket, tossing it at my feet, and struck a pose. As she moved position, her foot slipped, and she cried out before starting to fall –

My heart caught in my throat. But, as I reached out to grab her, she righted herself and looked back at me, laughing, the thrill of the near miss making us both giddy.

I took the photo, but no image would ever have done her justice. I wished I could capture her just as she was in that moment. If I'd had the skills, I would have carved her into a figurehead to guide me – more striking than any sea creature on the prow of a ship.

In the semi-dark, it was hard to see the magpie. But I knew it was there, the wing tips reaching out to her shoulders. A shadow across her back. We'd come so far, and this was the moment I'd been waiting for, the moment I'd find out once and for all how strong her commitment was.

'*Let's go,*' she said, before I could say anything. The wind was so fierce it almost swept away her words. She frowned. '*Didn't you hear me?*'

Things were worse when she spoke.

The reality of what was happening came crashing back.

Our perfect moment wasn't going to last much longer.

The adventure was ending.

'*Help me down from here.*' She reached out her hand to me.

But I didn't take it.

'*Were you serious about what you said earlier? About the Magpies?*' I asked her.

'*Come on. You don't really believe in that, do you? It's just a silly myth. A game we're playing. That's all this is.*'

The words were a slap in the face.

'*It's not a myth. Don't cross the Magpies.*' That much I understood and believed.

She rolled her eyes.

She didn't believe. Maybe she never had. She didn't respect the tradition. But, more than that, she wasn't going to *help*. And that betrayal was bigger than any that had gone before.

She understood, I think, in that final moment, the impact of her words. But it was too late to take them back.

'*No, don't! Please –*'

I stepped forward.

One shove was all it took.


It's strange. I thought I'd feel sad once it was done. *One for sorrow, two for joy.*

I keep waiting for the sorrow to come.

But instead?

Instead, all I feel is . . . joy.

# PART ONE

*One for sorrow,*
*That much you've learned ...*

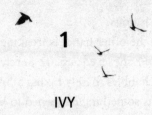

# 1

## IVY

Blood drips down from the cuts on my arm, still fresh from when the mirror almost crashed on my head. It's so bad I'm leaving red smears on the paper I clutch between my fingers. Audrey steps closer and reads over my shoulder. She wraps her arms round her body, trembling – whether from fear, or cold, I don't know.

> *Dear Clover,*
>
> *You are invited to become a part of* THE MAGPIE SOCIETY.
> *Do you agree to uphold the values of the school, protecting it from corruption, and keeping it and its students safe, no matter the cost?*
> *If so, sign here – and await further instructions.*

'There's no signature. She didn't sign it!' I flip the paper over, but there aren't any markings on the other side. I inspect the words, reading them again and again, trying to decipher some sort of clue as to who left the note.

One thing's for certain: the Magpie Society is real. It's not some relic of Illumen Hall's past. It's active, and they – whoever they are – wanted to recruit Clover into their group.

I'm almost jealous.

Audrey, on the other hand, is freaking out. 'What could this mean? Did she even see it? Surely she would have signed it,' she babbles, barely taking a breath.

'That means something happened to her.'

'Or did she choose *not* to sign and is now paying the price?'

'I don't know,' I say. 'I don't know anything.' I fold the letter up and shove it under my bra strap, being careful not to rip the lace on Audrey's dress any more. I send a text to Teddy.

> Tell Mrs Abbott to come to
> Clover's room in Polaris asap.
> Make sure she comes alone.

I wince when my hand catches on the clasp of my bag as I slip the phone inside. There's blood drying in the cracks of my palms.

'Be careful! We should get your hands looked at for shards of glass. Should I go get the nurse?' Audrey inspects my palms, which only makes them hurt even more. I snatch them back.

'No, I'm fine. The housemistress has a first-aid kit back at Helios. This is the least of my worries right now. Clover's gone!'

'How long will the cops take?' Audrey paces the room, stepping over the mess as she does.

'I don't know. Mrs Abbott should be here any minute hopefully. She needs to see this.'

I look around. It's disturbing to think of Clover struggling with someone here. I cast my mind back to the party and the flash mob of magpies. With all that chaos, it would have been so easy for someone to slip through the school gates and into the building. The people in the magpie costumes weren't Illumen Hall students either. Potential threats were everywhere.

'She's gonna freak out when she sees the note. Do you think the police will investigate the Magpie Society?'

'Well . . . we know Clover thought she was in danger – she warned us in her podcast that something like this would happen, didn't she? *One of you is next.* She just didn't realize that she was going to be the victim.'

'Jesus,' says Audrey. She looks like a trapped rabbit, wanting to run away, but unable to find a way out. The note scratches against my chest. My mind is whirring at a thousand miles an hour.

I exhale a sharp breath. 'Let's leave the Magpie Society note out of it for now. It'll only distract the police.'

'I don't know, Ivy. I think they need to be aware of everything.' Audrey bites at the edge of her nail. I'm not going to be the only one with bleeding hands if she keeps that up. 'I don't wanna hide evidence from the cops. What if – what if this is a potential murder case?'

'It's not a murder, Audrey. Clover is missing.'

She gestures around at the mess. 'You don't know what happened! The blood, her cellphone, that freaking terrifying recording she left? C'mon, this is bad!'

I take her hands, holding her gaze. 'Audrey, we need to be on the same page here. Telling them will only complicate everything. We want the police to focus on finding Clover, not on some secret society, right? If she still doesn't show up ... *then* we let them know.'

After a long second, she nods. 'OK. I'm with you.'

I breathe a sigh of relief.

'At least Mr Willis has gone,' she mutters.

'He'd be an idiot to ever show his face around here again now we know about the relationship he had with Lola. What a sicko.'

'But you burned the photo ...' Audrey avoids looking at me.

'Yes,' I answer quietly. 'He had a relationship with her, but his alibi proves he didn't kill her. That would have complicated things too.'

'But if it wasn't him then who *did* kill Lola? The same person who attacked Clover? I feel like we're sitting ducks right now. What if whoever did this comes back?'

Audrey's panic rises and she paces towards the door. As she reaches it, she comes face to face with Mrs Abbott.

There's a sharp intake of breath from the headmistress, who stares in horror at the room. She tiptoes through the piles of stuff and eventually reaches the desk.

'We called nine-nine-nine,' I say. 'The police are on their way.'

Mrs Abbott has her back to us, so I can't see her expression. But her shoulders tense beneath her blazer. 'Please go downstairs and meet the officers, then bring them to my office. I'm sure they'll want to talk to you first of all. I'll make sure no one disturbs this room. This is a crime scene now; we mustn't contaminate it.' She turns back to us. 'Have you touched anything?'

'Well, we –' Audrey starts.

I interject. 'No. We didn't touch anything. We just sat on the bed.' Audrey raises an eyebrow at me.

'OK, thank you, girls. I'm sorry – you must be so worried for your friend.' She frowns at me. 'Ivy, are you hurt?'

'I'm fine. We'd better go see if the police have arrived. They could be here at any moment.' I grab Audrey's arm, and we walk down the corridor away from Clover's room.

My head starts to throb. I start to feel faint, flashing back to narrowly avoiding being crushed by a falling mirror at the party, pulled through shards of broken glass on the floor.

It must be pretty obvious because Audrey grabs my hand and slows me down. 'How are you feeling? You must be exhausted. I bet you're still in shock.'

I put my hand to my head, and she rubs my arm.

'Got a headache and my hands sting. I'll be OK, honestly.' I smile, but I can feel my lips trembling. I know Audrey isn't convinced.

And neither am I. Suddenly the dress feels too tight, the drying blood now crusting over and making my skin crawl. I don't think this is the best look with which to greet police officers – covered in blood, even if it is my own.

'Actually, do you mind if I meet you downstairs in a couple of minutes? I just want to take this off and pop a few painkillers.' I start in the direction of the corridor leading to our room and Audrey hesitates.

'Shall I come with you?'

'No, I'll be quick. The police could be here at any minute. We shouldn't keep them waiting. You go ahead and I'll be right behind you.' I smile a lot more convincingly this time. She nods and carries on down the next set of stairs.

As I walk, I examine Audrey's beautiful black lace dress, now torn and much worse for wear. I feel terrible. I can only guess how much this would have cost and it's completely destroyed. No tailor will be able to fix it. I pull a small purple feather from the ripped lace near my collarbone. It must have come from the flash mob.

I can't wait to take the dress off and shed tonight's events. It hasn't gone as planned at all. As I walk alone along the darkened hallway to our room, I can hear laughing, singing and hollering from the rest of the Illumen Hall students continuing their Samhain celebrations across the school grounds. Most of them will have already forgotten what happened to me at the party, some won't care, and none of them have any idea that Clover is missing and the police are on their way. I twirl the small feather around between my thumb and forefinger.

The magpies are taking over.

I unlock our room with my pass, but instead of changing straight away I walk to the window. *Clover, where are you?* I think as I stare out across the grounds. I think I see a whisper of movement out of the corner of my eye – but it's nothing.

No, not nothing. It's a magpie. I bring two fingers to my forehead and give a small salute.

And I know in that moment that nothing is going to be the same again.

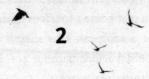

# 2

## AUDREY

I watch Ivy as she retreats towards Helios House and our shared dorm room, waiting until she's disappeared from view. I exhale sharply. There's a tightness in my chest that won't go away – but I know exactly what the cause is. I don't know Clover very well, but I heard that message on her phone's recording app: *Get away from me . . . No . . . stop . . . help!* I felt her terror. I hope we find her soon.

*Please be OK.*

I can't think about the blood in her room, or the warning that Clover left for us on her podcast. I wanna kick myself for not listening to her.

Maybe then Ivy wouldn't have burned the photo of Mr Willis and Lola. I hope he's running far, far away from here, and we never see him again. Yet two questions still ring in my mind:

*If Mr Willis isn't the murderer, then who killed Lola Radcliffe?*

*Who else is out there?*

I give myself a shake. The cops are coming now. They're the ones who need to sort this out. It never felt right – not going to the authorities and letting them deal with Mr Willis. Especially after what had happened to me back home . . .

I don't wanna be on the side of hiding things from the law ever again. Our part in this is over now. Ivy and I can concentrate on just being ourselves again, not mastermind detectives. For a moment, I let myself wonder what our friendship would be like without the Magpie Society. It could be something really great.

My legs are on autopilot as I follow the winding staircases down to the entrance hall. A couple of times I find myself turning round; although I know the school much better now, Clover's dorm is in a part of the building I haven't had much time to explore. I wish I'd stayed with Ivy. Seeing her so scared has spooked me.

It's eerie with no one roaming the hallways. Whenever I pass a window, I look out towards the rear grounds of the school. The Samhain party rages on, my fellow students milling around a huge fire pit. What are they all thinking? Do they have their own theories about the flash mob? I guess rumours will fly when the cops roll up to the front door.

I hate the way that the hallways seem to shift and change, so I'm caught by surprise when I find myself somewhere familiar: the main staircase. I breathe a sigh of relief.

I rush down the stairs, past the decorations – the pumpkins and the autumnal wreaths. It all seems so out of place now, with the harsh lights on, the atmosphere ruined.

'Audrey!'

I spin around as I'm crossing the tiled entrance hall to the front doors, my heels clattering on the stone. Teddy rushes towards me, concern on his face. 'Did Mrs Abbott find you?'

'Yeah, she did. In Clover's room. I've come back down to wait for the cops.' I can't seem to stop my hands from shaking.

His face drains of colour. 'The police? Why?'

I cast an anxious glance around us, but the hall is empty – apart from the strange sculptures of pumpkins and gourds, and the bushels of hay that are stacked in the corners. Suddenly I catch my breath as the bundles of dried grasses seem to sway as if there's someone there. But, as I stare, they go utterly still. I'm just imagining things. Paranoid Audrey.

'You OK?' Teddy reaches out and grabs my hand, bringing me back to the present. I blink.

I pull his hand close, and then he's engulfed me in a hug, his strong arms wrapping around my shoulders. I'm teetering on the precipice of a breakdown because this is how present-day Audrey reacts to trauma. She used to be strong, but now she can't keep a lid on her emotions. *Fuck her.* I have to be tougher than this. Somehow I wrench my emotions right back from the edge, gaining control of myself. There's no way the cops will take a sobbing girl seriously.

The first face that flashes to the front of my mind is Ivy's: strong and serious, but always ready for action. If I lose it, I'll be letting her down. So I pull myself together and push away from Teddy.

'It's Clover,' I say. 'She's gone missing.'

'Are you serious?' Teddy's eyes are wide. His hair is plastered to his forehead; he's obviously been running around, trying to act as a go-between for us and Mrs Abbott. 'I've been waiting for you girls to get back to the party. How's Ivy?'

'She's . . . shaken up. But we're not going back to the party. I'm to meet the police here and take them to Mrs Abbott's office.'

'I'll wait with you.'

'You don't have to do that. You can go back . . .'

He scoffs. 'No way. I'm worried about you.' He brushes the hair away from my face. I bet I look a complete disaster.

'Let's go check outside, see if the cops are here.'

He nods, takes my hand and pushes through the double doors.

It's cold outside – the frigid autumn air chilling me right down to my bones. I wrap my arms around my body. Beside me, Teddy shrugs off his jacket and throws it over my shoulders. I almost laugh at how stereotypical that is – but I'm not above accepting a little gentlemanly behaviour.

The front of the school is dark, the road stretching out into pitch-blackness before us. In the distance, across the field, there's laughter and music, smoke drifting up into the sky. Someone's passing around sparklers too.

'What do you think happened to Clover?' Teddy asks.

My head's a muddle. 'I have no idea.'

'Come on . . . you must know something. Or else why did you go to her room?'

I squeeze my eyes shut. That's the worst part of it. We went there to confront her. When all the while she was in danger. 'We think . . . we think she figured out the identity of Lola's murderer, and whoever it was threatened her. Attacked her.' I let out a sob. 'I'm so worried – she must be terrified. You heard her last podcast too.'

Teddy is quiet for a moment. 'Perhaps it's not as bad as you think . . .'

I blink at his cool tone. 'You're not worried?'

He grabs my hand. 'No, it's not that. It's just that Clover has done this before. Last year she disappeared for, like, three days. Turned out she'd gone up to Manchester to participate in a protest and just didn't tell anyone. It's kind of her thing. Her parents didn't even file a missing persons report.'

Now it's my turn to be quiet. Especially as the headlights of a dark sedan appear at the end of the long driveway. There are no flashing blue and red lights – but then there's no one else on the road for them to warn. My stomach turns – the alcohol unsettling me, making me shake. Ivy must have known about Clover's tendency to run away. This time was obviously different.

This time there was blood.

I step forward, creating space between us, and Teddy doesn't follow. The car pulls up, and two people in suits step out: a man and a woman.

'Are you the cops? I mean . . . the police?' I say.

'Yes. I'm DI Shing, and this is DC Copeland,' says the woman. 'We got a call about a disturbance and a potential missing person?'

I double take at the male officer's name. He was the one interviewed by Clover on the podcast. Then I nod. 'Please come with me.'

'Wait!' There's a shout from the darkness behind me. Bonnie sprints towards us, tearing across the grass. In her bright red party dress and heels, she looks deranged. 'What's going on? Why are the police here? Is it because of the podcast?'

'Go back to the party, Bonnie,' says Teddy.

The male police officer looks from me to Bonnie and back again. 'Please come with me,' I repeat. 'Our headmistress, Mrs Abbott, asked me to take you to her.'

He nods and they both start to follow me. Bonnie trots to catch up. 'What are you doing, Audrey?' she hisses. 'This should be Araminta's job. She's the head girl.'

'Araminta isn't involved in this. Tell her she should keep everyone outside for now.'

'I don't take orders from you.'

'Fine, do whatever you want, Bonnie. But I have one job – and that's to get these people to Mrs Abbott. I'll see you later.' I half turn away from her.

Bonnie is actually so furious that she stomps her foot. But she heads off in the direction of the party.

'Sorry about that,' I say to the cops.

They don't reply, and their sombre expressions sober me up as well. I pick up the pace, leading them through the big double doors and into the depths of Illumen Hall. I look up at the portrait that first greeted me only a couple of months ago. I know now that it's of Lady Penelope Debert, the daughter of one of the school's headmasters in the nineteenth century, who made sure girls could attend the school.

I pull up abruptly and the cops crash into my back.

'Audrey?' Teddy looks at me with concern.

I swallow. 'Sorry – this way.' But I can't ignore what I saw. Above the painted woman's shoulder is something I swear I've never seen before. A magpie.

And it's looking directly at me.

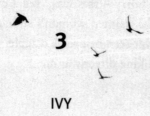

## 3

### IVY

I shrug into one of my old hoodies, the one where I've cut thumb holes into the sleeves that still smells faintly of Teddy's aftershave – like woodsmoke and sea spray – and pull on a pair of leggings.

I pick up Audrey's dress from the floor. It's a mess. I don't think any amount of dry-cleaning is going to save it: it's covered in blood and now it stinks like soap from the effort of scrubbing my hands. I stuff it in a plastic bag and throw it into the back of my wardrobe. Audrey is so rich she probably won't notice if she never gets it back.

My bed is really tempting. I feel like I've been hit by a truck. I could crawl under my duvet and sleep for hours. But I have to find Audrey and make sure I hear what the police have to say.

I check my phone in case Clover has managed to get a message out. But there's nothing.

I head down to the office where I'm met by the expressionless faces of two police officers standing beside Audrey outside Mrs Abbott's door. One is a fairly broad man, with his pen and paper at the ready (so old-school), and the other is a female officer with a slightly softer face, though still unsmiling. The office and its stark glass exterior is dark and moody. I feel a lump form in my throat as the seriousness of what's happening creeps up on me. A lump – or I'm about to vomit.

Audrey smiles as she spots me. 'Ivy, thank God you're here. Um . . .' She glances at the two officers. She's clearly forgotten their names. 'This is Ivy Moore-Zhang. She's my room-mate here. We were together when we went to Clover's room.'

'So you're the young lady who called the police?' the man says to me.

I nod. I hate that patronizing 'young lady'.

Mrs Abbott's heels click on the stone floors behind me. She shakes hands with the police and unlocks her office in deathly silence. I pull the sleeves of the hoodie down over my hands. I catch Audrey's eye, who wrinkles her nose as Mrs Abbott turns on the lights and ushers us all inside. Like she's smelt something bad.

'Take a seat, everyone.' Audrey and I sit together on the lilac velvet chaise longue next to Mrs Abbott's grand bookcase, and the police officers both sit in chairs in front of her desk.

The female officer speaks first.

'I'm DI Shing and this is DC Copeland. We're on the criminal investigations team for this area. We received a call about a missing student this evening, is that right?'

I raise an eyebrow. They've sent *detectives*? And not only that – the detective who Clover interviewed. There's obviously more urgency since Lola's death and they're taking no chances this time.

DC Copeland's pen is poised over his notebook, and he's looking at Mrs Abbott expectantly.

'Yes. Our Year Ten pupil Clover Mirth. As you can see, we are celebrating this evening with our annual Samhain gathering, and Ivy and Audrey here alerted me to the fact that Clover has gone missing during the evening's events.' Mrs Abbott speaks with her poshest, most formal tone. It's like she's trying to impress the detectives. It's immediately grating.

'Do you mind if we ask you a few questions, girls?' DI Shing turns to us.

'Uh-huh,' says Audrey.

'When and how did you notice Clover was gone?'

'We went to find her after hearing her latest podcast episode and realizing she wasn't at the party. When we got to her room, it looked completely ransacked,' I say without taking a breath.

'I knew that podcast was bad news,' DC Copeland mutters. 'And the theory about some bird group protecting the school? This is why we're the detectives, not teenage girls.'

'So it's only been a few hours?' DI Shing says, looking down at her watch.

'Not even that long,' says Copeland. He breathes out, clearly holding back an eye-roll. This man doesn't care one jot about Clover going missing.

His partner throws him a dark look; maybe she realizes he's giving totally the wrong impression. 'I think we'd better see Clover's room before all the students come in from the party. Looks like quite the event! We never had anything like this when I was at school. Then again, I was just at the local comprehensive. Nothing so grand as all this. Do you mind taking us, Mrs Abbott?' Shing gets up from her chair.

'Of course.' Mrs Abbott stands up too, ushering them out of her office. In the doorway, she turns back and stares at us. 'You stay here for now, girls. I'm sure the police will want to talk to you more when they've examined the scene.'

Once the door closes, Audrey and I both slump back down on the sofa.

'This is bringing back terrible memories for me, Ivy, I'm not gonna lie. Speaking with detectives like that. I've not done it since . . .' She gnaws on the edge of her thumbnail.

'Oh God, of course! I'm sorry this isn't great for you,' I say. 'We could have done with a few more shots earlier.' I smile at her, trying to be reassuring.

Audrey shrugs. 'What do you really think is going on here? Something just doesn't add up. What about the Magpie Society? They must be involved *somehow*. The magpie tattoo on Lola's back, that flash mob, Clover's warning on the podcast and now the invitation . . .'

I scan Mrs Abbott's office and notice a CCTV camera sitting pretty in the corner of the room. I nod over to it to alert Audrey that we are being watched in here. She catches sight of it and rolls her eyes back at me.

'We need to be careful, Audrey. We don't know who's behind this, or how powerful they really are. If we make things worse, we're next. You get that, right?' I drop my voice to a whisper. She holds my gaze, then nods.

We sit in silence for a while. I can still hear students outside and I gaze out of the window, hoping to see something to ease my racing mind. The stars are so bright this evening, and the moon is shining down on the perfectly pruned bushes lining the driveway. A perfect night for Samhain. But, just as I'm looking at the water fountain, I notice someone walking behind it. It's dark so I can't see properly, but it looks like . . .

*No.* It can't be.

I whack Audrey on the arm and point outside.

'Is that –?'

'Oh my God! That looks like Mr Willis,' she says with a gasp.

'Why hasn't he left yet? He literally said he was leaving hours ago!'

We watch as he opens the boot of his Mini, tosses something inside, then strolls off in the direction of the party.

'I feel like the timing of this is far too suspicious. We discover that Clover knows about Mr Willis and Lola's relationship, and now she's missing?'

'And he's back,' Audrey says ominously.

We jump as Mrs Abbott and both detectives arrive at her door and make their way back in.

I catch a look from Mrs Abbott that tells me she wants to ask us more questions – but when the police *aren't* around.

DC Copeland holds out his hand for Mrs Abbott to shake. 'As we've said, we'll be in touch if we need any more information or questions answered, but for now we've done all we can.' Mrs Abbott takes his hand and smiles back at him.

'Wait, you don't need to ask us anything else?' I say.

'No, not at the moment. We don't have any evidence of foul play here. I'm sure Clover will turn up eventually. We'll contact her parents and check she's not simply gone home, but ... Well, we see this a lot.' DI Shing puts her hands in her pockets.

'Especially at these posh boarding schools!' DC Copeland chirps. 'We might have to come and give a talk about wasting police time.'

'Hang on. You think we wasted your time?' Audrey asks despairingly.

'I'm sorry, our friend is missing and you're going to do precisely *nothing* about it? I know Clover – she wouldn't randomly disappear!' I say desperately. I can feel Audrey glance at me, but I don't look over.

'We'll do what we can.'

DC Copeland is starting to annoy me; he's so sure of himself and his crappy detective skills.

'We're just worried about our friend. Better to be safe than sorry, right?' I admit defeat. Clearly they aren't taking us seriously and I'm not about to put up a fight or give up all the information I have. They seem like they couldn't care less. The two of them turn to leave, and my shoulders drop.

'Well, that settles it then. If there's still no news tomorrow, let us know.'

'No – you can't leave!' shouts Audrey from behind me. 'What about the blood?'

## 4

### AUDREY

My heart is pounding. DC Copeland frowns. '*Blood?*'

'On Clover's desk –' I begin, but Ivy kicks my foot. 'Ow!'

Ivy looks up at the man and smiles. 'On my forehead,' she says. 'That's what Audrey means. I had blood on my forehead from when a mirror fell and knocked me over, but I cleaned up before you got here. I dripped on Clover's desk – honestly, I was bleeding all over the place.'

'We didn't see any signs of blood,' says DI Shing, looking from Ivy to me and back again.

'I told you – I cleaned it up,' Ivy says quickly.

'I thought you said you didn't touch anything?' Mrs Abbott says. A vein on her forehead is threatening to burst.

'The only thing I touched was my own blood. I figured I should wipe it all off since it wasn't relevant to Clover being missing and I thought it would just confuse things.'

I can't quite believe what I'm hearing, but I'm too stunned to contradict her.

'You know what? It's late; I'll show you out,' says Mrs Abbott, trying her best to lead the police away from us. DI Shing looks at me strangely. Mrs Abbott ushers her out the door, then turns to look at us. 'I trust you girls can make your own way back to your room?'

We nod, shuffling out of her office, and she locks it behind us. Ivy and I wait in the doorway until the police are out of earshot.

I open my mouth to speak, but Ivy stops me. 'Not here – come on.'

She grabs my arm and yanks me into the darkened room opposite Mrs Abbott's office. I stumble in, catching myself on one of the desks – this must be a classroom I haven't been in yet – then slump into a chair. 'What the hell, Ivy?'

She sits down opposite me. 'I panicked,' she says, biting her lip. Her eyes flicker from side to side as if she's trying to solve a math problem that I can't see.

'Why did you lie about the blood? It wasn't you dripping on the desk . . . that blood was already there. We didn't just imagine it! So how come it's gone?'

'I don't know.'

'But it was there, right?'

Ivy glares at me and rolls her eyes.

'So you agree. Good. Then I repeat: What. The. Fuck? Did Mrs Abbott tidy it up before the police got there? Because that's some cover-up. We have to tell the cops what we saw, exactly as we saw it, if they're gonna have any chance of finding Clover. I don't get why you stopped me!'

'Because – let's face it – they won't believe us. You heard them – they already have this vision of us as these prissy boarding-school girls who love drama. They'd think we made it all up for a laugh, or find some way to turn it round so that it's our fault.'

'We could tell them about the Magpie letter then. That *proves* someone else is involved . . .'

'We don't even know how long Clover's had that invite. What if it was research for her podcast? And come on – how do you think it would sound to the police? A secret society hiding in the background, protecting the school?' Ivy shakes her head. 'It sounds ridiculous. Maybe . . .' She takes a deep breath. 'Maybe they're right. Maybe we'll have heard from Clover by tomorrow morning.' She shifts in her seat and pulls her phone out of her pocket.

'She's done this before, right? Or something like this?'

'What do you mean?' Ivy asks sharply.

'Run away.'

'Who told you that?'

'Teddy.'

Ivy sighs. 'Yeah, she has. A few times. But I'm with you – I *know* something weird happened in that room. I feel like Clover's in danger. And I don't think this is something the police are going to help us with.'

'Why not? That attitude pisses me off. No one wants to go to the cops and everyone's first instinct is to cover shit up, just in case they end up in the spotlight or getting accused. But it doesn't work like that. I've *been* there, remember? The police know what they're doing. They will be able to help. If Clover is in danger, then we owe it to her.'

Ivy's eyes flash. 'They weren't much help with Lola's murder, were they? Why would it be any different this time? It's still a missing teenage girl. I can tell you exactly how many fucks the police are going to give.' She holds her thumb and forefinger up in a circle.

After a few beats, I nod. 'Fine.' Then I lean forward in my chair. 'So what are *we* gonna do?'

Ivy stands up. 'I don't know about you . . . but I want to go to bed.'

'But what about Mr Willis –'

'Audrey,' she snaps. Then she softens. 'I'm sorry. It's late. I was almost killed by a mirror. My body is aching everywhere. Let's take this up again in the morning. At the very least, my head won't be as fuzzy and we can make a plan.' She grabs my hand. 'And I promise there will be one. I won't let up until Clover's back safe and sound.'

I hesitate. 'OK,' I say eventually.

I follow her out of the room and almost crash into her heels as she comes to an abrupt stop. Mrs Abbott is waiting outside her office. I frown and wrinkle my nose as I'm hit by a smell again – like chlorine, as if someone's come back from a swimming pool. *Weird*.

'I wanted to make sure you girls got back to your room safely. But you haven't got very far.'

Ivy shrugs. 'Sorry, miss. I was feeling a bit faint. Audrey wanted me to sit down. But I'm feeling better now.'

'I'll go get her a soda from the canteen,' I say.

'No – you've had enough excitement for tonight, girls, and I don't want you getting wrapped up with all the partygoers returning. I'll have one of the kitchen staff bring something up.'

'Thank you,' Ivy says, and I nod. Then we dart around the headmistress, continuing back to our shared room.

'Something is definitely going on with her,' I say once we're safely out of earshot. 'Did you smell that? It was like bleach or something.'

'From Mrs Abbott, yeah? I smelled it too. But we mustn't

get ahead of ourselves. Like I said, let's wait and see tomorrow.'

Ivy climbs the first set of stairs, and then a voice comes down from above us.

'Wait and see about what tomorrow?'

Araminta's furious face appears on the stairs. Her usually coiffed hair is in disarray, her cheeks flushed with anger. In her sparkly dress, she looks like a furious angel. 'What is going on? Why were the police here? Why didn't anyone tell me?'

'Not everything is your concern, Minty,' says Ivy. I stand next to her, folding my arms across my chest. Tiredness has hit me like a ton of bricks.

'Don't "Minty" me right now. Tell me what you know. I'm the head girl! *Not* you, Ivy. Or have you forgotten?'

'Just because you're head girl doesn't mean it's your business,' Ivy says.

'Head girls are always in the know! Mrs Abbott used to turn to *Sadie* for everything.'

'Well, it's not my fault that you're such a failure.' Ivy storms up the stairs past Araminta.

'You've ruined my first big school event! I know your plan. You're going to wreck my whole year as head girl, aren't you? Ivy Moore-Zhang, I don't know what you have against me, or if you're really just so petty that you can't stand the fact that someone else is head girl instead of your precious Lola. But, I swear to God, I'm going to make your life a nightmare if you don't tell me what the hell is going on.'

Ivy narrows her eyes, and I take in a sharp breath. When

she speaks, her voice is cold. 'Lola made it her business to befriend everyone in the school – not make enemies. You act like you're better than everyone all the time. Maybe you should rethink being such a total bitch?'

Araminta reels back as if she's been slapped in the face. Ivy storms up the stairs, but as I pass Minty I touch her on the arm. Her round blue eyes are shiny – as if she's on the verge of tears. I almost feel sorry for her. No, scratch that – I *do* feel sorry for her. She's in the dark. I know what that's like. 'It's Clover,' I say to her quietly. 'She's gone missing.'

'What, seriously?'

'Yes. But the police are handling it.'

Araminta's eyes search my face, then she nods. 'Thank you for telling me. I'll go and make sure Clover's roommates are OK.'

'That would be great.' I hadn't even thought about them. My memory flashes back to a young white girl with long dark hair and thick glasses. She seemed sweet. Lyra something? She'd need someone like Araminta to reassure her that things were safe. 'I'd better go . . .' I dash up the stairs after Ivy, before Araminta can get anything else out of me.

'Did you really just do that?' Ivy asks me, without turning round, once I've caught up.

'I thought I should throw her a bone. She's had a rough night too.'

'She doesn't deserve it.'

'Maybe not. But she's gonna look after Clover's roommates. That will keep her busy – and out of our way.'

We stop outside our bedroom. It's hard to believe that

only a few hours ago we were coming out of here, laughing and giggling.

Ivy opens the door. 'Audrey?'

I follow her gaze. There are two letters lying on the floor with our names written on them in elaborate script.

I recognize the letters immediately. They're the same as the one we found in Clover's room.

Invitations to the Magpie Society.

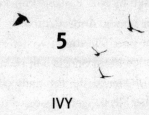

# 5

## IVY

We stand in silence, flipping the invitations over and over in our hands. They're thick with embossed lettering – they even *feel* important.

'What do we do?' Audrey holds up the card, her expression clouded with confusion. My own mind feels blank, and I struggle to focus on the situation in front of me. I rub my temples and exhale.

'I'm too exhausted to even think about it, if I'm honest. My head's still pounding. Let's put them behind the panel where we found Lola's diary and get into it tomorrow. Haven't we done enough for today?'

I take the invitation from Audrey's trembling hand. Kneeling down by the desk, I flick the wooden panel and it swings open on its hinges. I place the cards deep within the cavity of the wall.

'Let's get some sleep!' I fall back on to my bed without even taking my clothes off.

'This will all be OK, won't it?' Audrey says. She drops her expensive dress into a puddle on the floor, before collapsing into bed too.

'Honestly? I don't know. I just hope things are clearer in the morning.'

*

I feel as though my head has barely touched the pillow when I'm woken by Mrs Parsons knocking on our door.

'Time to get up and dressed, girls.'

'Where's the fire?' I mutter.

'You're needed in the sports hall right now.'

'But I'm not signed up for gym class,' Audrey says, mumbling in her sleep. 'Can't I sleep a bit longer?'

'Not today. The police are back – and they want to talk to you.'

That gets our attention, and the events of yesterday come rushing back. Mrs Parsons waggles her eyebrows and closes the door behind her.

I moan as I kick off the bedsheets and rub my swollen eyes. This feels relentless. The invitations we buried in the wall are crying out for our attention, pulsating like hidden heartbeats, but there's no time to ponder them now.

'The police came back?' Audrey jumps up and swings her feet into her pink fluffy slippers while heading for the wardrobe. 'They seemed pretty unconvinced last night that anything was wrong. I wonder what changed?'

'No idea. Maybe they found out something about Clover? I bet Mrs Abbott chose the sports hall because she wants to make a public display of how seriously she's taking this.'

'Or to make sure she's in control of how we receive information.'

I raise an eyebrow. 'You're catching on quick!' I throw on my grey jogging bottoms and matching hoodie, tie my sleek black bob into a low pony and run my fingers over my eye bags as I stare into the mirror.

'For someone who got absolutely mauled by a gilt mirror, you don't look so bad, Ivy ...' She shoots me a half-smile.

I sometimes forget how effortlessly beautiful Audrey is, but seeing her now, only awake a few minutes, she looks like she's already done a yoga session, showered, blow-dried her hair, had her morning coffee and eaten youthful glow for breakfast. I swallow my jealousy and remember I am the one who suffered a life-threatening accident yesterday. I can afford to look a little bruised.

As we head down to the sports hall, we join a queue of students. Everyone's buzzing like popcorn kernels in a hot pan. Full of nerves and adrenaline.

Grant Walker in Year Ten is just in front of us.

'What's going on then?' I ask him.

'It seems the police were here last night. They're back now, questioning students about the party,' he says.

'How do you know that?'

'From my mate down at Polaris House. I think it's to do with that podcast girl, Clover. Apparently she's gone missing! Proper dodgy stuff ...' He turns back to his friends who are now speculating about who could have been the last person to see Clover.

'So they're interviewing everyone? Seems like kind of a waste of time,' I whisper to Audrey.

Mrs Abbott is at the front of the queue, seeing students in one at a time. It dawns on me that Audrey and I are about to be separated. I hope she doesn't deviate from what we agreed. *No mention of the letter or the journal*, I want to remind her, but now there are other students filing in behind us. The door to the sports hall swings open and one of Clover's room-mates comes out – Lyra. She walks past us down the line, her head low, her face sullen and grey.

'This is going to take absolutely ages. They're interviewing everyone individually. C'mon, let's get some air. Smells like musty trainers and old PE kits here and it's making me feel sick.' I grab Audrey's hand and pull her from the queue before she can protest.

Outside, the air is crisp, and winter feels like it's just round the corner. It's fresh and the air fills my lungs and almost stings as it does. In the far field, I can see the groundsman's grandson, Ed, clearing up the bonfire from the party. There are clumps of students all around the courtyard. A couple of them are looking at me with concern.

I hate having their eyes on me.

Without even saying a word to each other, Audrey and I veer away from the crowds, drifting towards the woods where I go for my runs. I look back over my shoulder to make sure we're not being followed. Instead, I'm struck for a moment by how beautiful the school looks in the morning light.

There's a fallen log, which Audrey perches on. She takes her phone out and starts scrolling, gets bored and puts it away again. I sit beside her and trace my fingers along the ridges of the bark.

'Hey, what's that?' Audrey points at something hanging down from a tree behind us. It looks like black fabric. She stands up and pulls on it, holding it up by the shoulders. 'Looks like someone got a tad frisky last night at the party.' She tosses it back behind the tree.

'Wait, that's not a dress. It looks like a bit of that costume the weird flash mob wore, right before – you know – the mirror thing. The magpie outfits.' I kick at a pile of leaves, revealing a mass of black feathers and a mask with a long, sharp beak.

'Damn, you're right. These look expensive. I wonder who was wearing this and why they've tossed it?'

'Who *arranged* it? That's what I want to know. Whoever it was really rained on Araminta's parade.'

Audrey's eyes open wide. 'And caused the perfect distraction . . . What if *that's* when Clover went missing?'

Before I can answer, we hear footsteps running towards us.

'IVY! Mrs Abbott wants you up next!' shouts Grant. 'I've been looking all over for you two. You'd better hurry – she's fuming.'

Audrey and I exchange looks. 'Guess we can't avoid it any more,' she says.

I nod, although (much to Grant's annoyance) I don't race to meet Mrs Abbott's demand.

'Wish me luck,' I say to Audrey, leaving her at the sports hall door.

'Break a leg,' she says, a small smile on her face.

I knock. Mrs Abbott ushers me in. There's a table over the centre circle and on one side are the same two officers from last night, on the other an empty chair and the school counsellor, Dr Kinfeld. The hall is cold and echoey and my feet squeak as I make my way over to the empty seat.

'Nice to see you again, Ivy.' Detective Shing returns my

smile as I sit. 'Dr Kinfeld is with you today as a chaperone and of course it goes without saying that nobody here is in trouble. We're just asking some questions that will hopefully lead us to finding out where Clover is. It's important that you give us absolutely any information that you think might help. No matter how small. OK?'

I nod.

'Great. Then we'll just ask you a few questions, if that's OK?'

I smile again. This time I show my teeth.

The other detective shifts in his chair, narrowing his eyes at me. But I've been through this before, with Lola. I know how useless their questions can be. It's up to them to prove me wrong. 'What time did you notice Clover was gone?' he says.

I pause. 'Probably around ten forty p.m?'

'And why did you decide to go up to her room?'

'We noticed she wasn't at the party and thought it was a bit weird. Clover loves parties and she would never miss this one. But then we heard her last podcast where she said, "If you're at Illumen Hall, you're in danger." She sounded worried, so we thought we should check on her.'

'And what happened to your head and your hands? Those looked like nasty injuries.'

'Well, yes, a mirror nearly fell on me at the party. Someone must have overloaded it with decorations. But I don't know what that has to do with Clover going missing.' I laugh awkwardly.

'We just wanted to make sure nobody had done this to you intentionally – that's all.'

'What? No. I was having a panic attack, ran past it and must have nudged it.'

'Why were you having a panic attack?'

Suddenly I feel hemmed in. 'It all got a bit much – the music, the party, the crowd – then a flash mob turned up and I needed air. Instead, I found myself backed up against the wall and then the mirror happened.'

'OK. So then you decided to see where Clover was?'

'Right. We listened to the podcast, and Audrey and I ran up to her room.'

'Was there a reason you thought something suspect had happened to Clover as opposed to her just leaving of her own accord? Yesterday you seemed pretty adamant she wouldn't just run away.'

I roll my eyes. 'We heard how she sounded on the podcast so yeah, it was kind of worrying when she wasn't in her room. It isn't like her. She's the life and soul of the party; she loved Samhain and would have been there, in the middle of the dance floor. Also, her room was a *mess*. It looked like someone had been rummaging through her stuff.'

'Do you know if Clover's a tidy student, Ivy?'

'What?'

'Her room's usually spotless, I take it?' Detective Shing laughs.

'I don't really know. I mean, probably not spotless, but . . .' I twist my hands around in my lap as I begin to feel more and more uncomfortable.

'So then you can't be sure it wasn't just normal teenage girl mess? Maybe pre-party?'

DI Shing is talking down to me and I'm not enjoying it. Why aren't they taking me seriously?

'I assume Clover didn't show up at home then, since you're back today, asking more questions? You seemed pretty sure that kids do this all the time and that she'd just be at home, chilling with her family on the sofa,' I say forcefully.

'We can't disclose any further information at the moment. We're still investigating and taking it very seriously, I assure you. We understand she's your friend, and you're very worried. We are doing everything we can to get more answers.'

'You won't get them from that lot you're waiting to interview, just so you know ...' I point at the door. Dr Kinfeld tuts and gives me one of his looks that says, 'Not now, Ivy.'

'Does Clover have any other friends from outside Illumen? A boyfriend? Anyone she knows or speaks to off school grounds?'

'Not that I know of.' I shrug.

'That's all we need for now, Ivy, thank you.' Detective Shing puts down her pen and looks up at me, beaming.

'Er, thanks ... good luck?' I get up from the table, squeeze past Mrs Abbott, who is already ushering someone else in as I leave, and head back outside. Audrey's still there with Clover's room-mates, Lyra and Yolanda.

'How did it go?' Lyra asks me.

'Oh fine. I mean, I didn't have much information to give ...' I turn, wide-eyed, to Audrey to try and tell her that I didn't really give them anything. I can't tell if she gets my hint.

The quieter of Clover's room-mates, Yolanda, leans in. 'Did you guys receive one of those letters too?'

She reaches into her blazer pocket and my eyes widen as I spot the corner of a familiar embossed letter.

# 6

## AUDREY

Ivy and I stare at each other. Then she turns to Yolanda. 'Where did you find that?'

'Under my bed. I don't get it though. What does it mean? *The Magpie Society?* I thought it was a joke or something.'

Ivy shakes her head. 'Audrey and I got them too. We . . . we think they may have something to do with Clover going missing.'

'Shit! No way. Count me out.' She tosses the invitation away from her like it's on fire.

'Yolanda, calm down! Maybe they've chosen us because they know we care about Clover. You heard what she said. She thought the Magpie Society was protecting her,' says Lyra, scooping it back up off the ground. She looks worried. 'So what do we do next?'

It's a good question, but I'm not able to answer because I hear Mrs Abbott calling my name.

'Meet us by the fountain when you're done,' Ivy says, and I nod. With another sharp cough from Mrs Abbott, I pick up my pace, making my way to the middle of the sports hall where they've set up a small table and some chairs. The airy space hardly feels like an interrogation room – yet, in a way, it makes sense. There's nowhere for someone to hide and overhear us. My eyes dart to the ceiling, and I notice that there aren't any cameras covering the middle of the sports hall. Then I laugh darkly to myself. What kinda person have I become? Someone who checks for CCTV everywhere she goes?

'Something funny, Audrey?' The counsellor – I forget his name – looks up at me, and the sound of his voice wipes my smile away completely. The unsettled feeling returns – the one I'd worked so hard in therapy to forget. It doesn't feel long enough since I had to talk to the authorities about –

I squeeze my eyes shut. I can't think about that right now or else I'll break down – and I don't wanna do that in front of a cop.

I hear a vague offer of a glass of water, so I accept it to give myself a bit more time. I take a deep breath and look around the sports hall.

There's three people – two cops and the shrink. The same detectives as before, DI Shing and DC Copeland. DI Shing has her hair pulled back into a low ponytail, minimal make-up, a low-budget suit that hasn't been tailored quite right. She looks no-nonsense, but friendlier than the man. Her eyes have a touch of concern. The man's eyes are ... well, not mean exactly. Tired, perhaps. Weary.

'Please, have a seat, Miss Wagner,' says DI Shing. 'We need to ask you some more questions about the disappearance of your friend, Clover Mirth. Is it OK if we record this?'

'She wasn't my friend.'

'Excuse me?'

'No ... I mean, it's not that we didn't like each other or anything. She was lovely, as far as I know. Super cool.

Feisty. But we weren't *friends*. I didn't know her. I didn't . . .'
I'm babbling now and the police know it. The woman
smiles at me, which shuts me up, and I slump down in the
chair.

'We just have a couple of questions. Can you describe to
me what happened last night?'

I swallow. 'Sure. Ivy and I got ready for the party in the
evening . . .'

'Ivy Moore-Zhang?'

'Yeah. She's my room-mate.'

'And also Clover is her . . . fledgling? Do you know what
that means?'

I shrug. 'I dunno. It's one of those weird British boarding-
school things.'

'You're telling me,' mutters DC Copeland. He seems
annoyed. I wonder if it's because he's been played by Clover
once before.

I clear my throat. *Be strong, for Clover.* I need the police
to take the situation seriously – even if I can't say anything
about the blood, I can still try and help without breaking
my promise to Ivy. 'It basically means that Ivy is, like, her
mentor. She's on track to becoming a prefect, like Ivy is.
Maybe even head girl. Clover is super smart.'

Detective Shing writes down what I'm saying, even
though it's being recorded. 'Back to the night of the party.
Please continue.'

'Oh right. Well, we got dressed and it was kind of a
madhouse. There were people coming in and out.'

'Can you go back even further? What did you do during
the day?'

The question takes me by surprise. 'Oh.' I can't tell them about the Magpie Society – Ivy made that much clear. 'It was kind of a normal day, I guess. Woke up and had breakfast down in the canteen. Did some reading that I was supposed to catch up on over the break but didn't do . . . Then I went looking for Ivy to see if she wanted to borrow a dress of mine. She was in one of the music rooms, rehearsing. Then we went back upstairs to get ready. After getting dressed, doing our make-up, all that stuff, we joined the party and –'

'Back up one second, Miss Wagner. Did anyone see you during that time? Anyone who can corroborate. A teacher maybe?' asks DC Copeland.

I pause, biting down on my lip. My eyes dart to the female police officer, who nods at me encouragingly. I can't lie to them. I'm already omitting so much. This would be a step too far – especially as they've probably spoken to the teacher in question already. 'We saw Mr Willis. He's our history teacher, but I think he oversees the musical-theatre productions of the school too? So he was down in the music rooms when I found Ivy.'

'That matches up with what we heard.'

'If you knew already, why d'you ask me?'

'We're not trying to catch you out, Miss Wagner,' said DI Shing. 'We just want to make sure we get all the facts.'

It feels a lot like they *do* wanna catch me out. But I take a deep breath and continue. 'Like I said, we got ready for the party and then went down to listen to Araminta's speech – then there was this magpie flash mob – and then it was all kinda crazy, and a mirror almost fell on Ivy. It was all really shocking.'

'I can imagine,' says DI Shing.

'A notification popped up that Clover had released another podcast . . .'

'Oh yes, we've listened to it now.'

'Ivy was obviously concerned about Clover after hearing that, so we ran to her room – and that's when we realized she was missing.'

'Why didn't you think she was just at the party?'

I swallow, my mouth dry. I take a sip of water, but it doesn't help. I hate all this lying by omission. It makes my pulse race in my chest, and I feel like my skin is paper-thin, the detectives seeing right through me. 'I think Ivy and Clover's room-mates will be able to tell you more, but basically Clover didn't wanna go to the party. She was tired. And plus, you guys heard the podcast . . .'

They react to that, scribbling in their notebooks. I swallow, wondering what it was I said that set off their alarm bells. I hope my story is matching up with Ivy's. 'And, if she released the podcast, that means that she wasn't downstairs with us. Plus, there was the fact that –' *don't mention the blood, don't mention the blood* – 'it looked like there had been a struggle in her room. You know the rest. Ivy called you guys, we got Teddy to alert Mrs Abbott, and she directed us to meet with you. And now we're here.'

I breathe out, glad to have finished the story without revealing anything about the Magpie Society, the voice recording or the blood.

'I know we asked last night, but maybe you were in shock. Did you touch anything while you were in Clover's room? Move things? Maybe look for something?'

'No, not that I can remember . . .'

'Seriously? Nothing? Not even moved something out of your way to search the room?'

'Not that I know of. I mean, I think I sat down on her bed at some point – while Ivy was cleaning up the blood she'd dripped on the floor,' I add quickly, remembering Ivy's story from last night. 'But . . . why? What's this all about? Have you found out anything more?'

'When someone is taken, rather than just running away, they don't normally have time to grab their personal items. Because Clover's phone is missing, we presume she took that with her. It's all adding up as if maybe she wasn't taken at all and has just gone off on a jaunt somewhere.'

I swallow. I think of the phone on the floor. I'm sure that Ivy didn't take it. *I* certainly didn't. Looks like that was something else that the mystery cleaner tided up. 'If that was the case, then someone would have heard from her by now, right?'

DI Shing pivots in her seat, catching me off guard. 'Can I ask you why you're attending Illumen Hall, Miss Wagner? A bit far from home, aren't you?'

'What are you talking about? I only live a few miles down the road.'

'Forgive me, but you don't *sound* like you have a Kentish accent.'

'Oh right. Well, my parents moved from the States this summer and I came with them. Is that such a surprise?'

'Is that the only reason?'

I don't answer.

'We've done a little background checking and were curious to read about a news story featuring you and your family.'

I fold my arms across my chest, colour rising in my cheeks. Memories of being interrogated by the cops back home flood my senses. If they don't back off, I'm in danger of breaking down. 'I don't really see what that's gotta do with anything . . .'

'One teenage girl is dead in your home town, then you show up and another teenager girl goes missing.'

'I don't like what you're implying. Also, maybe you should be thinking more about what's going on in your own backyard. Especially as this whole thing started before I moved to this country, before I even knew about this damn place and Lola Radcliffe. *That's* a name you seem to have forgotten real quick. So you need to find Clover. Don't let her down. Don't let us down.'

Even the female police officer's gaze is steely. They're trying to make me squirm, I can tell.

But I can be determined too. 'Is there anything else you want from me? Or can I go?'

There are a few beats of silence. 'You can go. Our interview is over. For now.'

I stand, desperate to get outta there.

Detective Copeland stands too. 'Just so you know . . . maybe Lola did die before you knew about this "damn place". But your father – he's been here many times. We'll be looking into that too.'

I leave the room before he can see the colour drain from my face.

# 7

## AUDREY

After the police interview, I walk in a daze to the fountain outside, where Ivy had instructed me to meet her. She's already sitting there next to Lyra with Yolanda on the bench opposite. To my surprise, Harriet's there too.

'How did it go?' Ivy asks me before I can question this.

'It was pretty intense. I really hate that Copeland guy.'

'Me too,' says Lyra. 'He was so mean. Tried to make me say that Clover loved to run away.'

'Don't let him get to you,' says Ivy. 'If they're back, then they're taking Clover's disappearance seriously. I just wish they'd tell us why they've changed their minds and what clues they have. They didn't let on to you?'

'No,' I say, though a shiver runs down my spine. They might not have revealed anything to me about Clover, but they did about my dad. I didn't know he'd been to the school before – although, in a way, it makes sense. He wouldn't have moved us to a new country without doing a few recces first. *That's all it is.* I start thinking of how Ivy and I caught Mrs Abbott driving to my house –

I realize everyone is staring at me. I cough. 'So let me get this straight . . . We all received letters inviting us to the Magpie Society?' I ask.

'The only ones to admit to it so far, yeah,' says Harriet. So that's why she's here. *She got one too.*

'Anyone else in Polaris House?' Ivy looks at the two girls.

'Not that we've heard.'

'I mean it's not like we'll all go around shouting, "Hey, did you get that invitation to the secret society yesterday?"'

'I guess so. I'll ask some of my mates, see if any of them received anything out of the ordinary. But for now this has to stay between us.'

'What are we going to reply?'

'I'm joining,' says Lyra. Her face is flushed with determination. 'If the society has any clues as to where Clover is, I want to know.'

'What if they're the ones who *took* Clover?' I blurt out. Ivy shoots me a look. I know it's a long shot. Everything we know about the Magpie Society points to them as a group who want to protect the school and its students – not rile them up.

But what if it was a *student* who was threatening the school? Would they prioritize the safety of a fellow student? Or the preservation of Illumen Hall, the place they know and love?

'Let's make a pact,' says Ivy. 'Either we all join ... or none of us do. But I'm with you, Lyra. I think we should.'

'I'm in,' says Harriet.

Yolanda chews her lip. But, after the ordeal of being interrogated by the police, she seems reluctant to be left out in the cold. I can't blame her. She nods. I don't need to say anything – Ivy knows, whatever she decides to do, that I'm with her.

She digs in her bag, pulling out a pen. 'Let's sign now, while we're all agreed.'

She scribbles her signature on the letter, and the others follow suit on their own letters. I'm last – but it's not like signing our names is magic or something.

'So what next?' I ask. 'Where are we supposed to leave the letters? Were there any instructions about that?'

'We can't put them anywhere out in the open, where a teacher or the police might see. I think we should put them in our internal pigeonholes. If someone picks them up, then we'll know. Agreed?'

One by one, we all nod. I'm grateful for Ivy's leadership, even if I'm feeling anxious.

Just because something is old and established doesn't mean that you can trust it. I've learned that the hard way.

'Let's set up a group chat,' Ivy says to Lyra, bringing out her phone. 'That way you guys can let us know if you find anything or receive any more instructions.'

'Yeah, OK,' says Lyra, taking her phone out too. She looks up in awe at Ivy, and it makes me smile. It's amazing seeing the Ivy Effect in action. Because of Araminta's bitterness towards Ivy, I feel like I've gotten a skewed perspective of what things are like for my friend at school. But she's obviously really well liked and respected – you can see that in the faces of the girls as they look at her. And why not? Ivy has everything going for her. I've witnessed it first hand. She's smart and talented – being in her orbit is like bathing in her glow – and you hope that some of those smarts, some of that talent, will wash off on you.

'Shit,' says Harriet. 'I'm late for art. Mr Yarrow is going to have my head if I don't get back in time. Literally. I papier-mâchéd it the other day, and if I don't finish he's going to throw it in the bin. Someone better text me if anything happens with this Magpie Society thing.' She throws a sideways glance at Ivy. 'I'll see you later.'

'See you.'

Lyra looks up, her hand flying to her mouth. 'Oh my God.'

'What is it?' I ask.

'That policewoman is coming over.'

Ivy puts a reassuring hand on her shoulder. 'We'll talk to the police. You two go on. I'm pretty sure I saw that Ms Cranshaw had fresh cinnamon rolls baking. Tell her I sent you.'

Lyra looks relieved. 'Thanks, Ivy.' She and Yolanda run off down towards the kitchen without a backward glance.

A few moments later, DI Shing reaches us. 'Anything else you want to share with me before we head off?'

Both Ivy and I shake our heads. She sighs. 'That's a shame. Our interviews haven't revealed anything to make us think this is a suspicious case. I'm afraid if we don't get a lead soon my colleagues are going to think that this matter is over. They'll deprioritize it.'

'No, you can't!' I say. But Ivy is much calmer.

'You say your colleagues think the case is over. But *you* don't?'

DI Shing's eyebrow quirks and a smile plays on her lips.

'No, I don't. Because, unlike my colleagues, when I hear that a whole group of teenage girls are all saying the same thing – that their missing friend is truly in danger – I listen. I don't think you're making anything up. I believe *you* believe what you're saying is true. So, here.' She reaches into her pocket and pulls out some business cards. 'I know this might be a bit old-school in the age of social media, but take my card. If you think anything is relevant – big or small – you can come to me. And I promise that I'll listen.'

I take one, and so does Ivy. 'Thank you,' I say.

'You girls stay safe now.'

We watch as DI Shing climbs into the passenger seat of her car. I think I see her partner roll his eyes at her before they drive away. Once the cops are gone, it feels like the whole school heaves a sigh of relief. Everyone except Ivy and me. We're still wound up so tightly we're close to breaking point.

'What are we going to do now?' asks Ivy.

'I've been wondering something. I really should go see Patrick. Give him Lola's diary, like we promised.' I think of Lola's brother waiting anxiously for news.

'That's a good idea. He was working with Clover. Maybe she said something to him that will give us a clue as to where she really is.'

'I like the way you think, Ivy. I'll go this weekend. We'll see what Patrick Radcliffe has to say.'

'Good plan. I'd better shoot off . . . I really need to go for a run.'

'Wait, Ivy – can I ask you something? Why do you think Harriet got an invite?'

Ivy's voice drops down to a whisper. 'I think Harriet might have more to do with this than we know.'

'Seriously?'

'I know she comes off like a bit of a scatterbrain, but I've known her for a long time. She was really cut up after what happened to Lola.'

'Was she a good friend of Lola's too?'

'Sort of. But she has another secret to do with Lola's death. I swore that I wouldn't say anything, so you'll just have to trust me on this. She's terrified of the police. Maybe that's why the Magpie Society chose her. Because Harriet is more wrapped up in Lola's death than any of us.'

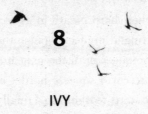

# 8

## IVY

I keep my promises, especially ones I make to my best friends. I don't reveal to Audrey what I know about Harriet. That's going to stay between her and me. I know better than anyone that she didn't *really* have anything to do with Lola's death, but the police might not see it that way if they knew.

For the next few days, all anyone can talk about is Clover's disappearance. The longer she's missing, the more worried we all become.

I hope she isn't in serious trouble. In her last podcast, she revealed she hadn't been able to identify Lola's murderer. Maybe she's just laying low for a while until the dust settles. If there really is someone dangerous operating at the school . . . then I hope they haven't found her.

The Magpie Society have gone quiet too and it's so unnerving. The invitations are still sitting in our pigeonholes. I hate waiting, feeling as though these things are completely out of my control. There's a tightness in my chest and I take a huge breath in. The corridor I'm in seems smaller than usual and students start filing down the stairs in the direction of their lessons. There's a large floor-length mirror on the opposite wall and, as students hurry past it, I imagine it falling and crashing like the mirror on the night of the Samhain party.

I take another sharp breath in as anxiety rises through my body, starting at my feet. I pinch the skin between my thumb and forefinger until the pain brings me somewhat back to the present. I squeeze harder and clench my jaw until the panic starts to diminish. I finally feel like I'm more in control of my body and start walking.

As I head to English, I notice a group of Year Nines staring at me, all raising their eyebrows and whispering. Did they notice my panic? Or is it because Audrey and I were the ones who discovered that Clover had gone missing? Either way, I curtsey as I pass them, smiling sweetly. Give them something to throw them off. They quickly disperse in embarrassment.

Ordinarily, I'd walk with Harriet between classes, but she had to visit the school nurse for an emergency tampon. Nothing about this surprises me as Harriet is one of the most unorganized, scatty people I know.

Harriet and I really are complete opposites and yet it works. As I turn a corner in the English block, I wind up face to face with Mr Willis who's walking in the opposite direction. It takes me so much by surprise that I halt and my entire body goes rigid.

It's as if he's still working here like nothing happened!

Audrey and I thought we saw him last night and this confirms it. He dodges me and tries to walk past. I thrust my foot out in front of his.

'You won't fly under the radar forever, you know. We haven't forgotten what you did.' I say it quietly, but loud enough for him to hear. He looks me square in the eyes and smiles. He's way too confident.

'I hope you're ready for your Christmas concert performance,' he says. 'Wouldn't want you to throw your entire future away.'

'I have no idea what you're talking about.'

'Oh no? So I take it you've stopped looking into that secret society then . . .'

My heart drops. How does he know about the Magpie Society?

'I'm late for class,' I say, pushing past him.

What an absolute tosser. Goosebumps rise all over my body as I think of the photo of him and Lola, and of her diary and her dark words. The despairing poems she wrote and the heartbreak on every page. *He* made her feel that way. He preyed on her, broke her, and yet here he is, still teaching kids and relishing a good career. Living and breathing each day, smiling and going about his business like nothing happened.

*It's my fault*, I think, but I push that voice down. I gave him the benefit of the doubt. He convinced me that he was going to leave. He is a master manipulator after all. Juggling Lola and his fiancée. Lola was no dummy and yet she fell for him.

I reach the door of Mr Bower's classroom where Harriet's waiting for me. We take a seat next to one another near the back of the room. It's clear the Clover buzz has spread – I suppose it's not every day the police show up at the school. I try and shake off my abrupt interaction with Mr Willis, but it's all I can think about.

'Do you think people will ever stop talking about this? First Lola, now Clover!' Harriet says as she rolls her eyes and takes her books out of her bag. 'This school is terrible for rumours, isn't it? Have you heard some of the crazy stories people have come up with?'

'Let's not pretend you don't revel in a bit of goss, Harriet!' I say with a grin.

'True. And I guess none of it's as wild as the real thing. Imagine if all these jokers knew about the Magpie Society? They'd be tearing apart the walls looking for it.' She laughs as Mr Bower claps his hands to disperse the chatter.

'Enough. Save your chit-chat for lunchtime, please, or at least talk about school-appropriate things like the Christmas concert, your mock exams . . . or your university personal statements. For now, though, open your textbooks to page one hundred and fifty and read that entire chapter to yourselves.'

I make a start on the reading but my mind wanders and, no matter how hard I try to focus on the words in front of me, nothing is making sense. I reread one sentence three times, but it doesn't sink in. My mind keeps returning to the Magpie Society and the letters.

'I can't believe the police are back,' says Harriet. She sounds subdued – so that's what's really troubling her.

I squeeze her hand. 'Don't worry. Your secret's safe with me.'

'What if they start digging again?'

'They won't. They have no reason to.'

'I guess so. And what will you do about the Christmas concert now Clover isn't . . . here?' Harriet whispers without taking her eyes off her textbook. Clearly she's not concentrating either. I sigh. Clover and I had a show-stopping piano duet that we'd been rehearsing together for the concert. Do I just turn it into a solo piece now? Do I wait and see if she comes back?

'Honestly? No idea!' I whisper back. Mr Bower catches me and frowns.

I bury my head back into the textbook, which may as well be written in Morse code. I scan the words and flip the page when Harriet does. She's doodling in the margins again. I feel my heart sink. *Where could Clover be?* I can't leave all the investigating to the police; I don't trust them. They'll just pigeonhole this as a teen girl running away. *No foul play.* Idiots. Clover could be in serious danger. I realize I've not blinked in ages. I rub my eyes and turn the page again.

A memory from last year hits me. Lola and I were walking back from town, fish and chips encased in greasy paper in our hands. I can almost smell the salt and vinegar now. The little wooden fork piercing the limp chips as we walked along eating, while Lola told me about a date she'd been on. How wrong it had gone, something to do with smoking weed and being caught ... I just remember watching her speak, occasionally biting down on an empty fork while she smiled, admiring how effortlessly beautiful she was and the radiance she projected. Her storytelling was so entrancing, you almost felt yourself there with her – and then realized jealously that you weren't. That your days never compared or even came close to her rich and exciting life.

She would go home at the weekends and do the craziest

things. Monday mornings in the common room became a cacophony of 'what did Lola do this weekend?' and she'd have everyone surrounding her as she spoke, mouths open, slapping their thighs and laughing. Those rare moments when only *I* got a story – well, those were special. I was always very envious of how quickly Lola made friends, and not the sort of 'on the surface' acquaintances, but head-over-heels deep friendships. People would do anything to be part of her circle. She had everything. She *was* everything.

Life was like that for her everywhere. Not just at Illumen Hall.

Whereas for me, once I left the safety of these walls . . .

Mr Bower's voice bellows and I'm back in the English lesson. A lump rises in my throat and I clench my jaw to stop a tear from falling. I want more than ever to slip on my shabby trainers and disappear into the countryside.

Running is my way of escaping my mind when it gets too much. It brings me back to the present. All I think about in that moment is the pounding of my feet on the ground and the sound of the blood pumping round my body. I want to run as fast as I possibly can across the school grounds, into the woods, past the old abandoned church on the cliffs. Letting the cold air sting the back of my nose and fill my lungs. I close my eyes to imagine it. My special place.

'Ivy?' Harriet thumps my arm. 'Are you going to share how you manage to astral-project yourself out of lessons so I can at least join you?" she whispers, laughing.

'Sorry, I guess I'm just not really with it today,' I say, as I smile back.

'As long as you're OK?'

'Yeah, I'm fine. Just a lot going on right now, isn't there?'

She nods and rubs my arm sympathetically.

'Girls, am I going to have to separate you so you actually get some work done?' Mr Bower shouts, making us both jump in our seats.

'Sorry, sir,' I mumble.

Harriet passes me a mint under the table, wrapped in a little doodle of Mr Bower yelling at us, looking like an angry Rottweiler. It makes me snigger. At least I know she has my back.

Like I have hers.

Always.

## 9

## AUDREY

Seagulls squawk overhead, their cries breaching the music blasting through my headphones. I stop in front of the intricate iron railing, running my finger over a patch of peeling paint, picking at it as I lean out and watch the sea. It's that roiling, murky blue-grey that seems to be constant over here. It never gets crystal clear, like it does in Georgia. The beach here is made up of hundreds of thousands of stones, uncomfortable and tumbling underfoot. I miss the golden sand, the soft, swaying grasses of back home. It's about the only thing I miss.

Not too many people are braving the beach this weekend. It's too cold, too wet and windy. Smart people are huddled up inside the coffee shops, or ducking into the cute antique stores on the high street. The thin overcoat I'm wearing isn't enough to keep my sweater from slowly being drenched with water. My jeans stiffen against my body. The strength of the wind has blown my umbrella inside out, so that's not much help either. I'm gonna look like a drowned rat by the time I show up at Patrick's. But there's nothing that can be done about it now. I decide to lean into the look.

My phone map indicates that his building is only a few

feet away, a little back from the seafront. It's one of those massive, tall-windowed buildings I've come to recognize as a hallmark of the British seaside. They look regal, steeped in history. Everything about this part of the world, this 'ancient Kent', reminds me how much history is buried here.

And, where there's history to be buried, there are normally stories too. Legends. Myths. I bet Winferne Bay has seen a fair few.

I can't put off my visit much longer – and besides I'm really starting to get drenched – so I run across the road. I hope that Lola's diary hasn't gotten waterlogged, although I had wrapped it up in a plastic bag before sticking it in my handbag.

I press the buzzer for Flat C on the top floor and, after a few moments, the door clicks open. There's no sound or camera that I can see, but I guess Patrick is expecting me. I'm only a few minutes late.

The hallway of the building is elaborately tiled in a black-and-white mosaic, and a spiral staircase circles up around a metal grid elevator. Patrick told me specifically to take the lift, but this one looks like it's been operational since the dawn of time. I'd hate to get stuck in there. I don't wanna take the risk.

Instead, I climb the stairs. There's a round, domed window above me, allowing soft, filtered light to pour in against the sandstone walls. It's beautiful. Peaceful.

Patrick is waiting for me at the door. 'I assumed when I didn't hear the lift running that you'd be taking the stairs. Didn't fancy it?'

He grins at me, and I'm struck once again by how fucking hot he is. If Lydia, my best friend from Georgia, had been here, she would be seriously swooning, especially now he's out of his suits. Well-fitted jeans and a sky-blue knit sweater with a pop of white collar works for him. I find myself regretting the drowned-rat look just a bit.

'It seemed a bit sketchy to me. I don't trust technology that was made before I was born.'

'I guess that's fair. But you missed the fact that it opens out into my flat. I mean, that's one of its most redeeming features. I'd give you a tour, but it's not that interesting. Your standard two-bed.'

I peer in through the front door. 'Doesn't look standard to me.'

He chuckles. 'Come on in. Can I offer you something? Tea? No, what am I talking about – you're American. Coffee?'

'Coffee would be great, thanks.'

He walks in, leaving me to unwind my scarf and hang my coat up on a hook just inside his front door. For some reason, I find myself moving extra slowly. The flat is bright and airy, but curiously soulless. From what I can see, there aren't any personal pictures or paintings on the walls, and everything is painted a bland shade of magnolia. But then I guess that isn't a surprise. He did say this place was temporary.

But, as I move further inside, I find myself asking: *Why?* It's freakin' gorgeous. The hallway opens up to a huge open-plan living room and kitchen, with a wall of windows looking out to sea. Each window has a little nook with a cushioned seat.

'Wow, this place is amazing,' I say.

'It's not bad. Does the job.'

'I could stare out at that view every day and never get bored. Even today – it's miserable outside, but it looks sort of . . . magical from in here, in the warm.'

Speaking of warm, I move towards the open fireplace in the middle of the room. It's one of those achingly modern ones that can be seen from all sides, and I stand beside it to dry off. The flames lick up at my clothes, fierce in their heat, and I take a step back. I twist my hair so that it's not such a mess.

'It's all well and good until night falls on a Thursday and you get drunken stag dos singing "Mr Brightside" at the top of their lungs – or on Saturday afternoons when gangs of teens are filming TikToks right below the window . . .'

'Oh, it can't be all that bad.'

'No, I suppose not. But I don't see the sea as a good place. After all, it took Lola.'

I swallow. I'd forgotten about that. 'Why would you wanna look out at it every day then?'

'It's a reminder,' he says. 'A reminder of why I'm here. What I'm trying to achieve. Justice for my sister.' He pauses. 'Besides, I only have the rest of this year.'

'What do you mean?'

'Oh . . . my parents want me to go back to uni. I guess I can't really blame them. They don't want Lola's death to derail my entire life. And I don't want that either. But I can't give up yet. Not when I feel so close.'

He looks fierce, standing at his kitchen island, his fist clenched around the handle of his coffee mug. I know his anger is there to hold back the tidal wave of grief that's going to follow – he's using his fight for justice to push the sadness down, delay those emotions until he's ready to deal. I can understand that. I went through the same thing.

'Did you hear about what happened at school the other night?' I watch his face for a reaction, but there isn't one.

'What, the Samhain party? It happens every year. It was one of Lola's favourite nights. She would have done an amazing job of hosting it. You know, the year that Kara and I hosted, we bought up all the fireworks in town and set them off throughout the evening. So you never knew when it was going to happen, then *bam!* Firework display. It was pretty epic.'

'Sounds like it.' I bite my lip, frustrated that I can't get out the words. 'But no, that's not –'

'That's what Illumen Hall should be about. But it's lost its way. It's not the school I used to know any more. Not that that matters to me now.'

'The party isn't what I wanted to tell you about,' I snap.

He raises an eyebrow at my tone. 'What is it then?'

I take a deep breath. 'It's Clover. She's missing. She might have been taken. The police have come to school to interview us and everything.'

'Oh, that. I did hear something about it.' Now he busies himself with the coffee, taking out a fancy milk machine and making up a cappuccino for me. It's then that he looks younger than I previously thought. But of course – he's only at college still. He's just a few years older than me, the same age as my oldest brother.

'I *know* you know her. You've been helping her out

with the podcast. It was you all along. We found the headphones that you sent her. Have you heard anything from her since the night of the party?'

'Whoa – is this some kind of interrogation? The police have already been here. They found the headphones in her room too.'

'They did? Why didn't you say?'

'I wanted to see what you were going to say first.'

I fold my arms across my chest.

'What, you don't believe me? Here.' He fishes around in his pocket and pulls out a small rectangle that I recognize – DI Shing's card. 'She and the grumpy bloke who headed up Lola's investigation came here. But I'm glad they're looking into Clover's disappearance. At least now the culprit knows there are eyes on them. People are watching. And we're not going to forget about what happened to Lola.'

'Aren't you worried about Clover?'

'Are you kidding? I'm very worried. I'm worried for all of you! Clover got so close to the truth. All she needed was a bit more time to investigate. There's someone dangerous at the school and she knows it.'

I teeter on the edge of telling him what we found out about Mr Willis, but I don't. We have no evidence – especially since Ivy burned the photograph.

'Anyway, you didn't come all the way down here to tell me about Clover. You said in your text that you'd found something?'

'Yeah. I finally looked in the room that you told me about. It turns out you were right. Lola had hidden something behind a panel in the wall. This.'

I bring out the diary, placing it reverentially down on the counter between us. Patrick slides it closer, taking it out of the plastic. He cracks the spine, taking a breath when he recognizes Lola's looped handwriting. His eyes flick up to me. 'Have you read it?'

I cringe. 'Some of it. Ivy and I looked through it to see if she'd left any clues as to what happened to her. Although she was in a bad headspace, we don't think that she killed herself. We believe *you*. We think someone murdered her.'

Patrick's blue eyes cloud over. 'Does she mention any names?'

'No. She'd definitely been seeing someone, but only used a nickname: *Goofo*. Didn't really give us much to go on.'

'That's frustrating. But it's something. Thank you. Thank you for this.' He stares at the diary intensely. The look sends a shiver down my spine, and suddenly I'm on edge.

'I think I'd better go,' I say.

'But wait – you didn't even have your coffee!'

'I know. But the bus leaves soon . . .'

'Before you go – one more thing. I know I've asked a lot of you already. But there's something else – and, now you've given me this journal, I feel like I can trust you properly.'

'You didn't before?'

He leans in. 'You have no idea. Every time it feels like Clover and I get close to the truth, we're thwarted. It's as if . . . someone knows our every move, before we're going to make it. Maybe you can help us get ahead for once.'

'What do you mean?'

'It's about the Magpie Society. Remember how I asked you to look into them?'

I almost laugh. The Magpie Society occupies way too much of my brain space. But I keep my face straight for Patrick. I wanna know what he's after.

'We need to find a list of people who've been part of it. See if any of them are still alive today.'

'Right . . . and how am I supposed to do that?'

'Clover thinks there are hidden rooms in the school somewhere. She was trying to find them, but a lot of the passageways are blocked off. Just . . . don't tell anyone you're looking for it. And I mean *anyone*.'

'Well, I'm obviously gonna tell Ivy.'

'No!'

'Why not?'

'I trust you because you're new to the school. You're one of the few people who couldn't possibly be a suspect! You were a thousand miles away when she died.'

I cross my arms. 'Ivy was one of Lola's closest friends, and now she's mine. I can't keep things from her. I mean, we live together.'

Patrick sighs. 'OK. Fine. You and Ivy can know. But don't tell anyone else – especially not any teachers.'

'Oh, don't worry. We don't trust them. I have my eye on everyone.'

'Text me the moment you find anything.'

'I will. But a secret room in the school is pretty vague. If I don't find it . . . don't be mad.' I get to my feet. 'I'll let myself out.'

'Sure, sure.' He stares at the diary again, caressing it gently.

I run down the stairs, taking them two at a time. I don't know what spooked me – but I think it was sitting with Patrick and his grief. It's almost overwhelming. But why didn't he seem more concerned about Clover?

When I'm back down on the beach, I look up at the building. I see the window where a shadow of Patrick appears. He moves across the living room, through one of the doors at the far end. He pauses. I wonder what he's doing. Is he calling someone? Reading the diary?

But then a curtain twitches a few windows across – and I think I see the brief flash of a face. But it can't be – can it?

I look again and catch my breath.

*Clover*.

Before I can think, I run back to the apartment block, pressing the buzzer for Flat C again and again. I stand back, waiting for an answer. Patrick doesn't let me in.

I fumble for my phone, but when I dial his number it goes straight to voicemail. 'Patrick? Hi, it's Audrey. I think I forgot my notebook in your apartment. Can you let me up again to grab it?'

I pace in the doorway, feeling like a fool, praying for someone to come out of the building so I can sneak inside, like in the movies. But no one goes in or out. My heart is racing inside my chest. The longer he ignores me, the more certain I am that he's hiding something. I just didn't think it was such a big thing: our missing student.

I take a few steps back and look up at the window. The curtains are deathly still.

*

I hang around for almost half an hour, waiting to spot some evidence of life inside the flat, occasionally buzzing the front door, willing him to let me up. I feel like I've lost my mind. Do I really think Clover is inside the apartment? Maybe my imagination's getting the better of me.

I'm finally about to give up when the hood of a car pulls out of a concealed underground lot, the other side of the building. Instinctively, I hide, ducking behind a low stone wall. I lift my head just enough to try and peer into the window as the car – a brand-new-looking Tesla, sleek and low to the ground – races by without a sound. Patrick is driving. And there's no mistaking it.

Clover is in the passenger seat.

# 10

## IVY

'Hey!' I pick up the phone to answer Audrey. 'Hang on a sec – I have to get out of here. The signal's really bad.'

Down in the music room, the thick walls allow me to practise as much as I want – but don't let me hear my phone very well. I was finished anyway, and soon I'll have to make my way up to the assembly hall for an emergency first rehearsal called by Araminta. She's really been on my back lately.

In the corridor, I almost have to hold the phone away from my ear, Audrey's screeching so much.

'Calm down!' I say to her. 'I can barely understand you.'

There's a pause as she tries to collect herself. 'It's Clover. I found her. She's at Patrick's.'

'*What?* She's at Patrick Radcliffe's apartment?'

'I saw her at the window and in his car,' Audrey says. 'It looked like she was there voluntarily – not held against her will or anything. What should I do? Shall I call the police and tell them?'

'Come back to school. I'll text Clover and tell her we know where she is. Maybe she's still on the trail of Lola's killer and, if we warn the police now, they might stop her. We can come up with a plan together.'

'OK, shit – I can't think straight!'

'Just get back here.'

'Will do.'

I hang up, leaning my head against the wall. Clover's safe. She's alive. But why was she with Patrick Radcliffe?

There's a clattering of papers on the ground behind me. I spin round and see Mr Willis scrambling on the floor, collecting up fallen sheaves of sheet music. I catch his eye, wondering just how much of the conversation he might have heard. I press a few buttons on my phone.

He coughs. 'Have you picked the new piece for your concert performance yet? I really need to review it so I can fit it into the schedule.'

'I haven't exactly had much time to think about it, *sir*. And, besides, what's to say Clover won't come back in time for the concert? I mean, that's what we're all hoping, isn't it?'

'Sounds like you know more than me.'

'What's that supposed to mean?' I shoot back.

He sighs. 'Nothing. Look, Ivy, I was in a panic when I said to you before that I was leaving. You've got the wrong end of the stick. I had nothing to do with Lola, and absolutely nothing to do with her death. So let's just drop this whole thing, don't you think?' He starts to move like he's ending the conversation, but I'm not finished.

'What about the photograph, huh?' I cross my arms, my frustration growing.

'I don't know what you think you saw, but it wasn't Lola in that photograph.'

'Oh really? Who was it then?'

'My fiancée, of course. So let's try and get things back to

normal . . .' He takes a step towards me, and I skitter back, holding my hands up.

'Don't come any closer. When Clover gets back, you know it's going to be the end for you.' I almost spit the words I'm so angry.

His voice turns dark. 'I think we both know that Clover isn't going to be coming back.' He stalks away, pushing through the soundproof doors and up the stairwell to the assembly room.

I shudder and look down at my phone. I end the recording. That last thing Mr Willis said about Clover? That sounded like a threat.

*

Up in the assembly room, my mind is a whirlwind. I'm desperate to send Clover a message to convince her to tell us what she's up to. Part of me doubts Audrey really saw her – but she seemed adamant.

It's been a week now since Clover went missing. As usual, school life manages to carry on as though nothing has happened, so much sooner than is socially acceptable. The whispers and incessant chatter in common rooms and corridors have already slowed and gossip has moved on to new topics. After Lola's death, it really struck me how so many people can seem to be so affected, mourning and moping in assemblies and crying on each other's shoulders in lessons, and yet the next thing you know they're back to only caring about the same shallow, meaningless shit as before. The human race really can be that fickle.

It can't just be me and Audrey that care enough about these bizarre circumstances to want the truth. I often wonder if my fellow students would be so relaxed sleeping in this school if they knew what we did. If they were aware that there could be a murderer on school grounds.

The grand assembly room is an old-style theatre, with thick red velvet curtains and tiered seating – there's even a couple of box seats for VIP guests.

The place is empty, for the moment, with the exception of the performers, who are all gathered round the front of the stage. Mr Willis hasn't waited for me to arrive before addressing everyone. The sight of him makes my skin crawl. I feel sick when I think that I used to stay extra late, donating my time and expertise to other students to spend a few more hours with him.

Not any more.

I slip into a seat near the back, trying to remain as much in the shadows as possible. I should be watching *Lola*, not Araminta, give a rousing speech. My mind should be preoccupied with the notes I've got to play, not puzzling over a myriad of different mysteries. I remember when I used to admire Mr Willis, even crush on him a bit. The thought makes me shudder – now I just feel rage and disgust towards him.

I also feel anger rise when I watch Araminta. There are only about fifteen performers here, but Araminta is making sure to assert her authority over everyone and take charge – green juice in hand, of course. She rants about her green juice and the fact it tastes like sewage, but she's still going to drink it because it's so expensive.

The Christmas concert is one of Illumen Hall's most

prestigious and longest-running traditions. It's the biggest event of the year and the audience is always packed with parents and family members. The school choir is one of the most esteemed in the south of England, and I have to admit it's an incredible thing to hear them belt out 'Carol of the Bells'.

Some of the stories to come out of these evenings are legendary. Not only do the relatives of the students gather for the evening, but talent scouts, music producers, composers and musicians also come along. Many students have been singled out after the concert and offered some incredible opportunities for university funding, apprenticeships and even jobs. I might be noticed by some big-time producer; this could be *my* year. I've worked so hard on the piano and, without Clover, this will be my first solo piece. I just have to decide what it will be.

The founders of the school fund the evening and they put on a champagne reception that lasts until 2 a.m., along with canapés, and grazing boards so big you could play football on them. Most students don't have the privilege of joining in – only the prefects and head students. It's more a chance for the wealthy to mingle and one-up each other on the rich scale.

Araminta is supposed to be doing a big number – as is the tradition for a head girl – but, of course, she's kept the details a secret so far. I can see her glance over at me. She wants something, I can tell. I wonder if she's dying to ask for an update about Clover. She hates that she wasn't interviewed by the police, even though it was a ball-ache for those of us who *were*. She just has to be in the middle of any drama.

'OK, everyone, up onstage and prepare your instruments!' Mr Willis shouts out. I move to the piano. Sitting on the little bench, everyone else polishing their instruments and changing their reeds, the nerves start to build. When it comes to playing the piano, I very rarely get nervous. It feels like a second way of breathing to me, as if I'm so calm and connected to the keys that I almost melt into them. Now, though, I just want to melt into the ground.

'So, as you all know, I've decided that this rehearsal is going to be dedicated to my big solo number!' Araminta calls out to everyone.

'I thought we were here to practise our own pieces?' I say back.

'Well, seeing as you haven't even chosen yours, I thought you'd be happy,' she shoots at me. She turns back to the rest of the group. 'I don't have long so would appreciate us all coming together to do this! I've prepared the appropriate music sheet for your instrument and it's going to be *so* epic! Think proper orchestral bonanza.' She swallows the last of her juice and dabs her top lip with a tissue.

I look round at the other students, expecting someone else to say they weren't here for this. None of them do. They're all much younger than Araminta – and terrified.

'Minty, none of us have ever played together before. Don't you think singing to a backing track might be better with so little time until the concert?' I try again.

'A backing track for the Christmas concert? Are you crazy, Ivy? Why would I ever do that? I'd be booed off the stage.' She scoffs and folds her arms as Bonnie passes out the music.

The other students lay the sheets out on their stands and get ready to practise. I snatch my part out of Bonnie's hands and look down at it. It's 'Think of Me' from *Phantom of the Opera*.

'Big song,' I say, raising my eyebrows at her.

'You don't think I can sing it?' Her tone changes, and she strides towards me. 'Because I can. I can sing it and I'm amazing at it. If you'd like to start tapping away at the keys in front of you, you'll see for yourself.'

I hear a couple of sniggers from a few students behind her.

'I've no doubt about it. The only problem I have is you and your typical bullying way of asking me to be the piano lead in your musical performance.'

'I'm doing you a favour,' she snaps. 'I could have picked someone else, but I thought – no, I'm going to ask Ivy.'

'Well, how lovely of you.' I sigh as I arrange the sheet music on the piano.

She walks even closer and leans into me.

'Do not mess this up for me, Ivy. I'm trusting you. Just play the damn music.'

'Believe me, I have bigger things to worry about than fucking up your "big band moment", Araminta. Some of us are actually concerned about everything going on around here, not just ourselves and the Christmas performance.' I roll my eyes.

She smiles tightly and walks back to the front.

'OK, on one . . . two . . . and THREE.'

We play through the song three times. The first time Araminta realizes quite quickly that Benny in Year Ten is actually not that great at the violin or reading sheet music and asks him to pack up and leave. Once Benny is savagely out of the picture, we actually seem half decent playing together and Araminta does sound surprisingly good singing the song. Overly dramatic, of course. The only thing she needs to work on is her choreography skills. Her movement is really atrocious. She's just standing there like a limp squid, with Bonnie and Katie swaying in the background as her backup dancers. I don't know how she's going to get help with that – Mr Willis might be all right at conducting, but when it comes to acting he's hopeless. He spends enough time praising her though. 'Oh, Araminta, that was incredible,' he says, and I almost vomit.

Whenever I'm forced to spend this much time with Araminta, it makes me think about how amazing Lola would have been as head girl instead. Just as we're about to make a start on a fourth go at 'Think of Me' (I'm already sick of the song), I notice Audrey waving at me through the window. She's gesticulating wildly for me to come and meet her.

I shut the piano lid and grab my bag.

'Where are you going?' Araminta squawks.

'I don't know if you remember, but I came here thinking I'd get to practise my own piece. Now I've run out of time, and I have other stuff I need to do!' I wave airily as I pass her and the others.

'OK, well . . . same time next week?' Panic rises in her voice.

'I'll let you know!'

'Ivy, you won't mess this up for me!'

I hear Mr Willis call my name, but my head is down and I'm out the door.

I make my way to the front entrance, push through the double doors to Audrey. She looks worried and is pacing up and down.

'What's going on?' I ask. 'Is it about Clover?'

'I tried calling, but you didn't answer.'

'I was in rehearsals; my phone's on silent. What is it? What's happened?' I almost feel like shaking it out of her.

She lets out a huge sigh and puts her head in her hands.

'It's not about Clover, Ivy. I've heard from the Magpie Society.'

# 11

## AUDREY

As I peer through the window, waiting for Ivy to notice me, it's strange to see Mr Willis standing there, acting like everything is normal. It turns my stomach. Whether or not he had something to do with Lola's murder, to know that he's still a predator who's roaming these halls ... well, it makes me sick. It puts everything into context, especially the fact that he's acting as the supervisor for the school concert. Seeing him in a tête-à-tête with Araminta ... I might not like her, but I don't want her to get wrapped up in whatever disgusting scheme he has going on.

She places her hand on his arm and he smiles at her, and I almost want to run in there right now and scream, 'HE'S A CREEP!' But *that* won't get me anywhere except a trip to Mrs Abbott's office, I expect.

Araminta gets up onstage as Ivy walks towards me. I feel a jolt, deep in my stomach. A yearning. Musical theatre had been one of my passions back home, where I'd filled my summers with amateur-dramatics performances in theatres in Savannah and around. It's a strange tug of nostalgia, so far removed from my real life now, which is more magpies than musicals.

Seeing Patrick again – and knowing Clover is safe – has brought the mystery of Lola's death back to the forefront of my mind. And, so far, only one thing has connected all the different threads together: the Magpie Society. That's why the surprise waiting for me when I got back from town made me so excited. Our first break.

I manage to catch Ivy's eye and frantically wave her over. 'What's going on?' she asks when she finally reaches me. 'Is it about Clover?'

'I tried calling, but you didn't answer.'

'I was in rehearsals; my phone's on silent. What is it? What's happened?'

I let out a long breath. 'It's not about Clover, Ivy. I've heard from the Magpie Society.'

Ivy's eyes open wide. 'Shit. I shouldn't leave rehearsal right now, while you know who is here. I want to keep an eye on him. But . . . what did they say? Wait a second – are you OK? You look like you went for a swim or something.'

'It's pouring with rain, you ass.'

'Oh right. And I want to know all about your visit to Patrick.'

'Can you believe that Clover's been there all along?'

'I hope she knows what she's doing.' Ivy looks over her shoulder. 'OK, let's go. Come on, tell me . . . what did the Magpie Society say?'

'Let's go somewhere private,' I say as a stream of Year Sevens crowd round us, waiting to get into the assembly hall to practise their carols.

'The library? There's no one there at the weekend.'

There's a different atmosphere as we walk round the school. People are looking at us like we might actually be guilty of something. I know who's behind *that*. Araminta and Bonnie and her crew, trying to ostracize Ivy and me.

My plan to spend the last two years at school flying under the radar has gone out the window. But I guess I signed up for that when I became friends with Ivy. Yet somehow I'm pretty sure this year hasn't gone the way Ivy wanted either. I can see the tension in her, bubbling away under the surface. I know her clear dreams for this year – and next – are clouding over. I wonder if her vision of the future is crumbling . . . or just changing.

I know mine is changing. I've never known what I wanted to do after graduation. My future had been so cut off after Alicia's death, it's like a curtain had been thrown over it. No vision board or meditation could cut through that thick black fabric. Thoughts of theatre school, or college, or even a year off backpacking around Europe . . . they all seemed so far away. I'd decided to keep it that way, to focus on the present. But now it's like my friendship with Ivy is slicing its way through. Maybe I'll go to the same college – sorry, *university* – as her. Find a way to forge an actual lasting friendship.

But first I need to get through two years at Illumen Hall.

When we get to the library, we head up to one of the booths. Because it's the weekend, there's no teacher manning the front desk, and there are hardly any students milling about.

It's a good thing too because, when I show Ivy what the Magpie Society left, she gasps.

'A phone?'

'Yeah. It was in my cubby. Hidden behind my fake one so that no one would have known it was there.'

'Have you looked at it yet?'

'I turned it on because I didn't know where it had come from. When I realized, I came straight to find you. We do this together, right?'

Ivy squeezes my shoulder and grins at me, then we huddle over the cellphone. The lock screen responds to my thumbprint. I don't want to think too hard about how they – whoever 'they' are – got my fingerprint in order to control the access.

The screen unfolds to an animated silhouette of a magpie, feathers splaying in slow motion.

'Wow. That's incredible.'

There's only one app on the screen – a little blue square.

'What is this?' Ivy asks. She presses on it, and it opens up to a giant floor plan of the school.

We zoom in, scrolling around the building. It seems to go on forever, with multiple floors and buildings jumbled together. The floor plan seems cobbled together from different blueprints, some newer, with crisp lines, some positively ancient.

'It'll take forever to search through all of this,' I say, feeling dejected. 'It's so detailed.' In every room, we have to zoom in to read the tiny writing indicating what the room is used for. Most of them are classrooms or dorms, but there are also lots I didn't realize existed: storage rooms, janitor's closets, kitchens, staff washrooms . . . you name it, Illumen Hall seems to have it. But, if the Magpie Society are trying to send us a message, I'm not getting it. 'What are we even looking for?'

'No idea. Some kind of sign? You're good at this, remember – you found that edge painting!'

There's a little button in the corner. 'What's that?' I ask. I tap it before Ivy can stop me.

The screen jumps to the library – to our exact position in fact. A little blue dot appears, indicating our location.

'Wow, that's cool,' I say.

'Audrey, this isn't just an ordinary floor plan.'

'What do you mean?'

Ivy points at the part of the library that we're in. 'Look – according to this map, behind that wall there's a hallway. But . . .'

She stands up, pulling books off the shelf. I help her. When everything is down, we're staring at white drywall. Ivy runs her hands along it. 'It looks like it's all blocked off now. Maybe once upon a time this would have led us somewhere.'

'Oh wow.' It takes me a moment to digest what this means. It's incredible. 'So this is a map that includes all the hidden passageways in the school. Maybe it'll lead us to where the Magpie Society meet . . . in a secret room somewhere.' I'm in awe of what the Magpie Society has done for us already. Then the favour Patrick asked me pops into my mind: to find a list of society members. Maybe I'll be able to figure it out after all. Had Clover gotten this close?

A prickle of fear spikes at the base of my spine. *Are we in danger too?*

'That's got to be it. But I wonder how many of them are going to be bricked up like this one?'

'OK, well, it's clear what we have to do. We have to go back to where we know there are tunnels,' I say.

Ivy's scrolling across the map, tracing around the perimeter of the school. She's gazing at it intently, particularly at one tunnel that seems to lead off the school grounds. But the map there is blurred and unclear – as if it's been scanned from a really old blueprint. There's no way of seeing where the tunnel starts or finishes.

'Ivy?'

'Yeah, OK,' she says, finally tearing her eyes from the screen. She passes me the cellphone. 'Let's go.'

We race down to the kitchens. They're not nearly as quiet as we need them to be and it's odd now that it isn't just the two of us, like it was during half-term – Illumen Hall isn't just a domain for us to run around in any more. However, somehow we manage to slip through the gaggle of feathers and locate the wooden panel in the laundry-room walls, with its telltale magpie carving. But at least we don't have to waste any time seeking out the entrance. We know exactly where it is.

We can breathe a bit easier once we've slipped through the wall and back into the bowels of the school.

'Is it weird that this is starting to feel normal?' I say to Ivy, even as I wipe off a cobweb that has entangled itself in my hair.

'Ha, no. To be honest, I never expected my sixth-form year to be dominated by hunting down a killer and trying to solve the mystery of a secret society working behind the scenes at the school, but, you know, what else is new?'

'OK, let's check the cellphone.'

We pause when we reach the open beams and all the doors leading off in different directions. One of them we know goes to the cave in the cliffs. Another must lead to the Magpie Society headquarters. But which one? I think again about the cave we found at half-term, with the sleeping bag and evidence of food wrappers. The shelf that included Lola's earring. I shiver. We definitely should have taken that piece of jewellery with us as evidence.

Ivy sits down on one of the beams and I look over her shoulder. The little blue dot on the map has followed us. We zoom in, and the lettering is old, cramped and hard to read – another place where an old map has been copied and then scanned a few too many times, and the technology can't handle it. But that makes sense, since this is probably one of the oldest parts of the building. It's clear that we're in the spaces in between the old servants' quarters and the main house. There have been so many extensions and add-ons that there are pockets that haven't been developed. Maybe the grand facade of the school is just for show – when really so much of the building is unused, falling into disrepair, or just . . . empty.

'Look!' Ivy says, snapping me out of my daydream. 'There. What does that look like to you?' She's traced the path from one of the doors across a few beams from us, and it looks like it leads to another room with a symbol on it.

I squint. 'I think . . . oh my God, I think that's a magpie.'

Ivy claps her hands together. 'We could have scanned this map all day and never found it. This was such a good idea to come to the tunnels! Come on, let's go through that door.'

A loud bang directly behind us makes us both jump. It came from the door that led towards the cave.

'What was that?' Ivy says.

'Maybe the cave-dweller is back?' There's a jolt of fear in my belly. 'I thought you said that you'd get that gardener man to close up the entrance?'

The banging starts again, louder this time. With caution, we approach the door that leads to the cave.

Ivy reaches forward and throws it open . . .

And we stare straight into the eyes of Ed Tavistock.

# 12

## IVY

'SHIT!' I jump backwards, almost tripping over my own feet.

Audrey screams and grabs my arm.

The light is dim, but I know that wiry brow and those dark green eyes belong to Mr Tavistock's grandson, Ed. You can just about make out his pulled-back ponytail and fluffy stray hairs poking out at all angles too. His eyes are framed because of one panel of wood he hasn't yet nailed up. The rest of the space is covered already by wooden boards. He's raising the last piece of wood and his hammer to complete the job just as he notices us too.

'JESUS CHRIST!' He frowns fiercely. 'What are you girls doing? You shouldn't be there!'

I back into Audrey.

'Wait, Ivy? Is that you?' He presses his eyes closer to the open panel as he speaks in his raised but husky tone. 'Are you still messing about with the Magpie Society? You have to stop; it's dangerous. Go back now.'

He doesn't even wait for a response before nailing the wooden board over the remaining gap. Audrey digs her fingernails into my arm. 'He knows we're looking into the Magpie Society?'

'Looks like. I guess his granddad told him we were asking about Lily Ellory and they put the pieces together.' I stand and watch in silence as the nails go in with such force that dust falls from the ceiling above us.

'What on earth is his problem?' Audrey turns to me.

'Had a shock, I suppose. I don't think he expected to come across anyone. I guess Mr Tavistock is too old to be coming down here to block off the cave himself.'

'At least I feel better knowing that the entrance is shut up. I didn't really like the idea that someone was camping out there, so close to the school,' says Audrey.

'Same.'

'Here – this door looks like it leads towards the room marked with a magpie,' Audrey says. 'It's a bit confusing as it seems to go down through several levels of the building.'

'Maybe it's underground.'

Audrey reaches for the door and tugs on it.

'Look who's getting confident now!' I laugh as I take the phone from Audrey and study the map for myself.

'Yeah, well, seeing Ed has got me fired up. If we don't do it now, he might come back and close up even more passageways.'

'I hadn't thought about that. After you.'

The door leads to a narrow and very low-ceilinged corridor. It smells damp and musty, and the scent lingers in my nose. It reminds me of an old church basement that's not been used in years.

'This school is like a labyrinth! There's so much of it that I never knew existed.' I brush a cobweb from my hair and follow closely behind Audrey. We head down a series of stairways, creaking and rotten in places. We have to be extra careful where we step. It's getting distinctly colder, and I shiver. The cave in the cliffs was high above the beach. This feels like we're headed much, much deeper underground.

We arrive at another door. This one is much more solid and takes some heaving from both of us to get it open. It's very intricately carved and the wood is really heavy. The hinges squeak like it hasn't been oiled in an age. The door creaks open and Audrey steps inside first. There's a set of very narrow stone stairs winding down. The stones are uneven and worn in the middle – they've been well used over time.

'This looks kinda terrifying! It's darker down there – do you have a flashlight?'

I take my phone out of my pocket and flip the torch on. The stairs don't go on for too long and we instantly see the bottom.

'It's so cold!' Audrey shivers as we both stand at the top of the stairs and a breeze blows up into our faces from below. 'Let's go down then ... I guess?' she says as she steps on to the first stair.

I follow closely after and the door shuts behind me. It's not long until we're at the bottom.

Audrey stumbles, resting her hand against the wall, but just as quickly she pulls it away again.

'What is it?' I ask.

'Look!' Audrey gasps.

I turn my camera light to face the wall. As I shine the beam up and down, we realize that we've entered a kind of grotto that is absolutely covered in tiny shells.

'This is the most beautiful thing I've ever seen.' Audrey's mouth is open, her eyes shining.

'I've *heard* of places like this.' My voice is full of wonder.

The shells have been deliberately placed in intricate patterns, in swirls and mosaics. They're colourful too – pink and pale green, ivory white and shimmering purple. It's somehow both beautiful and eerie.

'It's incredible!' I say.

'This must have taken years! Imagine the effort, the skill! I've honestly never seen anything like it.'

We stand for a moment and take it all in, running our fingers along the wall, touching each shell delicately. We then start walking round the corner cautiously and the shell-covered walkway continues. After a couple of minutes, we reach a much larger room. Huge grey, chalky stones curve overhead, framing the entrance. Inside the room, there's a small flickering light on the wall and more shells, but this time they've been arranged in the shape of a three-metre-high magpie. Its wings span the entire width of the wall. Deeper shades of navy, periwinkle and emerald shells glimmer in my phone light as I glide it across the wall before us. On the other side of the cave there's a huge bookcase that's filled with files, yearbooks, folders and paperwork. The scale of it almost takes my breath away.

Audrey turns to me. 'I think we've found the Magpie Society headquarters.'

# 13

## IVY

I take a step towards the bookcase. The first thing I notice is how clean everything is. Although it's clearly been here for decades – centuries even – someone is keeping on top of it as there's no dust, no cobwebs and it's very orderly and organized. Will someone turn up while we're here?

Clearly Audrey is thinking the same thing. 'Someone's been here recently. What if they come back?'

'Good. I have so many questions I want to ask . . . whoever it is. Someone's been orchestrating this – after all, who sent us all those letters? Who left the phone? The Magpie Society isn't dead. It's alive and thriving and this is the proof!' I gesture around, and Audrey tilts her head back, staring at the twinkling shells. 'We should start looking through some of this. There might be something really important that will help us discover what exactly the Magpie Society want.'

Audrey nods. 'Actually, this is kinda perfect. Patrick asked me to look for something.'

'Oh wow, I've been so wrapped up in our search, I hadn't even asked you about that. Can you believe Clover has been there this whole time? What's his place even like?'

'His apartment is beautiful – it has this huge open fire and big windows looking out to sea.'

'He didn't show you to the bedroom . . .' I waggle my eyebrows, and Audrey grimaces.

'No. He's still really obsessed with his sister's death. He didn't seem that surprised about Clover's disappearance, but then I guess he wouldn't since he's been hiding her all this time.'

'And you're *certain* you saw her.'

'Hundred per cent.'

'Shit. Have you told anyone else?'

Audrey shakes her head. 'No. I came straight back here, then found the cellphone and now we're here . . . D'you think I should? Should I have gone to the police already?'

I frown. 'I don't know. She hasn't replied to my text yet. But, if she's OK, she obviously doesn't want to be found. We should let her continue her investigating.'

'Patrick did say he thought she'd been really close to the truth. Actually, he asked me to look into the Magpie Society again. He specifically wanted me to find a list of members' names. He said it was a final piece of the puzzle. Where else would it be than here?'

'Let's look. Then we can decide about Clover.' I step up to the bookcase and gasp.

'What? What is it?' Audrey says, running over.

There, face out on the middle shelf, is an envelope.

'What the hell?' I open it, examining the contents. It's for us; there's no mistaking it. In swirly, handwritten letters, it reads:

*FAO: The New Magpies*

'It was just here on the shelf.'

'They obviously expected us to get this far. Should we open it?' I say cautiously.

'Yes, we have to find out what they want us to know!'

I start to peel back the envelope and slide out a single piece of cream card. I read it out.

*Once upon a time, the Magpie Society stood for justice. We protected the school from corruption and scandal. Yet over the years our little society has been whittled away to nothing.*

*The school needs us now more than ever. But it's impossible for us to help. It needs to be you. Are you up for the challenge of starting the Magpie Society once again?*

*Illumen Hall's future is in your hands . . .*

Audrey and I lock eyes. 'That's kind of a lot to put on us,' she says.

'You're telling me.' I set the letter down, then pull out a book from behind it that catches my eye. It looks to be A3 size, and it's red-leather bound with gold etching on the spine that reads *History of the Magpies*. I open it out on the floor and take extra care when peeling back the pages. Audrey kneels down beside me and holds up my phone while I do so.

It's an entire catalogue of black-and-white portrait photos, dating back to the 1800s. There are sketches too. Men and women all smiling at the camera or artist that drew them. Underneath are their names.

'Alexandra Downland, head of housekeeping,' Audrey reads over my shoulder. 'They're all people on the school staff. Do you think that's how the Magpie Society recruits?'

'It must be. Oh my God, look! Mrs Trawley's name is on this list. And Mr Tavistock too!'

Audrey's eyes open wide. 'No way. Mr Tavistock makes sense, he's the groundskeeper. But wasn't Mrs Trawley a student? She never worked at the school, did she?'

'Maybe over the years it evolved to include students too. I knew that crafty woman knew more than she was letting on. Didn't she say she was the granddaughter of Lily Ellory? Yes, look! Here's another Ellory. Clarissa Ellory, horsemistress. She sounds like a cool lady. Maybe Mrs Trawley's related to her?'

'Or this Ellory – Hetty Ellory, feather.' I point at another one further down. 'Wow, I didn't realize the domestic staff here have been called feathers for so long.'

'Maybe Hetty and Clarissa were sisters? Like looking after Illumen Hall is a family business.'

'That makes sense,' I say softly. 'If the Magpies wanted to keep the school safe, they would probably only trust family members.'

We flick through more pages dense with text about the history of the society and what they've accomplished, and see a variety of different faces staring back at us. Everyone looks so happy.

'Correct me if I'm wrong, but these people don't look ... sinister? They seem like your average, friendly neighbourhood folk.'

Audrey's right. These people are the sort you'd go to for

a cup of tea and a listening ear. They're proud to be a part of whatever this is. There are so many of these photos printed through the book that eventually they start to look more modern. The photographs develop colour and clarity, and the clothes and fashion become more up to date – well, if you consider bell-bottom jeans and peasant blouses up to date. We reach the last page, but there are still lots of empty pages left to fill.

'It stops in the seventies,' I say as we reach the end of the book. 'And Mr Tavistock has his name crossed out here.'

'That's weird. Do you think there have been no new members of the Magpie Society since then?'

'I guess. Remember what Mrs Trawley told us in town? "When they're needed, they rise up again." Maybe the Magpie Society is trying to restart?'

Right at the end is a list, like an index, detailing all the names in order under the heading OFFICIAL MAGPIE SOCIETY MEMBERS.

Audrey rubs her temple. 'Oh my God, so many questions. If that's the case, *why* are they needed again? And who of all these people wrote the invitations?' She runs her finger down the list.

I stretch, admiring the space around us, some of it in darkness, some with sparkling shells stealing the attention. A breeze comes in through gaps in the bricks and I get a chill. I wrap my arms round my body and shiver.

'So the only names we know are still around are Mr Tavistock and Mrs Trawley,' I say. 'But Mr Tavistock's name is crossed out, and Mrs Trawley doesn't live on the school grounds any more.'

'Do you think Mr Tavistock is the one who's been coming here to look after the place all this time?'

'Maybe – but I don't think he set up the fancy GPS phone device.'

'That's true. What about his grandson? D'you think Ed is tech-savvy enough to do this?'

I frown. 'You heard how hostile he was towards us. Why would he lead us here only to shout at us? We'll ask him for sure, but I don't think it's him.'

'OK then, someone could have remarried ... like Mrs Trawley, or her mother must have done to change her name from Ellory. She's got ancestors all the way back to the start of the Magpie Society, but we would never have known that had we not spoken to her. Anyone could be a Magpie. Ms Cranshaw might be one!'

'That's true. OK, instead of who, let's try and find out *why*. That might give us more of a clue. We should keep looking through these files and books. There's bound to be something that tells us more about the Magpie Society and what they stand for.'

There are still too many missing pieces.

The list of names continues over on to the next page. I spot Audrey taking a photograph with her phone, and my heart starts racing in my chest. I take a deep breath.

Then at the end it says MAGPIE SOCIETY – DISBANDED JUNE 1975. After that, it's completely blank. No more names.

'Ivy ... the Magpie Society seems like it was made up of good people. I don't think they would have been involved in a student's death. The Magpie Society *was* really about protecting the students and exposing corruption, wasn't it?'

'Seems that way. They really thought this school was something special. Something worth protecting,' I say.

We continue to rummage, but all the articles are historic. Nothing from the present day that could be a clue as to why Clover ran away or who killed Lola. No trace of who could be behind the Magpie Society now.

'Right, I think we should probably go,' I say.

Audrey gets up off the dusty floor, wiping the back of her jeans as she does. She goes to put back the book and inhales sharply. 'Wait, have we seen this already?' She points to a large folded piece of paper sitting on the same shelf as the note had been.

'No . . . I hadn't noticed that. What is it?' I pull the piece of paper off and lay it out on the floor. I hold my phone torch closer so we can see. 'Looks like a blueprint.'

'You're right. I've seen a few of these as my dad works with them a lot.' Audrey traces her finger round the page.

'Wait, Audrey, this is Illumen Hall. But it looks different.' I gasp. 'Oh my God. These are plans to turn it into a *luxury hotel*. Mrs Abbott is going to sell the school!'

# 14

## AUDREY

I grab the blueprint out of Ivy's hands, my eyes raking the long sheet of paper. There are lines scrawled all over the old framework of the school, adding extensions, changing classrooms to bedrooms, making alterations to the grounds . . . It's a complete overhaul. At the bottom are the words *Illumen Hall: A luxury spa hotel on the stunning Kent coast.*

'They can't do this,' Ivy says. She's almost shaking with rage. 'This is one of the oldest boarding schools in England. It was among the first to accept women. It's a part of history. It's got to be a listed building or something. They'd never get permission. What about us? The students, the boarders? This is our home. And what about everyone who wants to come here in the future?'

I swallow. 'Like who?'

'Like my sister. I was hoping she'd start here when she was eligible next year. Illumen Hall is a *haven* for people like me. It always has been. All this stuff –' she gestures around – 'proves what I've always known. That Illumen Hall is different. It's special. It's not just some home for privileged, rich white kids – no offence.'

'None taken,' I say.

'Look at this.' Ivy flips through the history book again. 'In the 1950s, they said that someone was embezzling from the school. A headmaster. Look at this guy.' She thrusts the newspaper clipping in my face. 'They threw him out – but still managed to preserve the school's reputation. So often people in power get corrupted. But Illumen Hall has always managed to rise above, to provide a safe place for the students. The school makes it so that no one has to worry about whether they can afford the best education. Especially not someone like me. So to sell it . . . to turn this incredible institution into some hotel . . . it's unthinkable.'

'Who would do this? And what on earth does this have to do with Lola?'

'I don't know. But the Radcliffes have been principal donors of the school for years. They wouldn't allow this to happen. If Lola knew about this, she would have done anything to stop it.'

'I could ask Patrick if he knows about it when we go confront him about Clover. Do you mind if I take this?' I ask. Ivy shakes her head. I roll up the blueprint and slip it into my bag. I only pray that Ivy didn't look close enough to note down the logo of the company who made the plans.

Because I sure do recognize it.

My dad's company.

I had no idea that he was involved in buying the school. And I definitely don't want Ivy to find out. 'So what do we do now?' I ask.

'Well, I think it's obvious. We have to do what that note said. Start the Magpie Society up again. Protect the school. We can't get the elite involved – that's why Araminta and

Teddy mustn't know anything. But those of us who received letters, like Clover's room-mates and Harriet? It's up to us now.'

'But we need more than this. I think we should go talk to Mrs Trawley and Patrick. Maybe if Clover knew about this she'd help us? She could use the podcast again and get the word out about the school closing. We can go tomorrow,' I say.

'Yes! Love a plan.'

'And then we bring the others in?'

'Right.' Ivy's phone buzzes and she groans. 'Shit. My schedule just landed for the next few days. Then there's exam prep, concert rehearsals, plus I'm supposed to be composing a piece for my next music exam. There's also all the stuff from Araminta like the yearbook, prefect duties . . . She even wants me to practise next weekend.'

I raise my eyebrows. 'Looks to me like they're trying to run you into the ground.'

'Probably to stop me from doing anything . . . well, anything exactly like what we're trying to do right now.'

'Start up a new secret society, you mean.' I chuckle.

'Yes. Exactly that. I bet Mrs Abbott is behind all these extra scheduling additions. Remember that "let's get everything back to normal" speech?' Ivy rolls her eyes.

'Yeah, that was kinda intense. Well, no one's trying to pack *my* schedule. I can take the lead on this. I'm on it. Don't worry.' I hope I sound reassuring.

Ivy takes my hand. 'Thank you.'

'No problem.' I squeeze her fingers.

I lean back, taking in our surroundings once more. I

reach out my hand and run my fingers over the ridged edges of the shells. 'This place should be a museum.'

'They'll probably turn it into the hot-tub room.'

'Oh my God. Mud baths among the shells.'

'Seaweed wraps.'

'Maybe Botox.' I pull the skin of my face taut and make fish lips. Ivy laughs at me and snaps a photo. 'Hey!' I say.

'You still look gorgeous.'

'I look like a goofball.'

'Guess you don't want me to send this to a certain Teddy then?'

'You wouldn't!'

'No, I'm not that mean. Don't worry.' Her phone buzzes again. 'Shit. There's a prefects' meeting. I'd better go – it might take us ages to get out of this place.'

'I'll head back to our room and do some digging into the blueprint.'

Ivy smiles at me. 'Audrey – I know this isn't your fight. I know you haven't got a reason to care about Lola or about the future of this school. I know you could happily sail through the rest of this year and not give a damn about any of this. But thank you for being here with me.'

I pause. She's not *quite* right. My dad's company logo burning a hole in my pocket has given me some personal stake in this. But I'm not ready for Ivy to know that yet.

'Ivy, you don't have to worry. You didn't drag me into this. I came here of my own free will. I mean, come on – this is making my school year a whole lot more interesting than just reading some stuffy British history book. But that's not the only reason that I'm interested. I care about you, Ivy.

You're my only friend here. And I don't say that lightly. I used to have a lot of friends back in Georgia. But honestly I didn't feel the same connection we have with any of them – and I realize we've only known each other a short time, but heck – I crawl through spiderwebs for you.'

'So we're Magpies together.'

'Magpies.'

There's a stamp on the desk and an inkpad. Ivy takes my hand, then guides it to the desk, sliding the sleeve of my sweater up to the crook of my elbow. She presses down on the inkpad and stamps the dark purple ink on the pale skin of my arm.

Next she passes the stamp to me. I roll the base of it in the ink as she pushes up her sleeve. Her freckled olive skin is lined with pale green veins. The magpie has a sharp, pointed beak that looks like it would draw blood if it was real. We both pull our sleeves down.

We're branded now, but only we can know it.

We mark the location of Magpie Society headquarters – the shell grotto – and head back into the dusty passageways. Thanks to the location marker on the cellphone, we can see that the tunnels lead off to different parts of the school, meaning we can get to our separate destinations even faster.

'Can you believe this? If the Magpie Society knew about this underground network all this time . . . that means that they could get all over the school without anyone knowing about it,' I say.

'I wonder where this one leads to.' Ivy points to a tunnel that appears to come out in the grounds. But it's hard to contextualize without any visuals. Even Ivy, who knows the school and the grounds like the back of her hand, can't place it. It's not the tunnel that ends up at the blocked-off entrance beneath the little hut where we found the old yearbook. We can see the trail that leads to that.

'We'll come back and see where that goes later on.'

'There's just so much to explore.' Ivy slips the phone in her pocket.

'Ivy. You know what this means though? That Lola's killer is still on the loose. Combine that with the fact that Mr Willis, a dangerous predator, is continuing to teach like everything's normal. I'm worried about you.'

Ivy nods. 'I know. I'll be careful.'

'I know it sounds . . . weird. But keep in touch, OK? And don't go places alone. Especially on your runs. If you can't drag me out there, maybe Harriet will go with you?'

'I don't know. Training is my one sanctuary right now. And Harriet doesn't like to run.'

'OK, you get *one* sanctuary. But, Ivy, you're my lifeline here. I don't wanna lose you.'

She looks me dead in the eye. 'Don't worry, Audrey. I'm not going anywhere.'

I watch her disappear down the passageway, then follow my own. When I emerge back into the school itself, I exit out of a panel into a darkened classroom. I'm glad no one saw me, or else I'd have a lot of explaining to do.

I brush off my clothes, displacing some of the dirt and dust. Then I pull out my cellphone. There's a long voice note on my WhatsApp from Teddy and it makes me smile. But I don't respond straight away. Instead, I switch to my photos app.

I open up the picture of the list of Magpie Society members that Patrick asked for. I edit it, obscuring some of the names. Then I send it to him.

> Patrick. I have what you asked for. If you want the full
> image, you have to meet with Ivy and me tomorrow. I
> know Clover is with you. We want answers –
> otherwise we're going to the police.

## 15

### IVY

I'm barely listening at the end-of-week prefect meeting, as all I've been able to think about is everything we discovered this afternoon. For once, even Araminta's taking a back seat, and Xander is up at the front, yammering on about how to regulate the annual communal-area kitchen clean-up.

Teddy is across the room, trying to catch my eye. But I studiously avoid him. I can't allow those feelings to creep back in, especially if the school is at risk of closing. I can say a swift goodbye to any hope of things ever progressing with him like they were before, or with anyone for that matter. I'll probably be shipped off to some all-girls' boarding school where they swan about in big, gossipy groups, tinting their brows and fake-tanning.

It all feels a bit like a dream. I can't stop thinking about the fact that tunnels and corridors leading to the Magpie Society headquarters are running beneath these very floors that we walk over every single day. Since Audrey mentioned the run, I'm even more determined to get my trainers on and pound the ground for an hour, so I drop Harriet a text to see if she'll come with me after the meeting. Running has always been a part of keeping my master plan on track. To my surprise, she agrees and we decide to meet by the oak tree next to the tennis courts.

When the meeting ends, I notice Teddy is coming over. We've not seen much of each other since the night of the party. And, honestly, I think I've been doing much better for it.

'Hey, creeper! Where you off to in such a hurry? One of your jogs?'

'You mean a RUN?'

'Yes, sorry. Jogging's not the same thing, I forget. It's only because I can only dream of setting a pace like yours!' He smiles and his eyes crease at the corners.

'You'd only do that by practising, Teddy. And I think you prefer more horizontal activities?'

'Steady on.' He cackles.

'That's *not* what I meant.' I roll my eyes.

'Seriously though, Ivy, have you heard any more about Clover?'

'No . . .'

'It's scary, isn't it?' he says. 'I'm just so pleased you're OK. I know this will really be worrying you. You know I'm only a text away if you ever need a friend, yeah?' He touches my arm and his face softens. I can tell he really means it, even if his emphasis on 'friend' stings a little.

'I know. Thanks.' I tuck the loose bit of hair behind my ear and smile at him.

'There it is! The creeper smile. Reserved only for special occasions, or special people, am I right?' He ruffles the top of my head and continues up the stairs. 'Catch you later, Creeps. Take care of yourself!' He shouts down over other students as he progresses up the staircase to the first floor.

I know he's trying to tone down the level of Teddy he's used to being around me but, as much as it's appreciated, I can't ignore our chemistry. What is it that draws me to that boy? I mustn't let this get complicated; that's honestly the last thing I need, especially as I know him and Audrey are becoming closer. I'm not one for a love triangle.

Once I'm changed, I head out to the tennis courts and there's Harriet, stretching against the giant oak tree. She's dressed in a lime-green tracksuit, with earmuffs, fluffy gloves and a huge bottle of water.

'I know, I know, all the gear and no idea . . .' She spots me walking towards her with a face that says just that. 'I mean, I'm not even sure this is the right gear. We're going on a run, not hitting the slopes.'

I laugh. But I'm glad she's with me. She vowed that she would spend more time outdoors, doing some form of exercise, and prefers someone else to hold her accountable or she just doesn't do it. I enjoy our runs, even though her pace is much slower than mine, but she doesn't mind if I run a few circles round her every so often.

Before we begin, Harriet tugs on my arm. 'Have you heard anything from the police? Do they have any leads about Clover?'

I shake my head. 'Nothing. The detectives have gone quiet.'

'I'm so nervous. What if they start asking questions about the tattoo?'

'Harriet, calm down. Why would they? And you got rid of all the drawings, didn't you?'

'Yeah, I did. But the original is still missing. What if Clover found it and is going to use it to frame me for Lola's death?'

I shake my head. I still remember when Harriet came to me in a panic, the day after the party on the beach. We were all in shock, of course, but Harriet had even more reason to be.

*'Ivy – you have to help me. One of my drawings was taken from my art book. The one I was working on for my final project.'*

*'The one you'd been keeping a secret from everyone? Including me?'*

*'That's it. It was a magpie. Somehow ... somehow an exact copy of it ended up on Lola's back.'*

That revelation had freaked Harriet out, but I'd kept her calm. I knew she hadn't been involved in Lola's death – she'd been at the party the entire time. But the drawing could implicate her.

'You can't think like that,' I tell her now. 'Come on, let's go. Running will help clear your head – it always helps me.'

We pick up the pace and pass through the grounds, up over the first field behind the school. It's slightly colder today, but the sun is shining so it feels fresh and autumn-kissed. Dew on the grass instantly soaks our trainers.

'How is everything with you and Cassie, Hattie?' I say as we run alongside each other. She doesn't hear me because of her earmuffs.

*'Harriet?'* I shout and wave my hand in front of her face. She laughs. 'Sorry! What did – you – say?' she puffs.

'How are you and Cassie?'

'Yeah – we're great. It's actually our anniversary next

week – not sure what we'll – get up to – but – excited to –
see her – yanno?' she pants.

'Ah, cute!'

'Any lovers – in your – life at the – moment?'

'You know the answer already. Big fat *no*. I'm not
interested in that right now. I have too much resting on my
final exams.'

'Fair!'

Just then, I notice Ed chopping wood in the trees we're
about to run alongside. He's cutting down the old, dead
trees signposted by a loop of bright green ribbon. This is
my opportunity to speak to him after seeing him in the
tunnels. I just need to get rid of Harriet first.

'Harriet, I think I've pulled a muscle in my leg! I need to
stop and stretch it out . . .'

'Oh, I'm so up for stopping for a bit, no problem.'

'Nah, you keep going. I reckon this is your best pace yet
and you can't lose that! GO! GO! I'll catch up once I've
sorted this out.'

'Really? Oh my God. OK, I'LL KEEP GOING!' She
runs on, waving behind her.

'PROUD OF YOU!' I shout back.

This sparks Ed's attention and he glances over at me. I
walk towards him through the trees, making sure Harriet
isn't looking behind her.

'What do you want, Ivy?' he says sharply, going back to
cutting a log.

'Nice to see you too, Ed! What exactly is your issue?
I feel like you have a real problem here and I'd love to
know why.'

He sighs. 'I've got a lot of big jobs to do and somehow you seem to be getting in the way of them. What were you and Audrey doing in that passageway anyway? I've been trying to close them all up . . .'

'Honestly? We were led there by the Magpie Society. You wouldn't happen to know anything about that, would you?'

He raises a bushy eyebrow. 'Of course I do . . . but *you* shouldn't have anything to do with it.'

'IVY! Are you OK?' Harriet is heading through the trees towards us.

*Shit.*

'Can we meet and talk about this some more? Maybe I can bring Audrey and a couple of others too? We've all received an invite to the society,' I whisper.

'Fine. Meet at my house next Saturday at seven p.m. Granddad is out at that time. Don't be late though. Also, in the meantime, if you or Audrey come across any other tunnels that you think are being used, let me know, yeah?'

I nod, before he turns to chop more wood, and then head back up the trail to meet Harriet. Even though she got a letter, I'm not ready to do any explaining to her just yet. Not until I know more.

My phone buzzes. It's Audrey.

> Patrick has agreed to meet us
> tomorrow in town. He says he'll
> give us the answers we need.

**Good,** I type back. I sigh with relief.

'Everything OK?' Harriet asks me, frowning.

'Yeah. Mind if we head back now?'

'Are you kidding? I'm dying out here. Let's go.'

I'm uncharacteristically slow on my jog back, trailing at Harriet's heels. But I feel like my mind is weighed down by all the responsibilities that have landed on my shoulders. But tomorrow one thing will be lifted. We're going to find out what's happened to Clover – once and for all.

# 16

## AUDREY

> Meet me in the cafe in town at
> midday.

'Ivy!' I jump out of bed and pile on to hers, holding my cellphone out for her to see. 'We got another text from Patrick telling us where to meet him.'

Ivy sits up, bleary-eyed. She stares at my phone, then grins. 'Great. Tell him to bring Clover.'

I lean back against the wall by Ivy's bed and type out the message.

> We'll be there. Can you bring
> Clover too?

There's a long pause as Patrick types.

> She's going to meet us at the
> apartment after. She knows how
> to find the last bit of proof as to
> who murdered Lola. When we
> have that missing piece, we'll be

going to the police this
afternoon.

'Holy shit,' I say. 'Clover's gonna do it. She's getting proof.'

Ivy is wide awake now. 'Thank God. Maybe this nightmare will finally be over.'

'You must be so proud of her.' I grip her knee underneath her covers.

She smiles at me, but her expression is tight. And no wonder. Her phone is buzzing non-stop. She turns it over and groans. 'It's Araminta. She wants me to run a prefects' meeting this morning.'

'But what about our visit to Mrs Trawley?'

'Are you OK to go by yourself? I'll meet you at twelve in the cafe with Patrick.'

'Are you sure?'

'Yeah. Might as well kill two birds with one stone.'

Which is what leads me, a couple of hours later, to be standing outside Mrs Trawley's house on my own, staring at the pretty, wisteria-covered cottage. It doesn't seem that long since Ivy and I had been at her market stall surrounded by painted vintage mirrors, learning about the Magpie Society properly for the first time. We're still no closer to knowing what the link is between Lola and the Magpies, but I have a feeling Clover is gonna unlock that mystery for us this afternoon.

I take a deep breath and pause before I knock on the door. My sweater rides up on my wrist, and I see the magpie stamp, now faded after my shower. I wish Ivy was with me.

She's been run absolutely ragged by Mrs Abbott and Araminta, pushed from pillar to post across the school. Having to run a meeting for Minty on a Sunday morning: ridiculous.

Just before I knock on the door, I glance at my cellphone. I open my messaging app – but it's not to text Ivy.

**DAD. BEEN TRYING TO CALL YOU. PLEASE GET BACK TO ME ASAP.**

There's no answer. This is just one of a series of unanswered messages, WhatsApps, phone calls and emails that I've been sending him.

All of them have been ignored.

Normally, that would be my ideal. It's pretty typical behaviour from him – to disappear off the radar for a while. *Normally*, that would be how I prefer our relationship. Distant.

But of course now, when I actually *want* answers from him, I can't get any.

I put it to the back of my mind – and stuff my cellphone back in my purse. Then I take a deep breath and knock on the door.

I wait for a couple of moments, but there's no answer. I knock again, louder this time. Still no one appears. Not even a twitch of the curtains. I step back, calling out over the garden fence. 'Mrs Trawley? It's Audrey!'

I put my hand on the door to steady myself and, like something out of a horror movie, it creaks open.

I swallow. I don't wanna cross the threshold. *Come on,*

*Audrey, suck it up.* Holding my breath to hold down my fear, I step in, and the door swings further in.

Then I let the breath out in one long swoop. There's no dead Mrs Trawley. Actually, there's ... nothing but dust motes sparkling in the golden light, stirred up by the front door I've just opened.

No side table. No quirky coat rack with a million different wool coats, umbrellas and hats hanging off it. I walk in, my steps echoing down the hallway, its walls bare of pictures and photographs. There are shadows where the frames must have hung, darker patches of paint protected from the sun's harsh rays.

The front room is empty. The kitchen cold and dark.

Mrs Trawley has left the building.

I text Ivy straight away.

> **No sign of Mrs Trawley. It's like she's gone. Moved out.**

I get a reply immediately.

> **You're joking?!**

I snap a photo of the empty room and send it across. Well, not *completely* empty. On the kitchen counter closest to the window, there's a black leather portfolio. The last thing left.

I open it. It looks like an old contract of some sort. There's large, medieval-style writing at the top that looks like the word DEED or something – but I can't understand it.

There's a Post-it note on the top, written in cursive script.

*Hope this is helpful, C. Sorry I couldn't stay around to explain myself. I hope you succeed.*

She obviously meant for 'C' to have this . . . whatever it is. 'C' must be Clover, I'm sure of it. Does it have something to do with the Magpie Society?

I take a closer look. It appears to be some kind of property document. My eyes instantly glaze over, but I force myself to focus. The text is cramped, hard to read, like it might have been photocopied a few times too many so the lettering's not very clear. I can just about make out that this was the original document from Lord Brathebone bequeathing his manor house to the founding of the school – Illumen Hall.

The rest is complicated Victorian legalese that I have no hope of understanding. I turn the document over and I see that there's a handwritten amendment made to one of the clauses. It's signed by two people – Lady Penelope Debert and Lord Alden.

The clause reads:

*All head boys and girls will be allotted voting rights on the future of the school, and afforded all the privileges of other board members.*

That's interesting. There are more perks to being a head student than I realized.

The handwritten amendment continues:

*If a descendant of a Magpie were to assume one of these positions, they shall inherit the legacy of Lady Penelope Debert.*

My mouth forms an 'O' of surprise. I don't know exactly what it means – but it *must* be important.

**I'm coming now – managed to get away early,** Ivy texts.

I'm glad I brought my oversized purse with me as I slip the document inside. It's not stealing – I intend to give it to Clover when we see her. At least that's what I tell myself. I know Ivy will wanna see this first.

**Great – see you soon,** I reply.

I make my way over to the coffee shop, mulling over Mrs Trawley's absence. I wonder where she went?

I think about pulling out the portfolio and looking at the document again – but somehow I don't think Mrs Trawley wants me flashing it about in public.

Thankfully, I don't have to wait long. Ivy pushes through the door – and, not far behind her, Patrick comes in. He must have been hanging around, waiting.

They make their way over to my table. 'Have you –' Patrick starts, but Ivy cuts him off.

'No.' Her voice is sharp. '*We're* going to ask the questions. Has Clover been with you this whole time? Is she safe? Is she OK?'

Patrick's bright blue eyes open wide – I can tell he's not used to being interrupted. But I've got Ivy's back on this. I wanna know as much as she does.

Finally, he relents. 'Yes. She's fine. The night of the party, she was assaulted by someone in a magpie costume who told her to back off the investigation, and she felt like she was in real danger if she stayed at Illumen Hall any longer. The problem is it's harder for her to investigate "off campus", as it were. She's convinced Lola's killer is still on the loose. So she's been staying at mine while she figures out how to get that final piece – the nail in the coffin. Thanks to you, Audrey, she might have it.'

Ivy looks at me. 'What?'

'The list of Magpie Society members. I sent a photograph to Patrick. But I obscured some of the names . . .'

'Oh right,' she says. 'And that gave Clover a clue as to the killer?'

'I think so. She's been puzzling over it all night. But this morning she knew exactly what she had to do. She went back to the school to collect the final piece of evidence. So this afternoon I'm going to drive her over to the police station. Clover said you should both come too, so you can see Lola's killer brought to justice. You've been working so hard for me.'

Ivy shakes her head. 'We're just glad Clover is safe, but I can't believe you didn't let us know. Don't you realize how worried we all were? What about her family?'

'It's what Clover wanted. And, until we have Lola's killer behind bars, I won't stop. I'll do anything. I told you that before. And, if that means keeping Clover safe while she continues her investigation, then that's what I'm going to do.'

'So no one knows she's in your apartment?'

'I haven't told a soul. You two are the only ones who know. But I'm glad it's over now. By this time tomorrow, Lola's murderer will finally be behind bars.'

Ivy and I exchange a look. 'You really believe that?' I ask.

Then Ivy bites her bottom lip. 'Oh my God. We might not be the only ones who know.'

'What do you mean?' Patrick asks.

'I think someone overheard my phone conversation with Audrey yesterday. I was down in one of the music rooms. Mr Willis was right behind me and he might have heard. I don't know for sure though . . .'

Patrick stands up like a shot. 'I'd better go and check on her. She should be back by now. I'll call you girls when we're ready to go to the police.'

'We'll come with you,' I say. 'Should we bring her a drink?'

Ivy raises an eyebrow at me, and I give her the slightest shake of the head. It's the only way we can really be sure that she's OK.

'Yes, let's,' says Ivy. 'I know she's a straight-up Americano girl. No nonsense. We can get her a muffin too. Clover's always hungry.'

After a moment's hesitation, Patrick nods. 'Good idea. Let's hope the service is quicker than normal.'

I'm itching to tell Ivy what I found at Mrs Trawley's house, and I can tell by the anxious look on her face that she wants to ask me too. The black leather portfolio is heavy in the bag on my shoulder. I feel the first tingle of excitement – the answers we're looking for are so close. It's like an enormous jigsaw that was once a pile of unintelligible parts, but is now starting to form a coherent picture. *Nearly there.*

Coffee and muffin in hand, we walk out. I nudge Ivy's shoulder. 'I found something at Mrs Trawley's house. I'll show you later.'

'I can't believe this nightmare is soon going to be over,' she replies. Her shoulders are tight, her lips pursed, the picture of concentration.

The sound of sirens fills my ears, and we're forced to stop in our tracks as several fire trucks sweep past us, preventing us from crossing the road. They're heading straight for the row of buildings along the shore. Winferne Bay is such a small town . . .

My instinct knows something is wrong before my brain does. A deep pit in my stomach opens up, and dread fills it.

Patrick frowns. 'What the . . .' Then his face goes ashen.

I turn to Ivy, who shrugs. Then her eyes widen. I read everything in that expression.

Patrick takes off at a run, and Ivy and I aren't far behind.

Our worst fears are confirmed. The trucks are stopping outside of his building.

'No. No, no, no . . .'

He falls to his knees as we round the corner to where his apartment block is completely ablaze. Thick black smoke pours out of the windows on the top floor, interspersed with bright orange flame. Firefighters jump out of the trucks, connecting their hoses to the water mains and trying to access the top floor via ladders.

'Clover!' Patrick shrieks.

That's when nausea overwhelms me, and I'm almost sick right there on the sidewalk.

*Clover was inside the apartment.*

'Surely she got out in time. Surely!' I scream.

Ivy and I turn to each other in horror, then she reaches out and grips my hand. We cling to each other, helpless, as we watch Patrick's apartment burn.

# PART TWO

*One for sorrow,*
*That much you've learned,*
*Two for joy,*
*Who had to burn . . .*

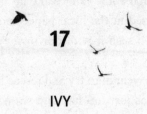

# 17

## IVY

The weeks pass by in a cold, hazy blur. Clover's death has sent shock waves through the whole school – she was such an institution.

Her memorial lands in the first week of December, when frost covers the ground like a shroud. Nothing can ever really prepare you for attending the memorial of a second friend in one year. The grim reality of stepping into a sombre crowd with another enlarged portrait of a student whose life was taken too young at the front on an easel. My jaw is already clenched, holding back any emotion that's been brewing since Clover's body was discovered last week.

As we walk into the Great Hall, 'Build Me Up Buttercup' is playing – one of Clover's favourite songs. But it doesn't drown out the weeping and sniffing from the hundreds of students and family members. Although Clover has already had her funeral, Mrs Abbott wanted to do this, as she did with Lola, for all her teachers and classmates, and to commemorate Clover as an Illumen Hall student. Her parents are sitting at the front, wearing black. Her mum is wiping her eyes, but somehow still smiling up at Mrs Abbott who has taken to the stage.

It still doesn't feel real, what happened. It's like some fever dream that I just can't wake up from. Photos of the fire were printed in the local paper and broadcast on the news, but we'd seen it with our own eyes. Patrick's wails still ring in my ear.

Firefighters went in to try and rescue her, but it was clear the inferno was just too fast and strong. When the police discovered Clover's body in Patrick's flat, they arrested him immediately. Yet he was released only a day later. The fire was ruled accidental and there was substantial proof that Clover was not being held against her will – messages, voice recordings Clover had made that were stored on the cloud. Still, there were a lot of questions for Patrick to answer.

Now whatever information Clover had learned about Lola's killer is lost to the ashes. We'll never know what the vital piece of evidence was that Clover was going to hunt down that morning.

The atmosphere in the school hall is bleak. Although Mrs Abbott's sentimental words fill the room, they don't cut through the grief that I can feel from every single body in here. Clover's shocking death will affect a lot of people for a very long time.

*Two students dead within a year!*

It just sounds like the plot of some overblown action film, not the reality of life in a small Kent boarding school.

Yet the school's motto rings in my ears too: *Alis grave nil. Nothing is heavy to those who have wings.*

Survival is built into the school's foundation, as strong as steel. It's survived bombings, scandals and threats aplenty. Illumen Hall will survive this. It has to. As will we.

Lyra is stepping down from the stage after doing a reading. She's crying and her hands are trembling. Her friends gather her up in a group hug as she sits back down with them. My body tenses. This was such a needless death. I can't help but think: *Will anyone else in this room be a victim?* Whose face will appear next on the school memorial easel?

Mrs Abbott comes back on to the stage to conclude.

'This year has been turbulent, and together, as a school community, we must now unite and be there for one another more than ever before. We will get through this. The Christmas concert shall be a tribute to both Lola and Clover. Two very bright, musically talented pupils, who I know would have shone onstage this year. Let's all work hard to make this the best concert we've ever put on – for them.'

I almost expect Clover to swing in on a trapeze once Mrs Abbott has finished speaking, clapping and cheering. I can't believe I'll never see her face again, or share a piano stool with her, or taunt her about her absurd love life. She really was like a little sister to me and so much of this just doesn't feel real.

Even if the fire had been an accident, she'd been staying at Patrick's purely to continue her investigation; if she'd dropped it, she would've been back in Polaris House where she belonged. The very reason we're all huddled together in this cold hall, celebrating her life, is because she dared to look into who took someone else's. If only she'd been less involved, less nosy and just stayed completely out of it . . . then we wouldn't all be here. It crosses my mind that I'm on the same path, but I push the thought away. It's different for Audrey and me. We're careful.

When we make our way out to the fountain afterwards, teachers are doing the rounds, making sure that students are feeling OK and encouraging them to visit Dr Kinfeld if they need to. I can imagine that after Lola, and now Clover, he'll see a substantial increase in counselling sessions. How could something like this *not* affect you deeply?

Mr Willis hands a tissue to a sobbing Araminta while wrapping his arm round her, and I roll my eyes.

Audrey and I step to one side.

'That was heavy!' Audrey says and she gets her phone out of her bag and turns it off silent mode.

'Yeah.' I fold my arms, wondering what we do now. I doubt they'll expect students to continue lessons. Maybe they'll ask us all to study in the common rooms or the library for the rest of the day.

'Do you think the same person who killed Lola struck again?' Audrey whispers.

'I don't know . . . but I have a bad feeling. We'd better get back to the Magpie Society headquarters and see what else we can find.' I glance around the courtyard, pulling the sleeves of my school cardigan down over my hands.

'Do you think we should tell the others who received invitations? Lyra, Yolanda and Harriet?'

I shake my head. 'It'll be too much for them. For now, let's just keep it to ourselves.'

# 18

## AUDREY

'Miss Wagner? Do you have any interest in solving this equation for me?'

I nearly jump out of my seat. The teachers here ignore me most of the time – and that's the way I like it. But for whatever reason, since Clover's memorial, they all seem to be paying me extra-special attention. I wonder if that's Mrs Abbott's doing.

Ever since the fire, I know she's been keeping a real-close eye on Ivy and me. We were the ones who were there when the firefighters arrived on the scene. We watched Patrick get carted away in handcuffs. We were driven back to school in the back of a police car, driven by a stunned DI Shing.

We always seem to be at the centre of the school's drama.

It's not like we *planned* it that way. I keep running through different scenarios in my head, wondering.

If Ivy hadn't been so busy with the prefects' meeting, if we had gone to see Patrick and Clover first, then would we have been able to stop the fire? Somehow, every which way I turn, it feels like my fault. I'd *known* Clover was in that building.

I'd seen her in Patrick's car.

If we'd told someone . . . the police, her parents, Mrs Abbott – then she would be safe right now.

The thought makes both Ivy and me feel sick. We'd had separate counselling sessions with Dr Kinfeld, but it hasn't helped much. He recommended we keep ourselves busy, find something fun to do to take our minds off the horrific events. We've instigated 'old-school-cool' movie nights in our dorm room, just so we're doing *something* that isn't thinking about death.

Yet all I feel is numb. I keep finding flames licking at the edge of my vision, that beautiful fireplace that I had admired so much turned deadly.

In the weeks since it happened, after cutting us some slack for the first few days, now it's like all the teachers have been told to drill us into submission. As if hard work will make us focus on ourselves and forget that another one of our fellow students died a horrible death. But – for the others – it actually seems to be *working*.

I just can't seem to get my head on straight. Not even the distraction of movie night – and Ivy has chosen one of my favourites, *The Breakfast Club* – can save me.

I keep thinking about the conversation we had with DI Shing. 'You're certain it was an accident?' I'd asked her.

'The forensic fire services did a thorough investigation. They confirmed that the fireplace malfunctioned, causing the blaze. Trust me, we had long conversations with Patrick Radcliffe and – while we found it highly suspect that he agreed to keep Clover hidden – it appears from the saved text conversations we found to have been at her request.'

'Did he tell you that she'd been gathering evidence about Lola's killer? That she was almost ready to talk to you?

What if the fire was set by someone who wanted to stop her from speaking to you?'

'Unfortunately, we can't know what Miss Mirth was intending to do. All her notes and belongings were lost in the fire.'

*That includes Lola's diary*, I realize with a jolt.

Any evidence we might have had to point to Mr Willis is gone.

'Miss Wagner?'

Tom, who is sitting next to me, nudges my shoulder. I snap out of my memory. *Oh right. The equation.* 'Um . . . I'm not sure.'

Mrs Parsons sighs. 'OK, but this was your assignment for *last* week and it's going to show up on all the IB exams. If you don't have a handle on this, please come and see me after class.'

My cheeks burn with humiliation as other eyes in the class dart towards me. This is *also* the kind of attention I was hoping to avoid since getting here. In Georgia, my plan had been to rely on my (likely mediocre) SATs to get into a good college. Not quite Yale, like my brother, but a decent enough school that wouldn't embarrass my family. Somewhere warm, but on a different coast to where my parents were. I had been thinking somewhere in California. Live the dream there.

Once Mrs Parsons's attention is turned firmly away from me, I look out the window at the roiling sea. It's raining again – a long way from any sort of California dream.

But somehow I *do* like it here. There's something about the damp that clings to me. It should be unpleasant, but instead I find myself sinking into it, not unlike a mudbath. No wonder Dad wants to build a spa here. Because even on days like today – days that would otherwise be classed as utterly miserable – there's something comforting about this place.

It sucks you in and you find you don't wanna leave.

Maybe it's magic.

*No*. I grit my teeth.

Thinking of Dad reminds me that he is still ignoring me – even with the fire drama – but, to my surprise, at that very moment I get a text from my older brother, Edison. He's asking to meet on the weekend in London. I reply with a tingle of excitement. Of all my family members, Edison is probably the one that I get along with best. And here's a chance for me to ask about the Illumen Hall hotel deal.

My cellphone buzzes again, but this time it's Ivy.

**MEET AFTER CLASS?**

I'm about to type a reply when a shadow looms over me.

'Look, Miss Wagner, I'm not stupid. I know you students smuggle phones into my classroom all the time, even though that's expressly forbidden. But at least try to be discreet about it? That's all we ask in return. And since you haven't been discreet . . . hand it over.'

'But . . .' I haven't replied to Ivy. I don't know where in these enormous grounds she wants to meet. Mrs Abbott has been assigning her tasks all over the school; Araminta's been demanding her time; we haven't been able to arrange one single special place.

Mrs Parsons snatches it out of my lap. 'You'll get this back at the end of the week.'

'But that's still three days away!'

'Just be glad I'm not reporting this to the headmistress. Then you'd really be in trouble.'

I slump back in my chair, studiously avoiding the gaze of everyone else around me. My secret cellphone, confiscated. God, how stupid am I?

All I know is that Ivy is gonna be mad that I'll miss our rendezvous. Especially as I can't get back to our room during class hours to leave her any sort of message.

When the bell rings, I grab Tom. 'Can you text Ivy and let her know I'll be down in the canteen?'

'Sure. But I gotta run – I'm supposed to be at PE next and I have to change.'

'That's fine. Just let her know where I'll be. Since Mrs Parsons took my phone . . .'

'She was in a shitty mood today. That was bad luck. Maybe ask her tomorrow if you can get it back. Use some of that Southern charm.'

'I'll try.'

I'll just have to head down to the canteen and hope that Tom remembers to pass on my message.

# 19

## IVY

I send another message to Audrey asking her to meet me on the edge of the woods. As I'm waiting for her, the trees are bustling and swaying in the breeze. The rain has just stopped, so droplets slip off the tips of the few remaining leaves and it looks so pretty and ethereal. I've always felt very comforted by trees. I love how they breathe and grow, shed their leaves, then work so hard to sprout them back every year.

There was a willow tree in the local park next to my flat when I was a child, and I would peel back the weeping willow leaves and enter into what I always felt was a safe haven. I'd go there to read my books, to write in my diary, to hide and to climb. I'd often sit in a low-hanging branch and dangle my legs over the edge, letting my imagination run wild. It felt like the tree was my guardian, that I was protected by its branches hanging round the trunk and almost touching the ground to make a bubble. I loved discovering which birds had nested further up the willow and watching them go from eggs to tiny chirping babies, to then taking their first flight. I miss that kind of childhood magic. I get a pang of nostalgia deep inside my stomach.

The main thing disturbing my tranquillity is my phone.

It seems to be buzzing with notifications left, right and centre. I think all my friends – especially Max, Tom and Harriet – have been especially instructed by Mrs Abbott to look out for me. Unfortunately for them, that tactic has the opposite effect. The more they pester me, the more suffocated I feel, and the more I want to push them away.

*Lola, Clover* . . . anyone who gets close to me seems to end up dead. My friends would be better off staying away.

I swipe away all the notifications without even looking at them. I don't want to hear from any of them – only Audrey. And, ironically, she's the only one who's not responding.

I send her another message, pinpointing exactly where I am in case she got lost. I sit on my coat and stretch out my legs.

The past two weeks have been a whirlwind. We've been kept so busy, we don't have any time to think about investigating and we haven't had a chance to get to the Magpie Society headquarters again. It's not for lack of trying. But I end up crashing out in my bed each night, absolutely exhausted.

Today was the first opportunity I had to think. I was really hoping we could both pop over to Mr Tavistock's house during our free period and catch up with him. Besides, it's been a while since I've seen him. He's usually very keen to overshare when it comes to me. I often catch him gasping and clutching his mouth when things come out that he knows he shouldn't be telling me. I'm actually shocked he was able to keep the Magpie Society a secret from me for so long. I guess some things people guard with their lives.

Just as I open up my timetable on the school app, I hear a loud cackle echo through the silence of the field and I immediately know who it belongs to. My phone is swiped from my hand by Harriet and, a second later, she, Tom and Max are sitting on the grassy verge beside me.

'We're taking this hostage until you stop ignoring us!' She shoves my phone down the front of her shirt.

'We just tried to message you to see what you were doing this free period. Wanna sneak off and grab some fish and chips from town? Play a card game . . . *anything*?' Tom smiles forcefully.

'We literally sat and watched you swipe our messages away, you cheeky bitch!' Harriet chimes in, laughing, but with a serious undertone.

'Sorry, I just . . . there's just too much going on right now and I think I want to be alone a bit more than usual.' I pull my coat on as I become more aware of the cold now my phone isn't distracting me. 'Though I did want to see Audrey – anyone know where that girl is?'

'Aha!' says Tom. 'That's why you need to read your messages. I texted you that Audrey got her phone taken by Mrs Parsons. She's waiting for you in the canteen.'

'It's always Audrey, isn't it?' says Harriet, a touch of hurt in her voice.

'Well, we just want to check you're OK. It's freezing out here, Ivy. Your blood must run ice-cold to be able to withstand this arctic weather in just that thin coat.' Max puts his arm round me. I tense up. Friendly displays of affection are not my forte at the moment. I think he senses I'm uncomfortable.

'We understand this is a hard time, babe, but we're here for you and we care about you.' Tom leans over and cuddles me into him on the other side so I'm now sandwiched between the two of them.

'And, even though you rarely show it, we know you care about us too.' Max smiles at me, his dimples creasing his cheeks.

'Honestly, guys, thank you. I will be fine. I think I just need a bit of alone time, that's all.' I feign a smile. They hesitate. 'Honestly. I'm OK. Love you all.'

Harriet slides my phone back out from the depths of her bra and hands it to me.

'You promise that you'll at least reply to a couple of the hilarious memes we've been sending you? You didn't even acknowledge the video I sent of Tom faceplanting on his board while doing a trick in the skatepark. He had a face like a squashed squirrel.' Harriet laughs out loud and elbows Tom.

'You swore you'd deleted that!' he gasps, all faux concern.

We laugh together, and I take the phone from Harriet and place it in my bag.

'I promise!' They all lean in for a group hug and Harriet plants a freezing kiss on my cheek before they make their way back to the main school building. I appreciate their efforts to cheer me up and raise a smile, but I just need a bit of silence and time to gather my thoughts. I relax back into my spot on the verge and take a couple of deep breaths.

As I sit there, other students huddled in groups make their way to their next classes across the school grounds, linking arms and laughing. Some are clearly using this five-minute buffer to gather and catch up, or have a quick snack.

I spot a small group of Year Sevens nearby under a tree, sneaking glances over their shoulders. Looks as though they're skipping their lesson, or going for a crafty cigarette. We've all been there – it's almost like a rite of passage in this school. Smoking is obviously banned, but, like a lot of things in Illumen Hall, if you aren't allowed it, you're more determined to find a way to do it. As part of my prefect duties, I should probably head over and tell them off, or report them to their head of year, but this overwhelming sense of nostalgia has softened me and I just watch instead. I miss those early days when I could spend hours exploring the grounds of the school, getting lost in among the hallways indoors and the trees outside.

Two of the girls light up a cigarette, while one of the boys decides to try and climb the tree. Probably showing off. I can't quite hear them from here, but I can tell they're egging him on and he's making pretty good progress. I'll leave them to it.

The thought of the school not being here any more ... it's devastating. No, more than that: it's unimaginable. Next year Violet would be eligible to come to Illumen Hall. I was excited to have her watch me as head girl. But now that's all gone. Stolen from me.

*Stop thinking like that, Ivy*, I scold myself. Sales of big buildings like this could take years. There's no need to panic yet.

The bell rings through the school: the start of the next lesson. Just then, I hear what I can only describe as a loud crack and a bang. I turn back to the group of students under the tree – but now the boy, who had made his way a good three metres up, is lying face down on the ground with a branch on top of him. The two girls start screaming.

I run over instantly to check he's OK. He's clearly not. He's unconscious.

'OH MY GOD, HE'S DEAD!' screams one of the girls.

'RING NINE-NINE-NINE!' shouts the other boy.

Together we manage to pull the branch off him, but he's in and out of consciousness and bleeding heavily from the head. His leg juts out at an unnatural angle. This is bad. This is really bad. I turn to the other boy.

'Fetch the nurse. While you're there, tell them to call an ambulance. I need you girls to take off your blazers and lay them over him. What's his name?'

'Leo,' one girl sobs as she starts to take off her blazer.

'He was only messing around. There wasn't a ribbon on this tree so we thought it was safe!' the other one cries.

'Leo, I know you don't know me, but I'm Ivy, and I'm a prefect at Helios House. Everything is going to be OK. Help is on the way.' I look down at Leo who is opening and closing his eyes, whining in pain.

Within minutes, the other boy is running back over with the nurse and Mrs Abbott. The girl's right: this tree hadn't been marked as dangerous like others around it. Leo's parents will be straight on the phone to their lawyers, and the school will be liable for this injury. As Mrs Abbott gets closer, it's clear from her face that this is running through her mind too. I wonder what she's thinking. Would a scandal this big be enough to shut down the sale?

Or could it shut down the school, for good?

# 20

## AUDREY

After fifteen minutes, there's still no sign of Ivy in the canteen; Tom clearly didn't manage to get a message to her. We can't go back to our rooms during class time, so I decide it's better to stick it out here, in case she does show up, rather than spend the short break scouring the school grounds – I know Ivy's always sniffing around after one of Ms Cranshaw's doughnuts, so there's a chance she'll come of her own accord.

I'd normally make good use of my free time by texting Teddy. He's been extra attentive after what happened to Clover and, although we've hardly had a second to ourselves to meet up, we've been getting closer over text. I love listening to his long voice notes, singing (*so* off-key, but it's OK because it's *so* sweet) lines of songs that remind him of me.

As if my thoughts conjure him up, I hear a familiar voice call my name.

'There you are!'

I look up and smile. 'Teddy!'

'You don't normally hang around the canteen. I didn't expect to find you here.'

'Mrs Parsons took my cellphone away. The secret one.'

'No!'

'Yep. Ivy wanted to meet me, but I couldn't reply.'

'I'm sure she'll forgive you. We still need to sort out that date, hey? Are you around this weekend?'

'I'm not sure . . . I'll have to check.'

'With Miss Creeper? You don't need her permission, you know.' He nudges my thigh.

'I know. We've just got a lot going on at the moment.'

'Don't need to access any more secret parts of the school, do you? I swear, I brick it every time I walk past Mrs Abbott's office that she's going to pull me up on changing the security settings on your passes.'

I'd forgotten about that. 'No, no more favours like that, I promise. It's been difficult to move forward since Clover . . .'

Teddy shudders. 'So awful what happened to her. Hang on – where are they going?'

All around us, students are running out of the canteen.

I call out to one of them. 'Hey, what's going on?'

'Didn't you hear? An ambulance just pulled up at the front of the school. Someone's hurt.'

'Oh my God. *Ivy!*' I jump to my feet, racing after all the other students. They're headed to the forest at the edge of the grounds, where a sobbing girl is being comforted by her friends.

'Audrey, wait!' Teddy shouts from behind me.

My vision tunnels: all I can picture is Ivy lying on the ground, writhing in pain. So it's a huge weight off my shoulders when I see her standing in a crowd of students. I think the entire school is here. Since Clover's death, everyone's so on edge – anything unusual attracts loads of attention.

Mrs Abbott is in a huddle with Mr Willis. They look

very cosy from where I'm standing. I narrow my eyes. From across the field, Mr Tavistock is limping towards them, looking every one of his seventy-plus years as he leans on his cane.

'See? She's fine,' Teddy says.

'Thank God. Look, I was supposed to meet her – she wanted to tell me something. In private,' I say pointedly.

Teddy nods, resigned. He leans over and kisses me on the cheek. 'As soon as you get your phone back, text me when we're going on that date, OK?'

'You got it.' I wait until he saunters off before heading over to Ivy. 'Hey,' I say when I finally reach her. Her school skirt is covered in fallen leaves, her forehead damp with sweat. 'I'm so sorry I missed your message – Mrs Parsons took my cellphone. What happened?'

'A boy fell from one of the trees. I think he'll be OK. But it was pretty awful. I heard the branch crack and thought the worst.'

'Thank the Lord he's OK. Word spreads fast here, huh?' I say, looking at the crowd.

'You're telling me. I guess after what happened to Clover everyone's worried – even though it looks like things are back to normal. But this might be our opportunity to do a little digging.'

'What do you mean?'

'Look at those two.' Ivy waggles her eyebrows in the direction of Mrs Abbott and Mr Willis. 'Don't they seem like they're in cahoots?'

'She wouldn't be so fond of him if she knew what a creep he is.'

'What if she *does* know?'

I gasp. 'You honestly don't think she'd keep him on if she knew he was having an affair with a student?'

Ivy shrugs. 'Blackmail can be a powerful tool. She could get him to do anything she wanted to hold on to his job. At this point, nothing would surprise me. Anyway, it looks like we can get out from under her nose for a bit. I've been studying the map on the Magpie Society phone again. One of the tunnels leads to a door right by her house. Let's go and look!'

'Ivy . . .' I kinda thought that with Clover gone she'd drop the Magpie Society stuff now. Clover's room-mates don't want anything more to do with it and the mystery of Lola's death seems to have gone cold. But Ivy is a dog with a bone. She's not gonna let this go easily.

'Come on. We've got some time. Everyone's preoccupied. Let's go.'

I glance around. It's true; all the students and teachers are totally focused on the boy still writhing on the ground. But I do catch someone glancing at us: Araminta. She's already committed to going to the hospital with the student though, so she can't follow us, as much as I imagine she wants to. I can almost read her mind – she's thinking she's jumped on the wrong drama train.

Mr Willis's voice sounds across the crowd, and I feel Ivy tense beside me. 'Right, everyone, back inside. I'm sure you all have classes to go to. Break it up, people.'

I grab Ivy's arm before he can rope the prefects in to help, and we slip away.

We cross the grounds, moving quickly. My breath

streams out in front of me, the cold seeping in underneath my blazer and down to my bones.

Mrs Abbott's home is sheltered in the woodland, a gorgeous old cottage with dark wood beams against white plaster. She must have a fire going pretty much constantly in the winter months as there's a steady plume of smoke that rises throughout the day. I don't blame her – but she must go through a heck of a lot of firewood.

Ivy pulls out the Magpie Society phone and passes it to me. I zoom in. 'OK – so the exit from the grotto doesn't come out in the headmistress's house but near it. Looks like it's in a shed or something.'

'No, it's not a garden shed,' Ivy says. 'It's stables.'

We stop in front of a long wooden structure smothered in twisting trefoil leaves. Creeping ivy. It covers almost everything except for a small door.

'This must have been where the horsemistress worked,' I say. 'I wish they still had horses here.'

'My dad was a good rider,' Ivy says quietly.

'Seriously?' This is the first time Ivy has mentioned anything about her dad in my presence.

'Yeah. It was his one fancy hobby. He's a car mechanic and a bit of a loser, to be honest with you. Leaving my mum the way he did. But I remember that about him: he loved horses. He had a natural affinity with all sorts of animals. There's this photo of him that I love – he's got his arm round the neck of a huge draught horse, with this gorgeous black Lab at his feet. He looks like a country gentleman, even though I know he's nothing like that really.'

'Sounds amazing. Can I see the photo?'

She shakes her head. 'Oh, I don't have it any more. I accidentally left it at my mum's flat, in my favourite photo album. I keep meaning to go and get it, but then other things get in the way ... and Mum's too busy to send it to me.'

'That's a shame. You should have those memories.'

'It's OK. I'll get it next time I'm in London and show you.' Ivy tugs at a rusted old brown handle on the stable door, but it doesn't budge. In fact, when we lean down to inspect closer, it looks like some brand-new metal braces have been applied – sealing the way shut.

'Dammit!' says Ivy. We circle the perimeter, trying to find a way inside.

'Hey! What are you doing?' It's Ed again, a pile of chopped wood under one arm.

Ivy and I both jump, clutching each other. But, when Ivy speaks, her voice is strong and indignant. 'We could ask you the same thing.'

'I'm doing my job. Preparing firewood for Mrs Abbott from some of the dead trees around here.'

Ivy raises an eyebrow. 'You should've chopped down the tree near the fountain.'

'Why? What happened?'

'Didn't you hear the ambulance? One of the branches broke while a boy was climbing. It wasn't marked with a ribbon like the others. You know the Year Sevens love to play out there – it's practically an Illumen Hall tradition.'

'Shit. You're kidding.' Ed's face is ashen. 'I'd better go over and see what's going on.'

'No, wait – tell us about the Magpie Society. We know your granddad was a part of it. We've seen his name in the ledgers.'

'Forget it! Don't you see? That's why I've been running around, blocking off all these entrances. I'm trying to cover up all this shit! Bad things happen to people who poke around about the Magpie Society. Look at Clover! That society will ruin my family – can't you see that already?'

He looks furious, his fingers opening and closing into fists.

Ivy frowns. 'What, Ed? What do you mean they're trying to ruin your family? Mr Tavistock is like a grandfather to me – you know he is. If there's something going on, *tell us* and we can help. Right, Audrey?'

'Right. Anything.'

His eyes dart from me to Ivy. 'Not here. Let's go back to the cottage. But it might be all for nothing now. If Mrs Abbott has her way.'

'What about the tree?' I ask.

'I'll deal with that later.'

We trudge away from the stables, through the woods. I look over at Ed as we walk. There's something enigmatic about him, despite his rough image. With a little trip to the barber's shop, some tailored jeans, he could look borderline hot.

Once we get back inside the Tavistocks' cute, chocolate-box cottage, Ivy doesn't waste any time. 'Tell us what you know about the Magpie Society.'

'No. First of all you tell me why you can't just drop it like you've been told.'

'This is my life we're talking about here! This school is everything to me!'

'*Your* life? You're so selfish; you can't see that some of us are about to lose our homes if you don't stop chasing the Magpie Society!'

'You think *I'm* to blame for this?'

'Why do you think Mrs Abbott is clamping down on you extra hard?'

There's a stand-off between Ivy and Ed. They're staring at each other, Ed underneath his thick, bushy eyebrows and Ivy with her fierce brown-eyed gaze. There are so many sparks flying between them, I feel like the whole cottage is gonna go up in flames.

'OK,' I say. 'Let's cool this down. I think we all want the same thing here. Ed – you're right. We can't let this drop. Like Clover, we've been looking into Lola's murder and – also like her – we've been led to the Magpie Society. Ivy and I owe it to Clover's memory to see this through. We know Lola had a magpie drawn on her back. Why? We know there was someone else up on the cliffs with her – there was eyewitness testimony to that. Who? We found the headquarters for the secret society, thanks to clues that someone left for us. *Why?* We're coming up on dead end after dead end – sometimes literally. So it would save us a heck of a lot of time if you could just tell us what you know right now.'

Ed sighs. 'Fine. Fine. You'd better sit.'

I drop into the old leather armchair. But Ivy and Ed remain standing. I feel kinda awkward getting back up now, so I stay put.

Ed walks over to the darkened fireplace and leans against the mantel. 'This ... Magpie Society thing. It *was* real, OK? It was as much a part of the school as the star names of the houses or the topiaries in the grounds. You've probably read this already, but it was established by Lady Penelope Debert, who convinced her brother, headmaster Alden, to allow the first female student to start attending the school in the late 1800s. She asked the staff – the people who *really* run the school – to keep an eye on the girl.'

'Lily Ellory,' Ivy whispers.

Ed raises an eyebrow and nods. 'Protect the most vulnerable student. And that's what they did – and then continued to do. The benefactors, the headmasters and mistresses, they take care of the "front of house", so to speak. But the *real* caretakers have always been behind the scenes. The hidden pillars of support, never acknowledged but always present.'

Ed looks down at his calloused hands. 'Yes, my granddad was a part of it. As the senior groundsman, just like his father before him, he was inducted in. But it all changed after that headmaster – Gallagher, I think his name was – was fired when the Magpie Society exposed his embezzlement of the boarding fees in the fifties. While they were glad he was exposed, the school's benefactors, the parents, the new headmaster – they decided they didn't want some secret society making decisions like that. It felt out of their control. They started making changes. Firing long-term staff. Closing their homes on the grounds. It took them twenty years, but they managed it.'

He pauses. 'Only my granddad was able to cling on to a

job – probably because they thought he couldn't maintain the grounds *and* keep a secret society going. They were right. You've seen him. He's got enough on his plate without worrying about the students too. It's not like he has a whole staff, as his dad did before him. When my parents moved off the grounds and then my grandmother died, he was really on his own. The society disbanded in the seventies.'

'Why doesn't he ask Mrs Abbott for extra help?' Ivy asks.

'You think he hasn't tried? I mean, she was really reluctant even to let me take my apprenticeship here, although I barely cost her a penny. They wouldn't even let me go to school here, did you know that? Despite the fact that my granddad lives in the grounds.'

'Hang on, so is your grandfather the only official Magpie left?' I ask.

'That I know of.'

Ivy frowns. 'So *he's* been sending us the invitations? He was the one who set up a phone with a map of the school's secret passageways? Seems like a bit much for him.'

'No, see? That's my point. It's not him, I'm sure of it. And it's not me either. Once you reported the person living in that cave, Ivy, I tried to shut off all the secret passageways. I don't know who is impersonating the Magpie Society, but I don't like it. I don't know what their goal is, but it has nothing to do with the society's original aim: to protect the vulnerable students of Illumen Hall.'

I grip Ivy's hand, my eyes widening, and she squeezes back.

Ed sighs. 'I also know Mrs Abbott wants to find any reason she can to fire my granddad. But that would devastate him. This place is his whole world. If she makes him leave the cottage, where will he go? He'll probably end up withering away in a care home somewhere. I don't want that. Although, after what happened to that boy, it might be too late.'

Ivy's face drains of colour. 'You can't be serious. She can't fire Mr Tavistock!'

'You can't control everything that happens here, Ivy!'

Ivy starts shaking, and I pull her down into a chair.

'Do you have anything to drink? A glass of water or something?' I ask Ed. Ivy looks really distressed, and I think she might pass out.

Ed lumbers to the kitchen. I take Ivy's hand in mine, and her fingers are ice-cold.

'Look,' says Ed when he returns. 'There's clearly something going on with this newly formed *Magpie Society*. Whoever gave you that phone, whoever's leaving you those notes . . .'

'Whoever drew that magpie on Lola's back . . .' I say, and Ed nods.

'They're not *our* Magpie Society. Not this –' he points up at a group photograph that includes his grandfather – 'Magpie Society. As far as I'm concerned, whoever's started this up again has only done bad things. Lola. Clover. And that's why they're hiding in the shadows. Manipulating you into thinking that they're us. Because they're up to no good. And my granddad is going to be the next casualty.'

Ivy shakes her head. 'Mrs Abbott must be trying to push

Mr Tavistock out because of her precious sale. They want to turn the school into some kind of hotel–spa hybrid thing. Host *weddings* here and shit. Completely ruin Illumen Hall's history, change it from the safe haven it was. This is exactly the kind of thing that the Magpie Society would want to stop, isn't it? So maybe they've banded up again? Maybe they don't think they need to have a legacy connection to protect the school. That's so . . . old-fashioned anyway. Sounds to me like even your granddad's Magpie Society, good as its intentions were, needed shaking up.'

Ed pauses. 'Well, I don't trust it. From everything that Granddad's said, the Magpie Society always puts the students first. Students dying does not fit into that.'

Ivy stands up and gives me such a glare that I'm forced to stand too. 'Look, Ed. We don't know who's leaving us these clues. But we do know that something isn't right in the school. So we're going to go ahead with our plans. Can we trust that you won't stop us any more, or close off any more of those entrances?'

He lifts up his hands. 'Do what you want.'

'Good.' Ivy's eyes flash. 'Because it's our job to protect the school. *We're* the Magpie Society now.'

# 21

## IVY

Once we're back at school, we make our way up to the common room and find an empty corner table to sit at. It's getting dark, the sky littered with pinpoints of stars in the deep navy. Audrey pulls her chair in and places her head in her hands. On our way up here, Tansy in Year Twelve confirmed what we feared: that Mr Tavistock has been fired. She saw him leaving Mrs Abbott's office, looking really distressed. We sit in silence for a while to try and make sense of it all.

'Do you think it's true?' Audrey says quietly, without looking up.

'I wouldn't put it past Mrs Abbott, if I'm honest. A dangerous tree that was still standing has quite literally crushed a student. Even though the boy's going to be fine, Mrs Abbott will use this as ammunition to get rid of the last long-term staff member.' I rub my temples and Audrey picks at her nail furiously.

'I wouldn't even be surprised if she orchestrated the entire thing by removing the ribbon herself! Think about it, Audrey: this has been in the works for years. Anyone who knew of the Magpie Society, and the good they used to do, is gone. The feathers are now temps! Anyone hired as domestic staff is here for a year max and then they're gone. Turned over. If the society really used to stand for something, to protect the school, this hotel development is the last thing they'd want to happen.'

I check around to make sure nobody else can hear our conversation. There are only a couple of other students playing table football at the end of the room.

'The less old staff around, the easier it will be for the sale to go ahead, I guess.' Audrey sighs.

'What's going to happen to Mr Tavistock?' My stomach drops. The thought of leaving the school is something I only ever have nightmares about. The idea that, with a click of her fingers, Mrs Abbott can ask you to leave and never return – and change the course of your life. Mr Tavistock and I have a bond, one that I genuinely think is cemented by our joint love of this school. He's the only person I can really talk to for hours about it. Its quirks and its beauty. I know he loves watching the changing of the seasons in the grounds he's worked so hard to maintain. The thought of him wasting away somewhere, not able to use his green thumbs, makes me sick.

'Do you still have those blueprints on you?' I ask.

'Oh ... erm, I'm not sure. I'll have a look.' Audrey heaves up her bag and flicks through folders and papers hesitantly.

'I think that's it!' I say, spotting the fine black lines and architectural drawing in a flash of paper that she almost misses.

'Oh yeah, there it is!' She pulls it out slowly and hands it to me.

I double-check who's around; it's still really quiet. Most people will be heading down to dinner at this time. Cautiously and carefully, I unfold the blueprint and lay it out across the table. I notice a logo in the top right-hand corner.

'This must be the company that's buying and developing the school; we should research them.' I go to grab my phone.

'I can do it!' Audrey jumps in. 'I love playing detective with things like that. I'll have a look on my laptop later and get back to you. It'll give me something to do this evening at least.' She smiles eagerly.

'OK, great! Araminta wants another rehearsal so I won't have much time anyway,' I say, scanning the rest of the paper for anything else we can investigate. 'This all just looks so shit, doesn't it?'

They're planning to bridge together the old buildings by using all-glass tunnels and completely demolish the Tower Wing. The oldest part of the school! It also looks as though the woods will be totally flattened and made into extra hotel blocks. I can't bear to imagine all those beautiful old trees with so much history being burned in a bonfire and replaced by modern square buildings with tacky balconies.

'I'm going to see if anything comes up when I google the school and search propertylife.com. Maybe we can find something on the land registry site too?'

'Good idea.'

I open the internet tab on my phone. Nothing comes up, although I see that a few articles about the tree accident have already circulated online from local tabloids.

'It must have been a private sale. There's nothing up yet.'

'Hmm . . .' Audrey taps a finger on her mouth. 'If this is in any way connected to Lola, Patrick might know something about it. Remember how we were gonna ask him what he knew, but we got distracted grilling him about Clover instead? Their family are extremely wealthy after all. Could they be involved in some way?'

'Worth a shot, I suppose!'

'I'll ask him when I get my cellphone back.'

'I've been thinking . . . what with all these secret tunnels, and how desperately hard Mrs Abbott seems to be trying to keep us apart, we should think of a way to stay in touch with each other.'

'How about a shared location app on our phones? We can add each other?'

'Perfect.' I log into the App Store and search for a friend-finding app. 'What about this one?'

'I'll download it and add you.'

'And so we don't have to sneak around the kitchens all the time – Ms Cranshaw will definitely start getting suspicious – we can use Mr Tavistock's home as a meeting place after he's gone. If you can't find me, that's where I'll be. Sound good?'

'Perfect.'

'Hi, girls.' I hear the familiar husky, loud voice of Araminta behind me and instantly shut my eyes and freeze. I'm *so* not in the mood for this. 'I take it you're studying?' She tries to eye up what we're looking at and I notice her eyes wandering to my phone.

'Yes. What do you want?' I bark back as I lock my phone screen. She frowns, and Audrey cringes from across the table.

'Have you picked your new music for the Christmas concert, Ivy? Now that Clover clearly won't be joining you . . .' She flicks her ponytail.

'Minty, do you ever tire of being such a fucking insensitive bitch?' I say to her.

Her face turns beetroot red. 'Coming from you?' She laughs uncomfortably, tears pricking her eyes.

'Let's not argue. This is a difficult time for everyone and emotions are high . . .' Audrey tries to calm whatever's brewing between me and Araminta.

'You're right, Audrey. Some people can't seem to handle their emotions.'

'Oh, please. Go and find someone else to boss around, Minty. I'm bored of you.'

She glares at me for a minute, then turns and makes her way towards the door. 'You know what? If you're not serious about the Christmas concert, then I think I'll speak to Mr Willis about replacing you!'

'Do whatever you want!' I yell at her back, even though the door shut before she could hear me. 'Can you believe her?'

'I might go after her.' Audrey slings her bag over her shoulder and gets up from the table.

'God, Audrey, you really are such a kiss-arse,' I growl.

Audrey looks stung and stares back at me, unable to move or respond. Her eyes instantly tear up.

'Sorry. I didn't mean that. I'm just stressed. This whole thing is just . . . a lot.'

'I get that,' she says softly. 'But I'm not letting anyone else fall victim to Mr Willis,' and she walks away without a smile.

# 22

## AUDREY

Ivy's barb still stings, but I don't change my mind. I catch up with our head girl. 'Araminta, wait. Don't go to Mr Willis.'

'Why not? Ivy's not in charge here. I'm not going to let her ruin the Christmas concert like she did the Samhain party.'

'It's not that. You can go to any other teacher. Just not him.'

Araminta folds her arms across her chest. 'Explain.'

'He's a creep, OK? I'd stay away from him if I were you.'

Colour creeps into her cheeks. 'That's a pretty bold accusation to make, Audrey. You've only been here for what – three months? You have no idea what you're talking about.'

'Please listen to me. He's not a good person.'

'Do you have any proof?'

'No, but . . .'

'Look, I know you and Ivy are super close, but let me tell you something. Ivy has a massive crush on Mr Willis. Everyone knows that. Last year she was basically like his stalker – she made Mrs Abbott change her music mentor so that Mr Willis had to spend more time with her. She joined the Christmas concert just so she could be with him. Honestly, if anyone's the creep, it's Ivy.'

'OK, that doesn't sound true at all.'

'It is! He's too nice a guy to admit it or tell her to back off, but it's true. Ivy was the same way with Lola Radcliffe. If she was here, she'd confirm it. She was always moaning to us about how Ivy wouldn't leave her alone.'

I'm starting to feel really guilty about how much time I'm spending with Araminta because the version of Ivy I hear coming from Minty's mouth isn't the Ivy I know at all. Maybe I *am* being a kiss-ass.

What I realize is that I'm being a kiss-ass to the wrong person. I'm going out of my way to warn someone I know to be a bully and a fake. But it's Ivy who I really want to be closer with.

I wish there was something I could do for her to prove my loyalty. Hanging out with Araminta is *not* the one.

'Any plans for the weekend?' Araminta is changing the subject. 'If not, I was going to go down to Margate with Bonnie and Xander to check out this cute cafe there ... You could come if you want.'

'Actually, my brother's coming to town.'

'Oh really, is he cute?'

I grimace. 'Er – ew! Anyway, he wants to meet me up in London. I haven't been there since we moved, weirdly enough. It'll be strange being back in a big city.'

'Oh my God, I *love* London. Why don't I come with you? I'd get to meet your cute brother. And we could go to Oxford Street and shop till we drop.'

'What about your Margate plans?'

She shrugs. 'I can do that whenever. This'll be some me and you time! Oh, come on – it'll be fun!'

I'm such a people-pleaser, I almost can't bear to let down her eager face. And I don't think that Araminta is used to hearing no. I swallow, summoning up all my courage. 'No, really. I think I have to see my brother on my own. Private family stuff.' She can't argue with that, can she?

'Aw, seriously? Come on, please!'

'No!' I snap.

'God, touchy much? All right, Princess, I was only doing you a favour.' She rolls her eyes. Then, just as quickly, she smiles. 'OK, I'd better go and check Leo's settling in OK with his broken leg. There really should be better disability access around here. I bet Clover would be right at the forefront of that campaign.' Her hand flies to her mouth. 'Oh my God, Audrey, I'm so sorry. It must have been terrible to be there when it happened. She could be a pain, but she was like a staple of the school. I never thought something so terrible would happen to her.'

My mouth goes dry. Araminta pats my hand, then leaves me blissfully alone. Still in a daze, I head back to my room.

Araminta's right – things just feel so wrong. I'd pushed the fire to the back of my mind, tried to make the reality of Clover's death as small as possible, squeezing it into some dark corner I wouldn't have to look at too closely. I can't even imagine how Ivy must be feeling, considering how close she was to Clover. She's been through so much lately. I wanna do something just for her.

Suddenly a thought comes to me. While I'm in London,

I could go to her house and get that photo album for her. The one with the picture of her dad in it. *That* will make her smile.

But, to do that, I need to find out where she lives. I look over at Ivy's side of the room, trying to find a phone number or an email address for her mom. I do a quick Google search for Moore-Zhang in London, but there's nothing.

I don't wanna rifle too hard around her private things, but that's when I catch a lucky break. There's a to-do list pinned on Ivy's corkboard above her desk. It's not the huge amount of coursework that interests me, but what it's written on. The back of an old envelope. The return address is Illumen Hall. But on the front . . . I pull it down from the corkboard and gasp. On the front is a London address.

I type it into Google Maps and up comes an apartment block, not far from Brixton station. I'll have to change trains, but it's on a line down from London Bridge where I'm gonna meet my brother. I'm starting to think I could really pull this off.

I save the address and pin the list back exactly as I found it, hoping Ivy is none the wiser.

By the time the weekend rolls around, the tension between Ivy and Araminta seems to have eased. Ivy's chosen her new piece of music – something incredibly complicated-looking she composed herself. She really is a superstar.

It does mean that she's rehearsing all the time though, so I don't even get to say goodbye to her before I run to catch my train.

I relax as I watch the vast swathes of Kent countryside

rush past me on my way into London, the buildings rising higher and higher. The further away from Illumen Hall I get, the more the strangeness of the past few weeks comes into sharp focus. It's as if I've been living in a bubble where secret societies, hidden passageways, shell grottos, creepy teachers, angry head students and girls dying in horrible ways are the norm. All the people in the city are just going about their ordinary lives, blissfully unaware of mysteries and magpies. It makes me realize how isolated I've been. I don't even have any idea what's going on in the news or in world events – I don't know what the new songs are on the radio or what movies are out in cinemas. I don't even check in with my friends back home any more.

I feel like an alien emerging from a spaceship on to a new planet.

I get off the train at London Bridge, staring up at the gigantic point of the Shard piercing the bright blue sky. I try to follow the directions on my phone to the little cafe in Borough Market where my brother wanted to meet, but it's real confusing. I remember being in New York City and finding the neat, straight lines of the blocks so comforting. London is a mishmash of streets and train lines and tiny alleyways – of big modern buildings and ancient history. I turn along one street and come across a giant ship, then the ruins of some medieval palace that reminds me of Illumen, before realizing I've gone too far in the wrong direction.

Finally, I find the cafe and duck inside. Sitting at a table with two coffees ready and waiting is my older brother.

'Deedee! So good to see you.'

'Edison! Wow! So wild that you're in London.'

I give him a big hug as he stands up, wrapping his strong arms around me. He's almost six feet five, towering over most of the other customers, even managing to make me feel short – it's one of the reasons I love him.

'I got you the most sickly-sounding coffee on the menu . . . some kinda toffee-nut nonsense. Hope you like it.'

I take a sip, hopping up on to a stool. 'Yum. Better than that boring espresso.' *He'd get on well with Patrick*, I think with a jolt. 'What are you even doing here? Shouldn't you be partying it up in your frat somewhere?'

'I'm not part of a frat and you know it.' He leans forward, lacing his fingers around his tiny coffee cup. 'Anyway, have you heard from Dad lately?'

'No . . . actually, I've been trying to get in touch with him and he's gone completely AWOL. It's kind of annoying.'

Now that I have a moment, I take in what Edison is wearing. He's in a suit. I frown; that's not like him.

'Apparently, he's in crisis meetings about his new project. He thought it would be good to fill you in on what was happening, so he asked me to come here to tell you. He's planning to –'

'Buy the school he sent me to and turn it into some luxury hotel, upending my life once again and destroying the lives of many of my new-found friends? Something like that?'

For once, I've managed to render my brother speechless. It feels satisfying, until the reality of what I've said sinks in. I hadn't really thought about it that way before. But it's just freaking typical of my dad. To send me to the school he wants to buy, probably to save money – here I was thinking he was dropping thousands of pounds on my school fees when it was probably all wrapped up in the deal. He doesn't care one bit about my future.

*Because he doesn't have to.*

I've lived my whole life with a giant safety net. I could move schools again, or take a year off, or skip college altogether, and I'd land on my feet. My dad might not care about my future, but he would never let me drown – as much as it annoys me to admit it.

My big brother finally exhales a sharp breath, then takes a sip of his coffee. 'So you do know. But how? Dad said he hadn't told you yet.'

'He hadn't.'

Edison raises an eyebrow. 'This is big. No one's supposed to know yet. It was a condition of the deal that nobody was told until everything's finalized. If Dad finds out that there's been a leak somewhere, he is gonna be so pissed ... You have no idea how much of our future is invested in this.'

'Well, trust me, *someone* at the school knows about it. I've seen the plans. Maybe Mrs Abbott doesn't wanna sell after all?'

'Your principal?'

'They call it headmistress over here.'

'Oh right. Nah, from what Dad says, she's been the one driving this thing hard. She's come by the house to give progress updates and everything.'

'Oooh.' Now it suddenly makes sense why Mrs Abbott had visited my dad at home that time. I feel anger bubble up from my stomach.

'Deedee, look. If this gets out – it could be really bad.'

'If it was that bad, Dad would have told me about it before!

He wouldn't have wanted me to go off to some school and make friends that I could only ever have for a year.'

'How could he expect you to understand? It's a huge, ambitious project for him. Huge money for us. The biggest yet. You don't wanna ruin it for him, do you?'

I dig the edge of my thumbnail into my forefinger, so hard I break the skin. But I don't care. At least it means I'm feeling something.

'Honestly, Edison? I don't give a fuck what Dad thinks. But I don't reckon he should count on this sale going ahead. D'you think he even knows or cares about the history of the school? That place has survived revolutions, massacres, bombings, world wars. Trust me when I say that Dad doesn't have a chance against the forces that *really* run the school.'

Edison leans back. 'That's just it. That was the other thing I wanted to talk to you about. You're wrong. Some of the school's most important donors are behind this. One family . . . the Radcliffes? They're the biggest investors in this.'

'Wait, what?' My eyes widen. Ivy and I had assumed they'd be *against* closing the school.

'Oh – that's interesting to you, is it?'

'I . . . I don't believe you.'

'Here you go.' Edison pulls up a document on his phone. Sure enough, the Radcliffes' names are there on a document approving the sale of the school. It turns my stomach.

'The teachers won't agree to it then. They'll all be out of a job.'

'The teachers? They're gonna get a big severance payout; they'll be fine. More than fine. They'll probably be delighted.'

'What about the students then?'

'Your headmistress is sorting that out. Everyone will be looked after. Look, Dee, I kinda thought you'd be happy about this – happy to be involved. I didn't know you were so attached to the school. But I realize now why Dad reached out to me. He's working insanely hard to pull this deal off. He's managed to get so many obstacles out of the way – you have no idea. He's moved mountains for this project and he was hoping to count on your help.'

'My help? He thinks I'm gonna help him tear down the place? I don't think so. And maybe you have the backing of Mrs Abbott and the Radcliffes and the teachers, but that's not everyone. People are gonna protest, you know.'

'People might object, but schools close down all the time. This project is huge for us – don't you get it? For our family. The students will be fine. But we *need* this. And don't forget all that we've done for you.'

'So that's why you're here.' I blink. I thought Edison and I were close. But no – he's just like everyone else in my family. Using me for whatever they need, expecting me to bend to their will. 'You want something from me.'

'You've got access to a piece of information Dad needs. A document – probably in the school library or archives. It's the deeds to the school. There's a special clause in there that we need to check.'

'Why didn't he just ask Mrs Abbott?'

'He thinks she might be keeping it from him. He doesn't want anything to happen that might pull the rug out from underneath this deal at the last moment.'

I roll my eyes. 'Is this why you're wearing a suit? Do you work for Dad now or something?'

'Actually . . . I do. I know you've been distracted since the incident, but, if you'd been paying attention, you'd know I've taken some time off college to work for Dad's firm for a while. That's why I'm here in London.'

My jaw drops. 'What? What about Yale?'

'Yale will still be there next year. This is important.'

'So why doesn't he ask me himself?'

'He's busy. He's in some big meetings at the moment, trying to sort it all out. This is crunch time, don't you know. Construction is due to start in the summer.'

'In the summer?' My jaw drops. 'So I'm not even gonna get to graduate from Illumen Hall?'

Edison laughs. 'Since when do you care about where you graduate from? You know it doesn't matter. You can go to any college you want.'

'How about what I want? A bit of stability in my life? Friends?'

'That seemed to be the last thing on your mind back in Savannah.'

'Well, things have changed.'

'Come on. You'll be fine. Don't you wanna do acting anyway? You can come up to London, go to a more arts-focused school – or come back to the States! I'm sure Dad would get you an apartment in NYC if you help him out with this.'

'I can't listen to any more of this. Listen, Edison, I'm happy you're looking well and doing fine, but . . .' I slide off my stool.

'Dee, you can't be serious! I only just got here.'

'Yeah, well, I have other things to do in London, OK?'

'What, haven't had your shopping fix this month?'

I narrow my eyes. 'Don't be a dick, Edison. You don't know anything about me any more. I used to look up to you, you know? But now I realize you're just as bad as the rest of them. Go back to college and hang with your lacrosse buddies. *That's* where you belong.'

I storm out of the cafe, feeling a chill that has nothing to do with the fresh air outside.

# 23

## AUDREY

I head towards the river. Watching the water rushing by, the sun glinting off the surface, I start to relax. I half wonder if Edison's gonna follow, but after a few moments I know he's left me to my own devices. That's what I've always been to my family: the middle child, the one who gets overlooked, who can be pushed around with no concern for how I might be affected. I don't think they even noticed me until last summer, when Alicia ended up dead in our hot tub.

Yeah, that got their attention.

But I seem to have slipped back down the ranks. Out of sight, out of mind at boarding school. Edison is Dad's golden child, his heir apparent. Jason is Mum's little prince, allowed to skip as much school as he wants in pursuit of his passions. *I'm* the one who gets sent to a new school for a fresh start – when Dad knew full well I'd have to say goodbye to any friends I made at the end of this year and try again somewhere else.

*Be good.* Dad's last words to me before I arrived at school. What he really meant was: *Don't get in my way.*

All in all, it leaves me more determined than ever to help Ivy. She's saved me, even though I've only known her for a short time. Shown me that it is OK to care about something. And, right now, I care about helping her achieve her dream of graduating from Illumen Hall.

Dad can wait a year.

I know what he's after now. What he doesn't know is that I actually have it: the document that Mrs Trawley left for Clover. I know that must be the missing lease, with the clause about head students being able to vote on any decisions regarding the school. If a Magpie became head student, they would surely stop it and receive Lady Penelope Debert's legacy, whatever that means. But my dad needn't worry. Araminta and Xander aren't Magpies, and they aren't gonna vote against the sale.

Another dead end.

Anyway, I'm glad I have something else to focus on – another task that I want to complete so my trip to London isn't a total bust. I have to get that photo album for Ivy. A tingle of excitement flickers in my belly. I pull up her home address on my phone and take the Tube a few stops down the line into south London.

I emerge into a place full of hustle and bustle, with a teeming market packed with street stalls filled with mounds of fruit and vegetables, and bunches of flowers. I can't really picture prim Ivy growing up here; it's a place of such colour, crowds and energy whereas she is so organized and meticulous. Still, I move away from the vibrancy of the market towards a dingy concrete building. There's a big, bold NO BALL GAMES sign in huge letters and BROUGHTON ESTATE underneath. The word 'estate' makes it sound grander than it is.

I spot a group of children playing on a swing set, and I wonder if one of them is Ivy's sister, Violet.

I make my way towards Flat 23, which is bordered by neat flowerpots that bring a smile to my face. I take a deep breath. I can't believe I'm about to meet Ivy's family.

I knock on the door. I can hear a radio playing through the window, and the curtain twitches just a tiny bit to reveal a young face. It must be Violet. I grin and wave, and the face disappears just as quickly.

The door opens, a tired woman in a creased suit answering the door. Her long dark hair is pulled back into an elaborate-looking braid. 'Can I help you?'

'Oh, hi – I'm Audrey Wagner,' I say with my warmest smile.

'Sorry, we're not buying anything right now or interested in any charity donations.' She starts to close the door.

I place my hand on it, stopping it from slamming in my face. 'No, it's not like that. I'm from Illumen Hall. I'm Ivy's room-mate? I was talking to her and she mentioned this old photo album that she'd left at home, and how she really missed it. I thought it might be a nice surprise if I brought it back for her, so I came here to see if you still had it?'

The woman narrows her eyes at me. 'How did you get this address?'

'Oh, Ivy had it pinned up on her board.'

'I find that hard to believe. I'm sorry, I can't help you.'

'Please, Mrs Moore-Zhang . . .'

'It's just Zhang,' she mutters.

'Mrs Zhang.'

I put on my biggest pageant smile, oozing as much

Southern charm as possible. I've been told that I can turn it on and off like a tap, and right now I'm attempting to turn it on as much as possible.

'Please – I'm sure you're very busy and I'm real sorry I dropped in unannounced, but I couldn't find a number or else I would have called. Ivy's my friend. My best friend. I wanna do this one thing for her, and then I'll be out of your hair. I promise.'

That does seem to give her pause. 'She's your friend.'

'Yes, ma'am.'

'To be honest, I didn't think that was possible,' she mutters. I frown at that. Ivy has tons of friends at Illumen Hall. I realize that I'm so new that she might not have mentioned me. Then I hear another voice.

'Who is it, Mum?'

I try and crane my neck to get a glimpse of Ivy's famous sister. 'Is that Violet?' I ask with a wide smile. But Ivy's mom moves so that my view is blocked.

'Wait there,' she snaps. She closes the door, leaving me standing in the cold. Obviously, my charm isn't working that well.

A few moments later, the door opens again a tiny crack. Mrs Zhang slips the photo album through the gap. 'Here. Take it,' she says.

'Th-thank you,' I say.

'Don't come back here,' she says through gritted teeth. 'Besides, Ivy hasn't lived here in years. If you really are her best friend, God help you.'

The door closes in my face.

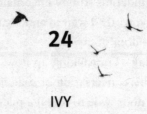

# 24

## IVY

It's a brisk early December morning. The wind blows through the trees and the final remnants of the dried autumn leaves are wafted through the air. I decide to make my way over to see Mr Tavistock and check if the latest rumour really is true.

I had hoped to go sooner, but have struggled to get away from rehearsals and revision over the past couple of days. Plus, I didn't want anyone seeing me walk to his cottage. He'd need time to box up anyway so I knew he'd still have a week or so on Illumen grounds according to school gossip. I've watched many staff pack up their stuff and leave this school over the years. Most just had to fill a box, some a suitcase, but never clear an entire house. It feels cruel in this instance. Where will he go? What will happen to Ed?

I knock on the door and Ed answers in a white vest and blue overalls, the top half knotted around his waist. His ponytail is tied loosely and the stray baby hairs around his hairline are frizzy with damp.

'Is your granddad here?' I ask without preamble.

'Hello to you too. No, he's in town at the moment. Want me to pass on a message or . . . ?' He leans his arm against the door frame and wipes a bead of sweat from his brow. There's mud under his stubby fingernails.

'When are you off?' I wait in anticipation, half expecting Ed to shut the door in my face.

'In a few days. I'm packing up now. You want to come in and have this conversation or shall we just stand here?' He opens the door wide to reveal a pile of boxes and a roll of bubble wrap. I walk in and perch myself on the arm of one of the remaining armchairs. Ed gets back to wrapping up bowls.

'Actually, it's good that you've come, Ivy. I was going to track you down, but it's just been too busy. I've spoken to Granddad, and he wants me to tell you something more. I was lying when I said the original Magpie Society have gone completely quiet.'

'I knew it,' I whisper.

'He's been aware Mrs Abbot was up to something dodgy – he just had no idea what it was. So, when I came here, he asked me for some help bringing the society into the twenty-first century, you know? Digitize the archive – or what was left of it – and find a way to keep tabs on the school. It looks like he was spot on with his prediction. She's implemented the final stage of her plan: that kid getting hurt was a stitch-up. Mrs Abbott wants us gone. And it was just the excuse that she needed.'

'What do you mean, a stitch-up?'

'That tree *was* marked as dangerous. I tied the ribbon on it myself. I know I did. It was dead; one gust of wind and it would have come down, let alone being climbed on. Trees are always marked with a green ribbon for cutting down.

Someone took that ribbon off the tree, knowing full well a student would climb it eventually and have an accident.'

'Mrs Abbott?'

'Or whoever she's got working for her. Maybe it's whoever's impersonating the Magpie Society? Like I told you, it wasn't me or Granddad who sent those invitations – I double-checked with him. That's why I've been closing up the entrances. You won't be able to access those headquarters again – at least not through the kitchens.'

'But . . . *you* haven't been fired. Why is she making you leave too? Can't you stay?'

If Ed leaves as well, it will just be me and Audrey trying to take on the beast that is this development. We could use his help.

'No. I'm just an apprentice. When the master goes, so do I. It's over for the school, Ivy. Mrs Abbott and the investors in the new hotel have won.'

'So what now?' My voice is small and meek. The rug has been pulled from under my feet.

'You really want to stop this, don't you?'

I nod. 'It's not just for me. I mean, of course I want to graduate from the school that I've dedicated seven years of my life to. But it's more than that. This school is part of *history*. It's opened so many doors – not just for me, but for others too. And I want younger students to have a chance to experience that as well. Illumen Hall is different. I feel that in my bones.'

'If only we'd been able to get a Magpie as head student.'

'What?'

'Oh – it was something written into the school code. Why

do you think I was never allowed to attend Illumen and instead had to go to Winferne Comprehensive? Normally, as the relative of a staff member, I'd have been given a place automatically, but not here. It's the one thing the headmasters – and mistresses, I guess – have made sure to control, especially since that headmaster got the sack. By not allowing people like me, descendants of Magpies, to attend the school, they made sure we could never enact that clause. If a Magpie ever did get through – like Maggie Trawley for example – they'd never choose her as head girl. It's rigged.'

'What would happen if a Magpie did become a head student then?'

'They'd join the board – like the other head students before them. They would have the right to veto the sale. And they'd be able to stop the sale of the school, of course. Rumours are they'd inherit a lot of cash too.'

He eyes me. 'I know what you're thinking, that I could get Granddad to make that Araminta girl an official Magpie. But they *have* to be a direct descendant. Typical rich-person obsession with lineage and bloodlines – Lady Penelope was a pioneer, but not about everything. So it's too late now.'

'It can't be,' I say, my mouth feeling dry.

'Well, you and Audrey will be the only two "Magpies" left at the school once we go and neither of you are blood relatives of the society so you can't inherit anything. And that applies to anyone else you recruit, of course. So come on. I want to show you something.'

He places the last bubble-wrapped bowl a box and walks through to the kitchen. He moves some boxes and slides the rug to one side, uncovering a hatch with a bolt. He pulls the bolt across and lifts the hatch, which then reveals a set of stairs going down into darkness.

'It looks dodgy, but trust me . . .'

I hesitate. I could walk down these steps and never see daylight again. I've seen the documentaries about young girls who are kidnapped and kept in basements for years. Ed holds out his hand and starts walking down the first few steps. I take it and follow him. As I do so, I take the Magpie Society phone from my pocket and check the map. This route isn't on here. Clearly there are still some things this school keeps hidden, but following Ed now it feels as though this might be the key to finally knowing all I can about the society and the secrets it holds. He turns on some lights and everything feels a little less like something from a psycho thriller.

The stairs lead to a dark tunnel. It's cold, damp and really muddy, but I focus on just putting one foot in front of the other behind Ed as he confidently makes his way along. We arrive at an old round stone structure with tiny little windows that have been filled in with mud. It looks like something that could have once existed above ground, but is now buried. Ed flicks a switch and lights pop on. There's a desk and a couple of monitors on one side of the small room. Heaps of wires and cords that are obviously connected to something spiral out of each corner.

'This is the Magpie Society tech base. It used to be their archive area, but when the society disbanded in the seventies they cleared out a lot of the old files. So, after I arrived, Granddad asked if I could hook us up to the existing CCTV and install a few cameras of our own so we'd have an overview of what was happening around the school.'

'How did you do this?' I stare in awe at what I'm witnessing.

'When you work on the grounds, you get a lot of access to things, you know? And I was able to add a few more cameras that even Mrs Abbott doesn't know about.'

'Can you only access this through the groundsman's kitchen? Where even are we?'

'No, there are a few different entrances. Although I've covered a lot of them over. My plan had been to remove the hatch and replace it with floorboards before leaving so nobody else could get in here, but I worry that me and Granddad are the last ones with access, so I don't want to do that. This leads underneath the old stables.'

'So are you saying that Mrs Abbott's house is directly above this?'

'Yes, it's pretty risky. You get to know her movements though.'

'Fuck. This is . . .' I pace on the spot.

'. . . a lot to take in?' he finishes.

'Yeah. I mean, I'm pretty clued up on the school cameras and corridors, but this is a new level of spying. How does it all work?'

'I can only show you this if you'll allow me to pass the keys over to you and Audrey now.'

I feel an overwhelming sense of responsibility. 'What do you mean?'

'We're checking out, Ivy, and there's nobody left. You are literally the only people I can hand all this over to.'

'Let me get this straight: you want ME and Audrey to take over and be a part of the Magpie Society? The official one, not just whatever we joined before . . .'

'Yes, because we're not going to be here. Maybe then you might have a tiny shot at stopping this development going through.'

'But what can we do?'

He stops me saying more. 'I don't know. Honestly. But this is the only thing I can think of. This is keeping centuries of good work alive.'

'OK,' I say confidently.

'OK what?'

'I'll do it – we'll do it.' I smile at him.

'Granddad will be thrilled. Let me show you how to log in to this.'

We sit at the desk and he goes through passwords and quick shortcuts that enable us to really quickly tap into the school cameras.

'Whoa. And you have sound?'

'Yes! We can listen in on conversations if we need to.'

'Surely that's not legal?' I say with caution.

'Nothing about this is legal, Ivy. You know that already.' He laughs. 'This is about doing whatever it takes to keep the school running.'

'Ed . . . how did you know you could trust me with this?'

'Because I knew, with all your digging around, that you were only inches away from discovering this for yourself.'

'And do you have access to the archives? Can you watch back CCTV footage from a certain date, for example?'

He makes a few clicks on his mouse and brings up thousands of folders ranging from today to months ago.

'It can only store a hundred and twenty-eight days' worth before it starts filming over existing files.'

'So nothing on the night of Lola's death. Can you check the night of the Samhain party? At around nine to ten p.m?'

'What for?'

'Clover.'

Ed frowns. 'We can check . . .'

We sit and go through a couple of angles and then we spot it. A certain camera that shows some of the main driveway by the side gate.

'Wait . . . that's her there! Can you zoom in?'

Ed zooms in on the footage and it's clearly Clover. She's talking to Mr Willis. It's dark, but the lights on the drive are perfectly angled towards their faces and it's as clear as anything that it's them.

'Do you have sound on this?' I ask. I want to know exactly what they're talking about. What could Clover have told Mr Willis?

'No, sadly not. These cameras are harder to update without it looking suspicious, so they're not as modern.'

'Dammit.'

We sit and watch as their interaction comes to a close. Clover is gesticulating wildly, and at one point it looks like Mr Willis is going to raise his hand to her. But then he walks out of shot and a car pulls up next to Clover. I write down the number plate. She then proceeds to get into the car and it drives out of the side gate.

'What the hell?' My mind is whirring. It must have been Patrick. But did Clover confront Mr Willis before running away? It certainly looks that way.

'That's pretty intense . . .' Ed looks up at me while I stare in disbelief. 'But at least it doesn't look like she was taken against her will. Poor girl. She didn't deserve what happened to her. She was like you and Audrey. Just trying to find out the truth.'

I raise an eyebrow. 'I didn't realize you knew her.'

'Ah, Clover was always hanging around, asking questions – especially after Lola died. For that podcast thing. She was impossible not to like, you know? She made it so you wanted to help her. She came to me for a few things – I think she suspected I was involved with the Magpie Society, but never asked me straight out. She was sharp.'

'Well, this footage is interesting. Mr Willis must be Clover's number-one suspect in Lola's murder.'

'I'm not sure . . .'

'Are you kidding? It's all right here. I have to show this to the police. It's vital that they see it, Ed. You know, you really should have shown this to them before.'

'I've been a little busy, you know? I don't have time to monitor every bloody camera angle. Do what you want. You run this gaff now. Just be aware that this is a camera that Mrs Abbott and the school security team don't have access to . . . so be careful how you word that to the Bill.'

He has a point. But this is so important for putting Mr Willis behind bars where he needs to be. What an absolute creep. Maybe I can run this by DI Shing on the down-low. She seemed willing to listen.

'Can you show me how to copy this across to my email?'

'Sure.'

Ed demonstrates how to send footage to my email address and we close down the software together. As we're turning off the lights and are about to head back out of the tunnel to the cottage, I have one more question for him.

'Do any of the cameras cover the area past the grounds and the woods?'

Ed looks at me strangely. 'No, the signal would never extend that far . . .'

'OK,' I say, smiling back at him and following him out into the tunnel. We emerge into a sea of boxes, and he hands me a set of keys. I stare down at them reverentially. 'So where are you and Mr T going to go? It will be weird not having you on the grounds.'

'Not far at first. We'll be in Winferne for a time while I send out applications to other big schools and country estates to try and get more gardening work.'

'Good. I have a feeling Audrey and I are going to have a lot of questions about all this.'

'Ivy, are you sure that you can trust Audrey?'

'Why do you ask?'

'Well, isn't it a bit weird that she wants to join you in the Magpie Society, considering she's part of the group trying to close the school? It just seems like she's playing both sides.'

I frown. 'I have no idea what you're talking about.'

'You don't? The company that's in charge of the redevelopment. It's owned by Audrey's dad.'

# 25

## AUDREY

On the train ride back to Winferne, all I can think about is my encounter with Ivy's mom. It's terrified me and I don't understand it. I can't make sense of it. Ivy hasn't lived at home in years? But she said that she went back every summer. What about at Christmas? Where did she go?

Something doesn't add up. I almost wanna get off the train, turn around and go back, demand some answers.

Ivy's mom clearly doesn't know her at all. What was it she said about Ivy having friends? *I didn't think that was possible.* What about Lola and Harriet and Tom and Max? What about me?

Ivy's the smartest person that I know. She must have her reasons for not wanting to be at home.

I run my hands over the photo album. I almost don't wanna open it. I don't know if I can even give it to Ivy. Somehow I don't think that she'll be all that happy that I went to see her mom without telling her. Not after how her mom reacted.

I don't want to invade her privacy even more than I already have. But still ... she's gonna be incredibly pissed off when she finds out *my* family's involvement in the redevelopment deal. I hope that retrieving the album will go some way to proving to her that I'm on her side. Fingers crossed I've got the right one, with the photograph of her dad and the horse in it, or else this will have all been for nothing.

I open the album and it lets out a satisfying crackle.

There are pictures of baby Ivy propped up on a cushion in between her mom and dad. Her mom isn't smiling – but her dad has a huge grin on his face. He looks happy and so does Ivy. He's wearing dark overalls, and they look stained – or at least well used. That makes sense. They're sitting in front of an auto repair shop called Moore's Motors.

I flip another page. There are more photographs of Ivy as a young child – she's always engaged in doing something, sitting at the piano or dancing. She has a pet – a little white rabbit. She looks so cute and innocent. Eventually, the pictures of her dad get less and less frequent, and then Violet starts showing up. As the years progress, it seems like Ivy's expression gets a bit more serious.

There's nothing in the photo album that seems to be that suspicious, or that Ivy wouldn't want me to see. It looks like a cute collection of family pics. I guess I'm wondering why Ivy's mom was so funny about giving it away. Finally, I come across the image that she'd described of her dad. It's exactly as she said – with a big horse at his side and a dog on his heel.

Then there are a few pictures towards the back that give me pause. Older images – a beautiful photograph of her Chinese grandparents, her grandmother in traditional dress, her lips lightly colourised in a pale red that jumps out of the sepia photograph. Then there's a picture of Ivy's other grandparents. They seem to be standing in a wood, the woman casually leaning against a tree, the man holding on to the reins of a magnificent-looking horse.

But I recognize that tree.

It's in the woods outside of Mr Tavistock's home.

I gasp in shock, and some of the other passengers stare at me. I hunker down in my seat, squinting at the photograph. Did Ivy's grandparents work at Illumen Hall? Did she know?

I lift the sticky-backed plastic carefully so as to not damage the photograph. On the back there's a little annotation.

**DM and CE, day before the wedding.**

I replace the photograph exactly as I found it, my heart beating rapidly. My fingers are shaking. It can't be true. Ivy would have said. There's no way she'd keep quiet about her family having a connection to the school. I'm starting to see suspicious clues everywhere; I think I'm going slightly insane. *Not everything is the plot of* Line of Duty, *Audrey.* Looking at it again, it could be a tree in a wood anywhere. But those initials. *CE*. That can't be a coincidence.

*Clarissa Ellory.*

Maybe there was a photograph of her in the Magpie Society headquarters. I'll have to check and compare it to the one in the photo album.

Regardless, now I can give the album to Ivy and be happy. She's got the image of her dad back.

I always wondered how Ivy ended up at Illumen Hall. I remember her telling me how her old primary-school teacher got her on to the scholarship programme here, but I wonder if Illumen Hall was really the only – or even the best – boarding-school choice. Were there no others closer to London? It seemed strange for her to be sent so far away. There's still much I don't know about her, even though I consider her my best friend.

*And there's a lot she doesn't know about you.*

I plug in my headphones, sticking on a podcast to try and while away the rest of the journey. I find myself navigating back to Clover's podcasts, just to hear her voice again. But, to my surprise, her last episode has disappeared from my downloads. I wonder if the police considered it too sensitive.

My phone buzzes. It's Ivy.

> Where are you?

> > Just on my way back from seeing my brother.

> Meet me in our room?
> I have something to ask you.

> > Will do. I have something you'll want to see too.

It's not just the photo album, which I'm itching to give to her. There's no way that I can wait a second longer to tell her about the document that I found left in Mrs Trawley's house. I know I should have done it sooner, but after

Clover's death I didn't want any reminder of that night. Especially now I know why my dad is worried about it. Lola might have been able to stop the sale – if she'd taken up her rightful place as head girl.

That's motive for murder.


When I finally get back to the school, a weight lifts from my shoulders. It's as if I finally feel at home here.

I pass by our housemistress, Mrs Parsons, who watches me with eagle eyes as I place my spare cellphone back in its little cubby, sighing audibly for good measure. Then I knock softly on the door of our room, not wanting to disturb Ivy if she's in the middle of something.

'Come in,' she says.

'Hey, just me. Sorry – nightmare journey back from the station. I missed the bus and had to wait.'

'Audrey . . .'

'Ivy . . .'

I laugh at how we both start at the same time, both super eager to talk to each other. But I jump in first because I have something heavy in my bag.

'I managed to get something for you, from London. I hope you like it.'

'When were you going to tell me?'

The tone of Ivy's voice stops me dead in my tracks. I look up at her, the photo album halfway out of my bag. Her face is stricken, but there's something else simmering under the surface. Anger.

She is so pissed.

'Tell you what?' I ask, still feigning ignorance, buying

myself time to catch up and figure out how I'm gonna deal with this, and emerge with my friendship to Ivy still intact.

Ivy scoffs at me. 'That your family's company is the one buying the school.'

'Ivy . . . I didn't know. Not until –'

'Well?'

'Not until I saw that blueprint.' I cast my eyes down. 'I admit it – I recognized the company logo straight away.'

'That's why you took it, isn't it? So you didn't have to confess to me. So I couldn't do my own research. How could you, Audrey? I thought we were in this together. And now I find out that you're part of the plot to tear down the only place I've ever truly called home.'

Tears well up in her eyes, and my heart breaks for her. It's only really come into focus exactly what she means by that since going to her home. It's clear that Ivy and her mom have some serious issues – and that tensions there run hotter than the Sahara. Illumen Hall really is her sanctuary.

Knowing that the school wouldn't be there for her to return to in the future . . . I can see just how much that terrifies her.

'I wanted to confirm with my dad first that he really was behind this . . .'

'And?'

I hesitate. 'He is. But wait, I also know –'

'God! I don't want to hear anything else about it! How am I supposed to trust you now? You'll probably make a shit-ton of money from the sale . . . You won't be interested in stopping the deal.'

'Ivy, that's not true. I don't wanna see this school shut down any more than you do. I know how much it means to you – and not just you, but all the students. And I know so much more about its history now. My brother confirmed everything for me.'

'Oh great – your whole family's involved.'

'But I haven't spoken to my dad yet. I'm really good at persuading him – you'll see. Even with big deals! You should have seen the size of the project he abandoned in Georgia after Alicia died. Anyway, it makes Illumen Hall seem like peanuts. And my brother accidentally let slip about a potential loophole. Let me talk to him before you freak out too much more, OK?'

Ivy is still glaring. But I can also see her wanting to trust me, her emotions warring under the surface. I sit next to her and take her hand. 'I promise you can trust me,' I assure her. 'Let me show you.' I jump up to go to my closet, where I stashed the file from Mrs Trawley. 'I have an idea how we can stop the sale . . .'

I turn to see Ivy looking at my bag, which is digging into her thigh. She frowns at the photo album that's still sticking out of it. 'What is this?' she asks.

I swallow. Revealing the album suddenly doesn't seem like such a good idea. But it's too late now because Ivy is already pulling it out of my bag. She makes a strangled noise in the back of her throat.

'Where did you get this?'

'When I went up to London, I stopped by your home.'

'You went to my mum's flat?' Ivy looks like she's in a daze, blinking slowly.

'Yeah.'

'And my mum . . . gave this to you? Just like that?'

'Basically.'

She snaps the album shut, then stares up at me. In her eyes is a look I haven't seen before. A fierce, incandescent rage. 'How dare you go behind my back?'

'What? Ivy, I saw how much pain you were in and wanted to do something nice for you.'

'How did you even find out my address?'

'It was on the back of one of the lists you pinned up.'

'So you went through my stuff, behind my back, betrayed my trust and invaded my privacy? What the *hell*? Get out!'

'What?' I blink. 'Ivy, I'm sorry you feel that way, but –'

'Didn't you hear me? Get out.'

I throw my hands up in the air. 'Get out? This is my room too, remember? Where am I supposed to go?'

'Fine. I'll leave then.' Ivy gets up and storms out.

I stare at the wooden door, which she slams so hard the picture frames on our walls shake and tremble. I wonder if we'll be getting a visit from Mrs Parsons after that outburst. More explaining for me to do.

Ivy took the photo album with her. But fuck it. If this is how she wants to treat me after I tried to do something nice for her, then so be it. I don't wanna deal with this. I don't wanna deal with any of this shit.

That is it. I am done with the Magpie Society.

## 26

### IVY

The fury and anger rise up inside me like bubbling acid, burning my throat and making it hard for me to breathe. I'm walking, but I don't know where to go. One foot in front of the other, I'm just trusting my body. How could Audrey have done this? What possessed her to go to my mum's flat and rock up there like a family friend on a sunny Sunday?

Just as I was beginning to let my barriers down with Audrey, to trust her and let her be involved in my life, I learn she's actually the enemy.

I'm a pretty guarded person: I don't open up with everyone I meet. Lola was honestly the last person I considered myself close to. Someone I would share even my deepest thoughts and feelings with. It isn't easy for me. I swallow my difficult emotions and shut them away inside my body. The less on the tip of my tongue, the better. It's how I've always been, but Audrey was beginning to see past that.

I sense the tension in my wrinkled forehead and rub it with my hand.

The one thing I had never gone into with Audrey, or anyone really, was the relationship I have with my mother.

It's complex and dysfunctional. I know that almost all families have skeletons in the closet and it's nothing new or ground-breaking, but my mum and I are two very different people. I didn't see much of her growing up; she worked multiple jobs to keep a roof over our heads and food on the table. When I did see her though, she wasn't really there. She suffered from very poor mental health when my dad left and after a while it was like she just . . . gave up being my mum. She made sure I was never at home. She put me in classes I had no interest in, made me do homework that she'd printed out from the internet, sent me to the library at weekends. At first I thought she was giving me the best possible start in life, but it became clear she just wanted me out of the way.

She didn't understand. I was bullied ferociously. Bullied for being half Chinese – never fitting in. Bullied for the cheap shoes she bought me – always oversized so I'd 'grow into them'. Bullied for what was in my packed lunch. Bullied for my second-hand uniform that never fitted right. I had absolutely no friends. I'd sit on my own every break, and the only people who paid me any attention at all were my teachers. I knew they just felt sorry for me. I never felt at home anywhere. But, if my Year Six teacher hadn't put me forward for a scholarship, I wouldn't be at Illumen Hall at all. I wouldn't have found the one place I could thrive.

If the school closes, I'll have nowhere to go, and I know I'm not the only one at this school with a precarious home life. My mum won't want me back. I'd be homeless. Even if I got placed in another boarding school – without a full scholarship, I wouldn't be able to afford it.

The more I think about the fact that Audrey saw my old flat, and had a conversation with my mum, it fills me with dread. What must she think of me now? I can picture Mum and how unfriendly she'll have been. Probably made out like I wasn't her daughter at all. The rejection hits me all over again. Years of abandonment cascading down on me. Illumen Hall is my only home. I feel safe here.

I've realized by this point that I have detoured towards Mrs Abbott's cottage. The trailing wisteria framing the door is now brown and lifeless. Grey smoke billows from the little chimney, spiralling up into the dusky sky and mingling with the stars above me. It's chilly, but there's no breeze and everything feels very still. The light is on in her living room and I can see her pottering around inside. I pound on her door and wait.

'Ivy! What are you doing here?' She seems flustered.

'I wanted to speak to you.' I smile and uncross my arms. 'If you don't mind?'

'Well, come on in. I can't have you standing outside as it's getting dark.' She gestures at a little tasselled footstool by the fire. I've been in Mrs Abbott's cottage a few times and it's always felt so homely but pristine. Today though I notice it's dusty and the rugs are dirty. Lots of mugs of half-drunk coffee are scattered across shelves and books, and paperwork is shoved into half-open drawers on her writing desk. I sit on the stool and she wriggles into one of her armchairs, moving her duffle coat from it as she does.

'So what can I help you with? Are you feeling OK? Do I need to set up some more sessions with Dr Kinfeld? I know you must still be in shock.' She crosses her legs and links her fingers, then places both hands neatly on her lap. I feel strangely calm now I'm sitting here with her in front of me like this.

'No. I just wanted to ask you why you're selling the school.'

There's a deathly silence and only the crackle of the fire can be heard for what feels like minutes.

'Ivy, I don't know how you've come to be in possession of this information. I can only assume Miss Wagner told you? But, yes, that is the plan. However, I do know how much this school means to you and I can promise you that this is a huge decision that hasn't been made lightly at all. Everything will work out well in the end.'

'For you, maybe. But what about the students who call this place home? The people whose friends here are their only family . . .' I clench my jaw to hold back a tear as I sense upset rising in my throat.

'I can assure you that every student here at Illumen Hall will be transferred to a suitable school befitting their personal situation. Absolutely *nobody* will be left with no home or education. Your future is safe, Ivy. I'll make sure of that.' She smiles sweetly and it instantly irritates me. 'I do ask though that you keep this between you and Miss Wagner for now. We're so close to having all these plans firmly in place and I'd prefer that to be the case before the entire student body is up in arms.'

'I thought you'd been so worried about the state of the school because you wanted to make sure the parents would invest again! Not that you were so afraid your special deal would fall apart.'

'Ivy, this is the only way we can secure the building's future. And the company has promised to find you all places at nearby schools, and pay for tuition if they won't match the scholarship. Let me be honest with you. The school was going to close either way and that's the truth.'

I know this isn't true and my fury rises.

'No! We would have found a way to keep it. Surely not. There'd be protests . . . We could arrange a GoFundMe or do some good old-fashioned fundraising. Host a car wash or something?'

Mrs Abbott shakes her head. 'It's too late for that.'

'It's not too late. Please give me some time –'

Mrs Abbott pulls herself up to her full height. I know exactly what this signifies. The deal is non-negotiable. I brace myself.

'This is it. This is the end of Illumen Hall as we know it. I realize it hurts to hear that, but this isn't up to you. End of story.'

'Fine.' I can stand tall too. 'But I know some people who won't stand for this.'

But Mrs Abbott just sits back down, her eyes on her desk again. I've been dismissed.

I spin on my heel and head to the door. It might be the end of the story. But not for the Magpies. I can't bear to listen to any more of this. I feel as though my heart is physically breaking. The decision has been made. I open the door, without saying a word, and I run. I don't know where I'm going, but I need to get away. From Mrs Abbott, from this decision and from my own thoughts.

# 27

## AUDREY

I wake up early, blinking in confusion. The last thing I remember I'd been on top of my duvet, staring at the ceiling, waiting for Ivy to get back. I must have drifted off. Mrs Parsons never came around to do her nightly inspection. Trust her to miss a day – and for it to be this one.

I shift in my bed, turning my head so that I'm staring at the other side of the room. Ivy's bed is still empty. She must have gone for one of her early-morning runs. She's crazy. It's so cold outside that frost is beginning to creep on to the windowpanes, its icy fingers creating unique patterns on the glass.

But then I frown and sit up.

Ivy's bed looks the exact same as last night – even the pen she dropped is still in the same position on the sheets. There's no sign that she slept there at all.

My heart beats faster, my brain immediately leaping to the worst possible conclusion. She's missing. She's been taken. She's hurt.

I quickly check my phone to see if there are any messages from her. But there's nothing. Even worse, I see that she's booted me out of the Magpie Society group chat.

You can be mad at me, but at
least tell me you're safe.

I text her, hoping to see her pop 'online' to view it, or to
see her typing. But there's nothing. I check the friend-
finding app, but her profile is dark. So much for that.

With all the worst-case scenarios running through my
head, trying to keep my anxiety on a leash, I pull on my
school uniform and head down to breakfast.

I catch sight of Harriet sitting at one of the long benches.
'Hey, have you seen . . .' The tail end of my sentence drifts
off as I see Ivy walking towards the table with a breakfast
tray.

Harriet shifts so that her back is towards me, and Ivy's
stare is as cold as ever. I swallow. 'Where were you? You
didn't come back to the room last night. I was really
worried.'

'Do you need something?' Ivy's voice is ice.

'No, I just . . .'

'Then let me eat my breakfast before you put me off it.'

Harriet crunches down on her apple at the same time,
the only acknowledgment of Ivy's display being the tiniest
quirk of her eyebrow. But I can see that they're putting up
a united front. I'm being left out in the cold.

My appetite is suddenly gone, and I have no desire to
suffer Ivy's bad mood. And this is a stark reminder that I
really have no friends here, other than the ones I've found
through Ivy. The dangers of pinning all my hopes and
happiness on another person. Hadn't I learned that before?

I head outside for some fresh air. At least the sky is a

bright bluebird blue. With the chill in the air and the leaves on the ground, it feels restorative. I might not be one for morning exercise, but this sort of walk I could get used to.

I head to the fountain, sitting down to peck at my muffin. Almost the instant I sit, a little magpie perches nearby. *One for sorrow*, I think. It jumps in my direction as I throw a little bit of muffin crumb on the ground. It approaches with caution, pecks at the muffin, then flies away in a hurry.

I wish I could say that the incident made me smile. But instead, deep in my guts, all I feel is dread.

There's a crunch of shoe on gravel. 'Everything OK?'

I look up to see Teddy standing over me. His hands are buried in his trouser pockets, and his head is tilted to one side adorably.

'Yeah, I'm fine.'

'Not eating with Ivy today? What did you do to piss her off?'

'Wow, word travels fast in this place, doesn't it? We only had the argument last night.' I hug my arms around my body.

'Um, it's kind of a big deal when two of the most visible girls in school no longer get along.'

I sigh, exasperated. 'Well, don't ask me – ask Ivy. She's the one who's mad. I tried to apologize – but honestly I don't see why I should. What I did was *not* that bad. Definitely not worthy of all this freezer treatment.'

Teddy slumps down on the stone next to me, then stands up again. 'That's freezing – how can you bear it?'

'Maybe I'm already turned to ice from Ivy's fucking Medusa glare.'

Teddy chuckles. 'Are you going to make me ask again?'

'What did I do? I made the mistake of *trying* to do something *nice* for her, and get her this photo album that she'd been missing. While I was up in London visiting my brother, I went to her flat to fetch it. Her mom is like the least friendly person on the planet ... which I guess is where Ivy gets it from. That whole family feels messed up.'

Teddy's face turns pale. 'Hang on. You actually went to Ivy's house? How did you even find out the address?'

'To her mom's apartment, yeah. I found the address on an old envelope Ivy had used to write on – it's not some major mystery I solved or anything. Everyone's acting like this is such a huge deal. I mean, you must have been to her place, right? You were her boyfriend for, like, two years.'

Teddy shakes his head. 'Never. My God, no. She wouldn't even tell me what part of London it was in! What was it like?'

He leans in eagerly, but something about the way his curiosity is piqued really illustrates how hard Ivy has worked to keep her home life a secret. After experiencing first-hand how hostile her mom was, I'm kinda not surprised. I don't want to betray Ivy's trust any further, even if part of me is tempted just to blow her whole world apart for the way that she's treating me.

I can't change how she is to me. But I can control how I act in response. I'd still like to be friends again with Ivy one day. And, to start with, that will mean keeping her secrets for a bit longer.

'Aw well, I didn't really get to go inside. I kinda sprung

the visit on her mom and they were busy, so she just grabbed the photo album for me and I left. I really should have asked Ivy if it was OK first.'

'She's not really the sort of person who likes surprises.'

I bark a laugh. 'Yeah, I get that now.'

Teddy squeezes my hand and I smile up at him. 'She'll get over it – don't worry.'

'I hope so.'

'In the meantime, I've been thinking more and more about our missing date.' He squeezes my leg, just above the knee. 'I know the last time you came on the boat was a bit of a disaster . . . but do you want to try again? I'm going to take her out on the water this weekend for a final spin round the coast before I put her away for the winter. I never get enough time to sail when exams are in full swing and my parents will kill me if I don't get the grades that I need. Come out with me? Don't make me beg.'

I pause, then smile. I'm not gonna invade Ivy's privacy any more than I have done already. But I *can* irk her a bit by agreeing to go out on Teddy's boat. 'Just no pirate outfit this time, OK?'

'So you'll come?' His face lights up.

'I'll be there.'

Distantly, we hear the bell signalling the start of class. He holds his hand out to me and I take it, allowing him to pull me up.

'Really sucks about Mr Tavistock, huh? I wonder who's going to keep the grounds tidy now,' Teddy says.

I'm immediately reminded of the Magpie Society. Even though I swore off any more investigating, maybe there is a tiny bit of Ivy's past that I want to pry into. 'Teddy, did Ivy ever tell you why she came to Illumen Hall?'

'She got a scholarship.'

'Yeah, I know that. But what made her choose Illumen? I know that primary-school teacher put her forward for it, but I mean there must be hundreds of boarding schools in the country, probably loads a lot closer to home. She could have literally chosen anywhere. What made her come here?'

Teddy frowns. 'I actually don't know. I came here because of the proximity to the coast and sailing – and the fact that my dad boarded here too. Most of the students who come here are legacies. But obviously not Ivy.'

'What do you mean "obviously not Ivy"?'

Redness rises in Teddy's cheeks. 'I don't mean . . . no, it's just, like, her family aren't exactly the type, let's say, to go to a school like this.'

'Too poor, you mean?'

'Wow, no. Hey, Illumen Hall has always had tons of bursaries. You'd be surprised just how many students here have a scholarship. In fact, one of the reasons the school fees are so high is because part of the amount is allocated to ensure that kids who don't have the same opportunities as we do get the chance to be educated at a place like this. Maybe *that's* why Ivy came here. Because this is one of the few schools that actually offers full scholarships, you know? From what I hear of Ivy's home life, it wasn't exactly a happy one. You don't seem to think any different. So she wanted an escape and came here. I can't blame her.'

'No, I can't either.'

'You're liking it here more?'

I grin. 'It has its perks.'

'Am I one of them?'

'You're pretty good. It's a shame we won't have next year together.' I snap my mouth shut, realizing that Teddy doesn't know about the school sale yet. But he grins.

'I won't be too far away. I'm going to go to uni in London – just a short train ride.'

Oh, that's right. He's graduating anyway, so the school sale won't affect him. I've gotten away with it, without revealing the secret. I lean into Teddy's shoulder. He thinks it's because I'm sad at the thought of us being separated.

A thought strikes me. Maybe Ivy doesn't *know* about her family connection to the school. If I can confirm it, then there may be a way to save the school after all.

'Much as I'd like to stay like this all day . . . shall we get to class?' Teddy asks. 'Walk you there?'

'No, that's OK. I'll see you later.'

He kisses my fingers, then saunters off. He sends me a text as he's walking away: **Miss you already.** Cheesy – but I can't help that it makes me smile. Part of me wants to follow him, drag him to the ground and kiss him passionately. But instead I turn in the other direction.

I'm not going to class. I'm going to the Magpie Society headquarters. If there are answers, I'll find them there.

# 28

## IVY

I know that in order to stop the sale of the school, I'm going to have to act now – with or without Audrey by my side. I can't sit back and let this happen. Ed said that it was in my hands, and I intend to do whatever I can to prevent the school closure. Although I know I should be focusing all my attention on my A-level studies and my music practice, this feels far too important for me to let slide. They might not know it yet, but the rest of the students' futures are currently in the hands of the wrong people, so the least I can do is try. For *all* the Ivys of the school, if nobody else.

Despite their reluctance, I've brought Clover's room-mates, Lyra and Yolanda, along with Harriet, to the Magpie headquarters via a new route I discovered on the Magpie phone. It suddenly dawns on me that telling them all I've found out about the society, when it was created and about the school redevelopment, is huge. I don't care what Audrey would feel knowing I'm here with them and she isn't. I spent the walk to the shell cavern filling them in as much as possible. Both Lyra and Yolanda, being Clover's best friends and room-mates, were a good choice as allies. I also knew Harriet would be someone I could trust with all this information too. There was a lot of swearing and 'Are you serious?' responses alongside gawps and gasps when entering the shell room.

'This is absolutely fucking nuts, Ivy ...' Harriet grabs my arm in excitement, her eyes wide.

'I realize we've already bombarded you with a million questions on the walk here, but ... HOW? WHY?' Yolanda looks round the room in bewilderment, reaching out and stroking the shells.

'I actually don't know much about the history of this place, when it was made or who by, but whoever it was it must have taken so long.' I sit on the floor and encourage the girls to do the same. 'So this is the headquarters!' I throw my arms up and gesture around the room and smile. I feel like I'm showing guests my new house, like a proud homeowner.

'Is Audrey joining us too?' Lyra asks.

I catch Harriet's awkward glance from beside me.

'No. Audrey isn't part of the Magpie Society any more.'

'How come?' Yolanda pipes up.

'She decided she had more important things to do.' The girls pick up on my tone and ask no more questions.

'Now that Clover is ... gone, I really feel like it's important to continue her mission. What if Lola was killed because she was going to stop the closing of the school?'

'Oh Lord,' says Harriet. 'That makes so much sense. Lola would have done anything to protect it.'

'Right? So now our goal is to stop the sale ourselves. I've decided that our best strategy moving forward is exposure. We expose the plan to the students, the parents and to journalists. We get as many eyes on this as possible because just the four of us against a big corporation will be almost impossible, but, if we can get more people on our side who don't want this to go ahead, we actually stand a chance.'

'Clover would have been amazing at this. She loved a bit of anarchy, protest and exposure.' Lyra laughs, but it's laced with sadness.

'Do you think we'll get in trouble for doing this?' Yolanda looks a bit nervous.

'That's the entire point of the Magpie Society. This school is what we stand for – it's a legacy. The Magpies wanted to protect vulnerable students, and up against this sale ... we're all vulnerable. But we can stay completely anonymous. Nobody will know it's *us* exposing the plan.'

It dawns on me that Mrs Abbott will immediately suspect me and Audrey since she's well aware we both know about the sale. I'm mostly just trying to reassure the others. With no proof, she can't say it's us for sure.

Yolanda and Harriet start flicking through some of the old books and photos of members of the society and Lyra pulls me aside.

'Ivy, I'm really worried about this. What if it puts us in danger?'

'Don't worry; I'm on it. I'm still in contact with the police. I won't let anything happen to us.' I smile encouragingly, although I know deep down I can't be sure.

After the meeting and the conversation with Lyra, Clover fresh in my mind, I decide to see if DI Shing can meet me so I send a text.

Very quickly, she texts me back and asks if we can get together in the local park, halfway between the school and the police station. I only have to wait around twenty minutes before I see her approaching. Her hair is more relaxed than last time I saw her, tousled loosely on her shoulders instead of tied back in a pony. She's wearing a beige parka jacket and I instantly think of Inspector Gadget.

'Ivy, how are you?' She sits down next to me on the bench, crossing her legs.

'Not too bad – you?' I instantly feel a little awkward. I've been so wary of the police throughout this, but I think it's about time to let her in on a bit more information to keep her interested in Lola's case. I feel like DI Shing is actually invested, and she could turn out to be very helpful.

'Before you begin, I must update you on your teacher, Mr Willis.'

'Yes, the creep.'

'We checked his alibi for both the night of your friend's death and Clover's disappearance. It all checks out. He wasn't involved, Ivy.'

I sit in stunned silence. How is that possible? 'It was him. It must have been him! I told you that he overheard Clover's whereabouts as well – he could have started the fire deliberately!'

'We're certain Clover's death was a tragic accident. And as for Mr Willis . . . Ivy, he's innocent.'

'What if I could show you something new? Say . . . CCTV footage of him arguing with Clover just before she goes missing? It looks as though she's confronting him about something. He seems angry.'

She frowns. 'We've checked out all the school CCTV and found nothing like that at all.'

'It's a different camera. One that the school don't own.'

'If that's true, of course I'd like to see the footage. I won't ask how you have ownership of CCTV footage on school grounds that isn't connected with the school itself, but you should know that anything you give me could be presented as evidence in court if needs be. You will have to explain how you have access to this camera.'

'Fine. If it goes to court, I'll share my secret.'

'Is this what you wanted to meet me about? Sharing the footage?'

'Yes! Shall I just email it to the address on your business card?'

'That's the best place. Thanks, Ivy. And I'll say this again: if there's ever anything you want to discuss, please just call. I don't like that you're off investigating on your own. I know Clover's death was an accident, but I don't want anything to happen to you or any of the other students.'

'OK, thank you!'

DI Shing then gets another call that she picks up and signals that she has to leave, miming goodbye and waving as she heads back to the car park. I hope I'm doing the right thing by sharing that footage with her.

As I meander along the road back to school, I spot Audrey and Teddy walking side by side, sharing a bag of chips and heading through the school gates. I feel a flash of anger.

As they cross the school grounds, they take a right. I follow some way behind and take a left. The only place I want to go now is a music-practice room. I want to sit at the Fazioli grand piano and pour everything I have into those keys and the song I've written for the Christmas concert. If this school is sold, I can only rely on my grades and talent to get me anywhere in life. I feel good that we have a plan, but there's still so much going on in my mind. It's almost impossible to focus. The only things I can truly think about right now are those that are important to me. The school, my grades, my music – and Lola.

# 29

## AUDREY

'Dammit!' I slam my fist against the wall.

'Excuse me, miss? You shouldn't be in here. Students aren't allowed.'

I spin around, finding myself face to face with a frowning Ms Cranshaw.

'I'm leaving, don't worry.'

I've come down into the kitchens, trying to gain access to the tunnel via the elaborately carved panel door. But it's been secured with a brand-new shiny lock. I know whose handiwork this is: Ed Tavistock. My access to the Magpie headquarters is blocked. Without the Magpie Society phone, which is in Ivy's possession, I can't find another way in.

Instead, I go up to the library, back to flipping through various yearbooks, attempting to find a picture of Clarissa Ellory. But nope, there's no sign of her. After the student called Lily Ellory from the late 1800s, I can't find mention of another person by that name either.

It's a dead end.

*Magpies are the feathers of the school.* The people quietly working behind the scenes. Unfortunately, they're *so* behind the scenes that most of the yearbooks don't have any lists of the staff members who worked there – at least not until a minor revolution in the 1960s. Finally, I find a page mentioning the school staff. I notice it because of the name Tavistock, and I'm curious about what the groundskeeper looked like when he was younger.

There's a grainy, hard-to-make-out group photo of the staff. All their faces sort of blur into one. But the caption is what interests me. Because listed, in very tiny font, among a heap of names, is *C Ellory – horsemistress.*

*Yes!* I stare down at the picture. The face is blurry, but definitely recognizable. Ivy's grandmother? It could very well be.

I exhale sharply, squinting to confirm.

Ivy *is* related to one of the original members of the Magpie Society after all. Does she know? I take a photo with my phone for later. Slowly, it feels like pieces of the jigsaw are coming together. Though it doesn't matter now. The sale is done. Maybe once upon a time something could have been changed, but it's too late now.

I have to concentrate on my own future.

I chew my fingernails, then make my way back down the to the lower floor of the library. As I'm walking through the stacks, I think I hear the sound of someone crying. I almost don't wanna look – I feel like I've been dragged into so much drama already. Then again, what's a little more?

I sigh before ducking around the stacks, searching for the noise. The library is uncomfortably quiet apart from the faint sobbing. Most students head to the common room on their free periods, or they're all in class.

Whoever else is out here was obviously looking for somewhere quiet to hide.

Just as I'm about to leave them to it, I spot the culprit. And my curiosity is instantly piqued. It's Araminta.

She looks up as I arrive, then buries her face in her arms, trying to look as if she was just searching for something on the ground.

'Everything OK?' I ask.

'I'm fine. Just leave me alone.'

'I can't do that.'

She looks back at me, surprised. Her eyes are red, but she's wiped away her tears.

'Why? Just want to report to Ivy?'

'I'm not Ivy's puppet. Besides –' I slump down on to the floor next to her – 'we had a gigantic fight. I'm pretty sure she hates me.'

'She can turn on you like that. In a flash. I've seen it before. With everyone ... It's not that much of a surprise though. She modelled her whole life on Lola.'

I turn my head to look at the head girl. I don't know what she's crying about, but I've a feeling she's not quite ready to open up.

'OK, look. You knew this girl, right? You must have spent the past six years at school together. What was Lola really like?'

Araminta sighs, tilting her head back against the shelves. 'Lola? She was everything. We all wanted to be like her. To *be* her. Me especially. She would have been an excellent head girl. Way better than me. She was ... she was like magic. You just wanted to be in her presence.'

Araminta has a faraway look in her eye, and I feel a pang deep in my stomach. I wish I'd been able to meet her, this person who everyone thinks was so dynamic and amazing.

All I've seen is a painting. A painting that weirds me out.

But maybe it's not the painting that's so weird. Maybe it's everyone's obsession with her. Including her own brother! His grief just seems – extreme. Even buying a flat in Winferne Bay, just to be close to the case. That's without getting started on Mr Willis. He'd have to be really stupid – or really infatuated – to have got it on with a student, not to mention one as high profile as Lola.

A dangerous position to get himself into. A massive risk.

'I guess she'll never have that chance now. And I have enormous shoes to fill.'

'Why is being head girl such a big deal anyway?'

'It's hard to explain. It's huge. It guarantees me a place at any uni that I want. Access to a whole network of amazing alumni of previous head students, in a whole variety of fields from acting or music all the way to top lawyers and bankers and doctors. I get to be involved in decisions about the school – we basically join the board for a year. It's not like at other places. Being head girl is a massive deal. Seriously, once this year is over, I'll have any internship I want at the snap of my fingers. It places me among the elite. But trust me, I know I didn't earn it like Lola did. I feel as if I'm reminded of that every freaking day.'

'You seem to be doing OK to me. So Ivy wants into that club, does she?'

'Of course. I mean, she *should* be in it. I know she's difficult, but also everyone knows how hard she works. I've always kind of hated her for that. Anyway, she'll be

OK. She's one of the proper go-getters in the world. I'm just . . . not. And now I'm going to fuck up the Christmas concert.'

I've seen where Ivy came from and now I understand what might be behind that fierce drive, what she's hiding from all the others. People like Araminta seem to think she's just determined. But, for Ivy, this truly could be make or break.

'Is the Christmas concert really that big a deal?'

Araminta rolls her eyes, like I'm supposed to be caught up on every stupid bloody tradition in this place. But then she smiles at me. 'It really is. It's like a world-class showcase for us. Parents come, many of whom are bigwigs in the world of art, music, theatre, film. Some of them are high up at universities. But Mrs Abbott throws the guest list wide – hoping to recruit new donors. She let me know that this year is going to be bigger and better than ever.'

I wonder if Dad is coming. I'm sure he wouldn't pass up a chance to show off the potential of the school. Maybe I can convince him to let us have just one more year. Give Ivy the chance to be head girl, claim her legacy, and get the place she wants at the uni she wants, then the school can be turned into whatever pleasure palace my dad has in mind.

'But anyway Lola would have done this incredible violin piece because that's what she was so great at. And I'm supposed to sing, but I just can't get it right. I'm never going to nail it.'

'What's the song?'

'It's "Think of Me" from *Phantom of the Opera*.'

'Ooh, tough one.'

'You sing?'

'Yeah, a little. Back in the States I used to do some community theatre.'

It was a little bit more than community theatre. But I didn't want anyone here to know that. I'd had enough of everyone staring at me.

'So you know – it's quite a hard song, with some big notes. Plus, I don't want to just stand there like a lemon so I'm going to have some ballet dancers in the background. But Bonnie and Katie aren't natural performers, and Mr Willis is shit at choreography, to be honest, and there's no other teacher with any real experience to offer any assistance or guidance. Also, my costume is just blah, some old tutu from a former production of *Swan Lake* or something. Terrible. So I've just been trying to wing it, and I'm not sure that it's working. No, scratch that, I *know* it's not working. That's why I'm here. Was hoping for a quiet place to cry since I can't go back to my room. Every time I walk into Polaris House, people stare at me.'

She looks genuinely distressed. And, despite everything, I feel sorry for her. I know this decision is gonna piss off Ivy. But maybe that's OK. Maybe I need to widen my friendship circle just a tad.

'Why don't you show me? I might have some tips for you. I actually helped with the choreography of *Showboat*, which was the last musical that we did.'

Araminta blinks. 'You would seriously do that?'

'Why not?'

'Um ... I can think of one short, dark-haired reason why not.'

'Like I said, I'm not owned by Ivy. And this is just a musical thing. It's not like I expect us to be "besties".'

I use air quotes around the last word, and Araminta laughs. 'OK, cool. But not here obviously. Come down with me to one of the music rooms. They're soundproof so at least no one else will hear me when I fluff the high notes.'

'I'm sure you'll do great. It's good to push yourself.'

'I'm going to throw myself off a cliff if I don't nail it,' Araminta mutters. Then she gasps. 'Oh my God, that's super insensitive of me. I'm sorry.'

I shake my head. 'Don't sweat it. But, Araminta, I have to ask. You've always been adamant that Lola's death was by her own hand – accident or suicide, but that she was up there on the cliffs by herself. Why do you think she would have done that? Sounds to me like she had a pretty perfect life. Not one that you'd want to run away from.'

Araminta looks around the library, searching for listening ears. 'She did. But she had secrets – and she found out other people's secrets too. She had a knack for that.' Her eyes are dark as she says it. Did Lola find out one of Araminta's secrets? What could she possibly be hiding? I change the subject.

'Is that really why you're so upset? Your solo?'

'No, you're right. There's more to it than that.' She pauses. 'Guy trouble. It's a long story and really embarrassing.'

'Tell me about it – trust me, I know what you mean.'

'Any more progress between you and Teddy?'

I look over at her sharply as we leave the library, heading down towards the music-practice rooms in the basement.

But there doesn't seem to be any malice in her face – only genuine, open curiosity. This is a different side to Araminta and I like it.

The bell signalling the end of classes rings and students begin to pour out into the hallway. It's the start of our lunch period now, but, since I won't be welcome with Ivy and her crew as normal, I might as well continue on with Araminta. As we walk, the crowd swells towards us, so Araminta grabs my arm to help guide me.

I look up and catch Ivy watching us.

Oh well, she's seen me with Araminta now. I'll let her draw her own conclusions about what's going on. She's the one who pushed me into this.

Now let's see what she's gonna do about it.

# 30

## IVY

It's raining and the drops hammer on the old, thin single glazing of Harriet's bedroom window. It's a Thursday evening. If I'd been with Audrey, it would have been movie night. On Mr Kinfeld's advice, we'd started alternating each week, picking a classic film to watch on our laptops. A film club just for the two of us. This week was going to be *Sixteen Candles* as Audrey had never seen it and it's one of my favourites. Instead, I'm with Harriet in her dorm room. She shares with a girl called Ruby who only boards three nights a week. She basically has her own space so I've been staying here. It's a bit smaller than the room I share with Audrey and has a sloping roof, which means you have to duck down slightly before sitting on her bed. She also has a lot of house plants scattered everywhere. Bushy ones, trailing ones and some that look like they were grown on another planet. She's a very good plant mum though: they're all so green and thriving. She bought me a cactus one year for my birthday and I couldn't even keep *that* alive.

'You seem different now that you aren't running around after Lola any more, you know . . .' Harriet says this out of nowhere while we're scrolling through Instagram, lying side by side on her bed.

'What do you mean?'

'I don't mean it in a negative way, and of course I'm really sad she's no longer here, but you seem more ... relaxed? More yourself without her around.'

It's a weird comment for Harriet to make, and one I wasn't expecting. Harriet never disliked Lola, but I do think she envied our friendship at times. I hadn't really thought about the impact not spending time with Lola would have on me as a person or how it might change me at all.

'You're probably right, you know. I hadn't really considered it.'

'And I know you loved her, and you were both so close, but I do feel like it was a bit –' she hesitates and reads my expression – 'unhealthy sometimes.'

'Maybe. Although she wasn't as perfect as everyone made out. We've all got our flaws.'

Harriet smiles. 'I know! I mean, as far as her prefect duties went, that wasn't always so great.' She laughs.

'Yeah, it was more a status symbol – she didn't really care that much. And I know it will absolutely shock you to hear this coming from me, but Araminta is actually a pretty decent head girl.' I almost choke on my own words and Harriet bursts out laughing.

'OH MY GOD! Are you feeling OK, Ivy? You're right though – she does take it very seriously, not that we'd ever admit that to her, of course.'

'Obviously!' I laugh along with her.

'Oh, I want to show you what I drew up on my laptop in the library earlier today.' She jumps up from her bed and grabs the bag that's hanging by the door.

'Here!' She thrusts a pile of A4 pages into my hands, her face full of anticipation. On the top page is a poster that reads:

## SAVE OUR SCHOOL: STOP THE SALE
## OF ILLUMEN HALL

She's drawn an incredible illustration of the front of the school, the same one you usually see on all our banners and on the website, except half the building has crumbled on one side and a bulldozer is poking out. She's added text too, explaining the plans and calling all students to take action.

'I thought we could distribute them round the school, put them in pigeonholes and lockers, slide them under dorm-room doors, pile them up in the library and common rooms and even throw them from the top of the staircases like they always do in American teen movies!' She grins at me.

'Harriet, these are incredible. You've absolutely smashed it.' In that moment, I just want to squeeze her.

'Glad you approve. Took me bloody ages drawing the school and that bulldozer on my iPad.'

'Well, your design skills have shone through.'

Harriet places all the posters in her desk drawer and lies back down beside me.

'How will you feel if we can't stop this sale? Have you thought about how it might affect your future?'

'No, not really . . . Hey, did you hear that Jacob in Polaris got sent to Mrs Abbott's office for plagiarizing?' I change the subject. I don't want to get into the future right now. I know the minute I open those floodgates it'll be hard to shut them again. But Harriet can see right through me.

'If that's what's more important to you right now, then . . . girl, you need to get out more!' She laughs and stands up. 'I've got to head down to the library. I told Mrs Engleson I'd join her creative-writing class this evening and, although I am largely regretting my decision to say yes, I also think she's providing tea and Wagon Wheels so I'm in. I'll bring you one back, if you like?'

'No, it's OK. I've got to pick up some stuff from the music room anyway so I'll just meet you here later.'

We both leave her room and head off in different directions. I decide I want to make my way to the Magpie Society CCTV room so start walking towards the groundsman's cottage, which is now completely empty. Mr Tavistock and Ed left a couple of days ago. I watched from the landing as they put the last boxes into their truck and drove off through the gates.

I pull my coat up over my head to shelter from the rain and walk quickly across the driveway, through the woods and into the cottage. It's weird standing here without any belongings filling the rooms. It feels sad and desolate. A wave of melancholy floods my body. This is all really happening and so much quicker than I first anticipated. I slide the kitchen rug off the hatch door in the floorboards, unbolt it and head down the stairs and along the tunnel. Once I'm in the round stone room, I switch on the lights and take a seat at the desk to look at the two screens showing the current goings-on over at the school. Not a lot is happening: it's late, dark and raining so most people are inside. I want to go back and rewatch the footage of Clover and Mr Willis, see if there was anything before or after the clip I emailed myself that we might have missed. I'm slowly going through it, frame by frame, and analysing the expressions I can just about make out on their faces. *What are you saying to him, Clover?*

Just then, I spot a file name I hadn't seen before. It has a weird extension that I thought was just a program or something, but then I realize that it's a chat log. I open it up and an archived chat appears, between Ed and Clover.

My heart pounds. It's from the day Clover died.

| | |
|---|---|
| Clover: | Ed? You there? |
| MSCCTV: | Clover! You're OK! Where are you? |
| Clover: | I'm hiding out with Patrick in Winferne. I'm OK. I just needed to get away from school and I can't come back until I know Lola's killer has been arrested. |
| MSCCTV: | Do you still think it's the same suspect? |
| Clover: | You know who I think did it, Ed. But I need proof before I dare tell anyone. I need to find Lola's phone. It's honestly the only way of confirming. |

So Clover was clearly in communication with Ed, something I had no idea about. I feel a tinge of betrayal. Why didn't he mention this to me? Why would he have let me believe she was missing? But the answer is obvious: it would have made him a suspect in her death.

| MSCCTV: | Where are you going to look? |
|---------|------------------------------|
| Clover: | I have the what3words of the phone's last-known location. I finally convinced the phone company to release the data to me. It's just off school grounds – I think in that abandoned church. I'm going to try and go there this morning. But, Ed, I need a favour. Mrs Abbott is on to us. We've already seen she'll stop at nothing to keep the school's reputation safe. She's been getting rid of anyone standing in her way – I don't want to be next. |
| MSCCTV: | I'll keep her distracted this morning by asking about hedges or something. People are really worrying about you here, you know? Maybe you should come back . . . |
| Clover: | We're so close now. I can't stop. Once I get the phone, I'll gather everything together to go to the police too. Tell them and show them everything I have. Then Lola will finally get some justice. |

As I read the exchange, my heart beats in my chest so hard I can feel it rattling my ribcage. The abandoned church. I know exactly where that is. It's too late to go there now. But, as soon as I have the chance, I know I'll have to.

I head to Harriet's room. She's still not back, so I lie on Ruby's bed, thinking about Clover and the chat I just read between her and Ed. How close she was to getting the proof. How determined she was.

It feels lonely just lying here, listening to the rain. In

another world, one where she hadn't betrayed me, Audrey and I would now be dissecting the film we'd just watched. Seeing her in the dining room earlier, linking arms with Araminta, it felt like she did it to spite me, on top of everything else. I must have got her so wrong. How much do I really know about Audrey and her family anyway? If Audrey can go digging into my personal life, I can do the same to her. At least I'll discover more about her dad, his company and this sale. If she's not going to help me, then I'll go looking for the answers myself. I know where she lives. I just need to work out how to get inside.

I drop Ed a text.

> **Ed, are you still in Winferne? The Magpie Society needs your help!**

# 31

## AUDREY

I'm sitting on a red velvet chair in one of the music rooms. There's a shiny black piano dominating the space, and a stack of metallic music stands in the corner. This is one of the places Ivy spends so much time in. And no wonder. It's far better than anything we had back in my high school. The facilities at Illumen Hall really are second to none. An even bigger shame that no more students are gonna get to enjoy them.

Araminta drags one of the stands out in front of me and arranges her music on it. With only a few weeks to go before the concert, I'm surprised she hasn't learned it by heart. That's one thing she'll need to fix before too long.

'Ready?' she asks me.

'Whenever you are.'

She nods, takes a deep breath and closes her eyes. When she starts singing, I sink back into my chair; she has a nice voice, but she doesn't have the balance of innocence and power that she really needs to play a good Christine. Still, with some dedicated practice on her breathing techniques, she won't be far off. And, despite her fears, she doesn't need a ton of choreography, so I'm able to offer a few suggestions to really help her get the most out of her performance. I give her some ideas as to what Bonnie and Katie can do behind her, to enhance the showmanship.

It feels so freeing to be creative again. I hadn't realized how much I'd missed it. It also feels good to be doing something that's not investigating a murder.

And I will be fine.

If the school closes – yeah, it sucks. But at least I have my life. My health. Friends. Family (sort of). Clover doesn't have that. Lola doesn't have that. Alicia doesn't have that.

There are things to be grateful for. I have to constantly remind myself of that.

When she finishes her first full run-through, I applaud. Araminta smiles at me gratefully. 'What do you think?'

'Honestly? You're almost there. I think I need to see it onstage though.'

'What do you mean?'

'In this room, it's hard for you to get into character properly. But also you're gonna knock 'em dead. You've got the voice and the look. Don't worry so much. To play a good Christine you have to allow yourself to really show some vulnerability. There's a lot of romance in the whole Christine story too. Is there someone you can think about, a relationship or something that you can focus on?'

I feel like I'm channelling my old drama coach. Drilling into me the scales, making me practise over and over until it became second nature. I hadn't ever really wanted to be a stage actress though. I like the accolades, the recognition – but not the hard work.

I've always coasted. That's been my way. And things have always come to me, despite my lack of effort. As if my laziness is rewarded just because of who I am.

Since making me a part of her Magpie Society, Ivy's given me something to work hard for. A cause. I rub at my wrist where the magpie stamp once sat. It's gone now. Faded to nothing.

'Audrey?'

I blink and look up. Araminta is staring at me strangely, and I realize she's been talking the entire time that I've been daydreaming. 'I asked if you wanted to grab some lunch?'

'Oh yeah. I'm starving. I didn't get much breakfast, probably why I spaced out. Let's go.'

Sitting in the cafeteria with Araminta, Bonnie, Katie and the rest of the group that used to be my 'enemies' is strange and yet also strangely normal. Across the room, over the crowded heads, I can see Ivy, Harriet and their crew. They're not paying me any attention, but it's the deliberateness of their averted gazes that shows me just how bothered they are.

I try and sink into the conversation at the table.

Bonnie is heads together with Araminta. She side-eyes me, loyal companion that she is, not trusting the newcomer. But I can also tell that Araminta is pleased as punch to have me on her team. I'm feeling a little bit like a prize to be won.

Araminta gives Bonnie a subtle nod of the head, and she dives in. 'How are things going with Hottie?'

'Hottie?' I ask, sitting forward to learn more.

Araminta quirks an eyebrow, then she giggles and leans back into me. 'I've been seeing this guy since Christmas last year. He is so hot, but it's all quite . . . hush-hush.'

Does no one have public relationships in this place?

'Is it someone I know?' I ask.

Araminta and Bonnie exchange a look and then giggle again. 'You've definitely met him.'

'Does he go to this school?'

'That, I can safely say, is a no. He doesn't *go* to this school.'

I flinch. *It can't be.* I try to keep my expression neutral. 'Ah, OK.'

'But you know him.'

'Bonnie!'

'What? I'm keeping the secret. But she does know him . . . I'm just being truthful.'

'Well, be quiet before you give too much away.' But Araminta doesn't seem *that* bothered. She flips her blond hair off her shoulder. 'There's only a few months left now before we can act like a proper couple. It's been great, especially since all the people trying to stop us are out of the way.'

Immediately, my heart starts to race in my chest. I try and keep my cool. Araminta won't open up to me if I seem too eager. This is a game, but one I'm a master at. 'Oh, nothing like a forbidden romance. Trust me – I know exactly what that's like.'

'Really? Tell me more . . .'

'Oh, it's a long story from back home. A stage romance with a director who was much older than me. He really didn't want anyone to know, but hey – got me the lead role.'

Araminta laughs, her eyes glinting. 'Sounds juicy. Was he hot?'

'Smoking. But honestly, when he left his wife and said he wanted us to go public, the shine kinda wore off. Plus, by that time, I was seeing Brendan – and he was mega hot, and didn't require any kinda secret. That's the problem with hidden romance stuff. Sometimes half the chemistry is wrapped up in the fact that it is hidden.'

'Oh, don't worry about that. What I have with Hottie is different.'

'It is *so* different,' says Bonnie, the classic sidekick. 'You guys are going to get married and have beautiful, smart, history-loving babies.'

'Bonnie!' Araminta says.

'What! And hey, Audrey, how are things going with Teddy?'

My heart is pounding wildly, but I stay calm. 'I'm supposed to be going out on his boat this weekend,' I reply. 'Y'all have any idea what I should wear on a boating date?'

Katie scrunches her nose. 'In this weather? I'd make sure you have your waterproofs.'

'I'm sure you'll spend most of the time taking things off, so I wouldn't worry too much,' says Araminta. Then her phone buzzes. 'Oh, speaking of, I'd better run. Got a little rendezvous before class.' She gives us all a wink. 'Audrey, thank you *so* much for your help today. And you're right about needing to see it onstage to properly appreciate it.

Can you come to our dress rehearsal next week? I'll have had some time to practise by then.'

'Sure, of course,' I say, suppressing a shudder. My mind is racing. I'm pretty sure I know who Araminta is madly, desperately in love with. And suddenly Araminta had a pretty strong motive for wanting Lola gone.

## 32

### IVY

It's Saturday and Harriet and I are meeting up with Ed to head over to Audrey's family mansion. The school always feels a little emptier this time of year. A lot of students spend weekends at home through the winter months as the school feels so bleak and cold. There are no activities running and people usually prefer to curl up by the fire in their stately homes and eat pheasant on a Sunday. At least that's what I imagine.

Before meeting Ed, I swing by my room to pick up some clean clothes, but I need to wait for Audrey to leave before going in. We're now completely avoiding each other and the fewer awkward encounters the better. I know she usually heads off around 8 a.m. for breakfast so I linger in the corridor out of sight and wait for our bedroom door to click open. Sure enough, at exactly 8 a.m., the door opens and out she comes. She's dressed head to toe in waterproof gear, fleece jacket and sturdy boots. Not your typical Audrey attire at all. She looks as though she's going for a hike! I wish more than ever that I could quiz her on what on earth she's doing and where she's going, but I can't and I don't. She's probably up to something with Araminta, therefore I don't care.

The door shuts behind her and she heads for the stairs. Once she's out of sight, I run into the room and grab a few bits out of my wardrobe to change into, making sure I don't make it too obvious I was here.

Downstairs, I join Harriet by the door and we make our way outside together. Ed is already waiting for us in his old silver Volvo in a lay-by.

'You took ages! I was worried someone would see me,' he says as we reach the car. 'You know I'm not allowed back here.'

'Sorry, we came as quickly as we could.'

'OK, jump in. Where is it we're heading again?'

'Coastal View, Klinedine Road. It's in a row of huge houses along the cliffside. Do you know the ones I mean?'

'Yeah, I know.'

It doesn't take us too long to reach the road of ridiculous houses, the kind you only ever see in films or Hollywood Hills. Ed drives slowly so we don't miss the big gates among other big gates.

'It's this one!' I shout as I recognize the entrance.

'You wait out here. Text if you need me,' I say to Ed.

'Likewise.'

Ed parks his car up on a grassy verge and Harriet and I jump out and ring the bell.

'Hello?' a woman's muffled voice answers.

'Hi, I'm Ivy, Audrey's room-mate! I'm here with my friend Harriet. Audrey asked us to pop in and pick something up for her.'

'OK. Gates should open for you now.' We hear a buzz and the gates start opening slowly. I don't know if this is

Audrey's mum or a housekeeper. I'm hoping the latter. The fewer people in the house the better.

We make our way along the driveway and knock on the door. To my surprise, Audrey's dad himself answers and holds out his hand.

'Hi, I'm Walter! Nice to meet you both.'

I shake it confidently, smiling and hoping this conceals my underlying anger.

'I've actually been here before, Mr Wagner.'

'Good to hear, good to hear. Well, what is it you need? I can ask our housekeeper to fetch it for you.'

'Oh . . . I think Audrey wanted us to get it from her room for her, along with some slightly more personal items.'

'Girl things!' Harriet pipes up.

'Oh. OK, well, whatever you have to do. I'm actually heading out now so grab what you need and the housekeeper will let you out. She's in the kitchen. Nice to meet you both.' He slips past us and beeps his car open. The man about to ruin my life. Harriet and I step inside.

The house is just as I remember it. Minimal and white. Barely a trinket in sight, just oodles of chic, expensive-looking furniture that you wouldn't want to sit in, just look at. The living area is full of bright light as the wall is just a huge pane of glass, with a view out to sea.

'I'm pretty sure his office was round the back. Let's go.'

We walk along the corridor. My feet bounce on the plush carpet. I pray to the Magpie Society gods that his office is open and that we can get inside. We pass Audrey's room and I see it's still as boring and sterile as it was. Untouched and unloved.

Before long, we're at the entrance of his obnoxious glass office, and it's open. Walter's desk is in pride of place at the centre, his huge Apple Mac sitting proudly.

'Right, so what exactly are we looking for?' Harriet asks as we stand and stare at the room before us.

'Anything to do with Illumen. Check all the drawers and that pile of papers. We don't have long and I don't want the housekeeper hearing us so we need to be quick. Take photos on your phone of anything you find!'

We both set to work, flicking through drawers and any papers lying on the desk, and it doesn't take long before we spot what we came for. There are so many documents relating to the redevelopment and the school sale, including an entire list of investors.

'Shit ... look at everyone who's throwing money at this!' I hand Harriet the piece of paper after I've photographed it on my phone. 'Looks like a big payout for a lot of the parents. And the teachers are all being given a huge severance package too. Keeps them onside, doesn't it?'

'And look, here's a printed email chain between Walter and Mrs Abbott with historical documentation about the school that she's clearly scanned in and sent over! "Here is everything I could find. As far as I can see, there are no restrictions or limitations on what we can do."'

'Interesting! Let's just take photos of literally everything in this pile and then we need to head out. We can look over it all later when we're back at Illumen.'

'I feel like a real-life detective right now ...' Harriet laughs. 'That or as if I'm doing something seriously illegal.'

'Yeah, best not to think about it too much. Right, you head out and speak to the housekeeper, keep her distracted. I'll tidy all this away and meet you in the drive.'

'OK, let me just pop all this stuff back.'

Harriet starts opening the desk drawers again to put the paperwork away, making sure it looks as neat as we found it and in roughly the same order. She forcefully yanks open one drawer that sticks and something slides forward from the back. It's a single shell earring. I feel a rush of blood to my face.

'That's Lola's!' I say. I shove it into my coat pocket and zip it up.

Harriet's mouth drops open. 'Why was her earring hidden at the back of this drawer? Does that mean Audrey's *dad* knew her?'

'I don't know. But I'm going to take this straight to the police.'

## 33

### AUDREY

We're out on the water, and Teddy is doing something complicated-looking with ropes and the big sheets of his sails. I'm not sure that I'm a hundred per cent comfortable with the fact that I'm on such choppy seas with this guy. I should have maybe done some research on how good a sailor he actually is. I wish I could have asked Ivy for some advice, but she hasn't been back to the room in days.

It sucks because all I want is a chance to explain – and to let her know that I haven't abandoned her and *definitely* didn't mean to betray her. While I feel the sting of losing Harriet, Max and Tom so quickly, I knew they were all Ivy's friends really. I wanna tell her my plan: to stay in Araminta's inner circle to try and find some proof of Mr Willis's guilt (or, potentially, Araminta's). But Ivy is the master at avoiding me. It's been a week and she hasn't slept in our dorm room once. I'm feeling desperately alone.

At least it meant I didn't have to explain to her why I was going out today dressed in some borrowed waterproofs and boots. Teddy said something about shoes with grip being helpful on a boat. Shoes with grip? Who did he think I was? Some kind of mountaineer?

'Can you pass me that rope?'

'Excuse me?'

'Over there! That thing coiled up by your foot.'

'Oh right.' The boat lurches as I move, and I let out quite an undignified squeal. 'Are we going much further? I think I'm starting to feel a bit sick.'

'Yeah, sorry – I didn't realize it was going to be *quite* this bad out here.'

'You *knew* we were going out in rough weather?'

He grins at me. 'It's more fun this way.'

'Jesus.' We crash over another wave, and the spray shoots up and over the side of the boat. I'd dropped my hood, thinking that it didn't do anything for my hair. But, now it's covered in salty water, I'm not sure that's a good look either. I can see Teddy eyeing me and, as much as I wanna pretend to be chill, I am very much *not* OK with this.

'Why don't you go down below deck while I steer us back in? I know a local cafe that will deliver us coffees to the dock when we arrive.'

'*Now* you're speaking my language,' I say to him.

I duck back below deck, using both hands to catch myself along the railings. It's pokier down here than I remember, and I have to stoop down to avoid bashing my head on the beams. I wonder if that pirate costume is stashed away somewhere.

The boat is pretty neat and tidy, with everything having its place. I browse the row of books – secured behind a neat wooden bar – to see what kinda thing Teddy likes to read. You can always tell a lot about a guy by his reading material. That he reads at all is a positive sign and it's surprisingly cerebral – lots of non-fiction. There's a copy of Homer's *Odyssey* as well. A story about a voyage. That's hardly surprising.

There's a slim volume that looks well used. I pull it out halfway and it reads 'Ship's log'. *Hmm.* I pull it out a bit further and then there's a noise behind me. I quickly hide it under my seat. For some reason, I don't want Teddy to know I've been snooping. I'm embarrassed, but there's an undercurrent of fear there too. I don't know where that's come from; he's never made me feel that way. I guess I'm just so on edge.

'You OK down here?'

'Yeah – feels a bit better. Shouldn't you be up there . . . driving or something?' My stomach churns and I hope I'm not gonna be sick.

Teddy looks breezy. 'Oh no, we'll be OK. I've dropped the anchor for a while. We're in a bay, which is sheltered, so it shouldn't be so rocky.'

'Oh yeah, that's probably why I've been feeling better too. I'm not used to this boat life.' I try a smile, and thankfully the nausea subsides. 'Have you been doing this long?'

'I had once hoped to go to the Olympics . . .'

'Seriously?' My jaw drops.

He laughs. 'Yeah, but I gave it up a little while ago. So fixing up this old boat has kind of been like my hobby. A way to keep in touch with my grandfather, but not have to focus so much on competition. My dad was pretty gutted when I packed it all in.'

'Why did you?'

He shrugs. 'Honestly? I just didn't enjoy it any more. All the early mornings and also the sniping behind people's backs. Honestly, the pranks we played on each other got more and more dangerous. When my teammate almost drowned after someone tacked up some of his rope . . . I'd had enough.'

I rub his arm. 'Sheesh. That must have been tough.'

'No kidding. Anyway, this is much more fun. Although I'm pretty sure that's one of the reasons Ivy wouldn't take our relationship seriously.'

I cringe. 'Really?'

'Is it awkward mentioning that? Sorry. It's just now that you know her . . . It's hard to talk about it with other people.'

'D'you still miss her?'

'Kind of. I don't miss the pressure she puts herself under. That's why, when I quit the Olympic training team, I think she saw me as weak. She can't really get over that.'

'Yeah, I can imagine. She's pretty unhappy with me at the moment.'

Teddy's eyes open wide. 'What were you thinking, going to her home without asking?'

'I was *thinking* that maybe it would be nice to do something for her for a change. How was I to know that her mom was a bitch?'

Teddy leans in. 'I'm so curious. What was it like?'

'She comes from a totally different world to us, Teddy. Maybe that's why she didn't wanna date you seriously. I don't think we could ever really understand what it was like for her. We have too much privilege. She's had to overcome so much. But, even though she hates me now, I'm glad I did it. Because I don't think I could ever truly understand her without knowing a bit about where she came from.'

Teddy puts his hand on my knee. 'You're a good friend, Audrey. She'll realize that and she'll come around.'

'I really hope so. I miss her.'

'Although maybe not if you keep hanging out with Araminta ...'

'Look, Araminta's been nice to me. But it's not just that ... I also think it might help to answer one of our major questions about Lola's murder.'

Teddy shifts in his seat, looking uncomfortable. 'Maybe I should go back upstairs and –'

'I think Araminta's having an affair with Mr Willis.'

Teddy freezes. 'What? I *knew* that guy was a pervert.'

'I think he has a type. We're pretty sure he dated Lola as well.'

'That's sick. Why haven't you said anything to the police?'

'We don't have any proof. We found a photograph of them together, but then it accidentally got destroyed.'

'*What?*'

'Well, it wasn't definitive anyway. All we know is that he's a mega creep.'

'If he could have been involved in Lola's murder, then that's huge! We have to do something.' Teddy seems way more riled up than I expected. He's pacing about the cabin, his fingers balled into fists.

'Whoa, calm down. It's not like he could have killed her. He had an alibi. He was on his way to Paris with his fiancée the night that Lola died.'

'How do you know that?'

'We just do, OK?'

Teddy stares at me until I answer. I rack my brain for something more credible than, *Well, we confronted him and he showed us the time stamp of his photographs.*

'The police confirmed his alibi. Something about the time stamp on his photo . . .'

'Well, time stamps can be faked – even just by changing the time on your phone you can trick the camera. They could have got a really early flight or train. Doesn't mean they left the night before.'

'What, you think he just brutally killed someone and then jetted off to Paris for a romantic post-murder weekend away?'

I chuckle. But Teddy isn't laughing. 'It could happen.'

'No. We know it's not him.'

'But I saw him that night. In town. He was getting coffee. There was a girl in the car with him. A blond girl. I assumed it was his fiancée too, but it could have been Lola.'

'What time was that?'

'Well, I was just on my way to start the bonfire at the party. So I guess around seven?'

He's right. The ticket Mr Willis showed us said his train left at 6.30 p.m. If he was still in Winferne Bay at seven, then he's been lying to us. I swallow. Looks like Mr Willis's alibi is off the table.

'Actually, I have a photo, I think.' Teddy gets his phone out, scrolling back to that night. 'Yes! There. See that Mini in the background?'

'Mr Willis's car,' I say, whistling through my teeth.

I immediately need to tell Ivy. But would she even want to hear from me? Then I frown. 'Why do you care so much?' I ask Teddy.

'Look, I wasn't Lola's biggest fan, but you guys and the podcast have kind of infected me with this drive to know what happened.'

'We're all like mini detectives now.'

'Exactly. So, if Mr Willis had some kind of motive for killing her, and tried to cover it up with a fake alibi, then I think that's important.'

'Well, I have a card for this female police officer. Maybe I'll call her and let her know your information.'

'Good idea.'

There's a moment of silence as we both think about what happened to Lola. There's something going on with Teddy that I can't read, an expression that I don't understand. I don't know him well enough. If I had to guess, I'd say he was holding something back, warring with himself over what to tell me.

'What is it?'

'Oh, nothing. Just thinking that you're really beautiful. And I love the sound of your voice.' He reaches out towards me, wiping some sea spray from my forehead.

Warmth rushes to my face, his words disarming me. Maybe that was his intention, but I go with it. I haven't flirted much with anyone since Brendan and I miss it. 'You're not so bad yourself.'

He sits down next to me, and finally we lean in to each other. Our lips brush together and he inches towards me, my back pressing against the bench cushions. I kiss him back eagerly, my hand reaching up and grabbing his neck, pulling him in. I haven't kissed anyone like this in months, and the intimacy of it is spreading warmth throughout my body. I can feel how much I want it, the urgency increasing. His body is firm and strong against mine, his hands tracing their way along the exposed skin of my neck and collarbone, and it is so good just to be touched. I shift so his finger slips beneath the edge of my shirt and, as I grip the belt loops of his jeans to press him closer into me, I know we're moving into dangerous territory.

Then the boat lurches, and spray attacks the window. It breaks us apart.

'Shit. I'd better go check on the anchor. We'll head back to shore now to be safe. But this business between us –' he reaches up and strokes my cheek – 'it isn't finished.'

'No. I don't think that it is.'

He grins at me, and it might be the cutest thing I've ever seen. But then he stands as the boat rocks and rolls again, my stomach flipping, and I'm glad that he's going on deck to sort out whatever's happening outside. I've had enough of being at sea.

When I move my feet, the ship's log slides out from underneath me and falls to the floor. I lean down to pick it up, then flip through it. It's just a long list of journeys and people who have been on the boat – a lot of Teddy out on his own, sometimes with his parents. In some of the entries, I even see Ivy's name a couple of times. No surprise there.

Then I flip back a few pages, to the start of the summer. And there's one name and date that catches my eye.

*Oh my God.*

On the date that Lola died, she was on Teddy's boat.

They say she fell from a cliff into the water. But she could just as easily have fallen off a boat and into the sea, washing up on the beach. In fact, that might be even *more* plausible.

My heart races and the fear I felt earlier returns. Is Teddy a murderer?

I think about confronting him, but I don't want to. Not while I'm so vulnerable – out at sea and far from anyone. My hands are shaking.

I don't know what he's capable of. I feel like I can't trust my own instincts about people any more.

Teddy. Mr Willis. Araminta. Mrs Abbott. All the different suspects swirl in my mind. But what strikes me now is that *anyone* who knew about the sale of the school had a motive for Lola's death. She must have intended to stop it.

Maybe Clover found out the same thing, and they needed to silence her too.

Which means I have a big problem. Because, in my mind, the puzzle has come together. Except, rather than seeing a clear picture of the murderer, I have a clear image of who the next victim is going to be.

And that's Ivy.

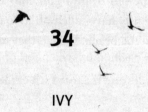

# 34

## IVY

Harriet and I are sitting in the courtyard behind the Tower Wing at Illumen, eating a late lunch and looking through the photos on our phones that we took in Audrey's dad's office.

'It was nuts that we were able to casually stroll into her house like that. I felt a bit like one of Charlie's Angels, except Ivy's Angels obviously.' She zooms into one of the documents.

'I know. Thank God he was going out.'

'So when did we decide to distribute my posters about the school closure?' Harriet crunches through her sad-looking salad box.

'We should do it soon. I feel like the rest of the students need to know this now.'

I look up and notice Audrey and Teddy together, wearing their outdoor gear. *Oh right*, I think, *his boat*. I've been the one in waterproofs, sloshing about on *Old Sheila* too.

Audrey has a slight tinge of grey to her complexion and, judging by the weather, it would have been very choppy out at sea. The idea of Audrey feeling sick on the boat comforts me slightly, though I really shouldn't care. But I do. I feel the anger rising inside me like lava. Is this just another thing Audrey's trying to rub in my face to irritate me? Now there's no way I'm going to share with her what I've learned about her dad or any of the Magpie Society stuff I've discovered over the past few days.

Audrey catches me looking. She hugs Teddy goodbye and starts approaching us. The hood of her coat is still up over her head, probably because her hair has been ruined. As she gets closer, I see that she doesn't look in the slightest bit remorseful or embarrassed. Actually, she seems eager, maybe a little nervous.

'Harriet, do you mind if I chat with Ivy for a bit?' She crosses her arms and gives a weak smile in my direction. I stare back blankly. Harriet looks at me for a sign. I nod.

'Be my guest!' She gets up and gestures at her seat.

Audrey sits down and waits until Harriet is far enough away that she won't hear her. I still say nothing and stare ahead.

'Ivy, we *have* to talk –'

I interrupt her. 'Let me guess. You're after some Teddy advice? You need help with Araminta? Your family are rich scumbags?' If this girl thinks she has the audacity to ask me for advice right now, I honestly think I might snap.

'That's not at all what I was gonna say. What is wrong with you? Why are you being like this?' She turns towards me, raising her voice slightly. I've never seen her like this, her voice wobbling.

'*ME* being like *THIS*? Are you serious? You keep the biggest secret from me about this development, something so incredibly important. You then go behind my back to visit my mum. Next you ditch whatever's left of our friendship to pal up with Araminta AND, finally, you spend an afternoon out at sea with my ex-boyfriend. You wonder why I'm like this? *Really, Audrey?* You aren't that fucking stupid, are you?'

I let loose. It's running out of my mouth and I can't stop it. 'Please spare me the grovelling and the shitty justifications for your actions, I honestly couldn't care less any more. Besides, it's the Christmas holidays soon so just stay out of my way, OK? I've already told Mrs Abbott you need to change rooms. Room seven was always supposed to be for prefects only.'

Audrey sits in silence and stares at me. She's searching for a tiny speck of hope for our friendship so she knows where to go from here. Her eyes start to water and her jaw is clenched. I can sense her desperation beneath the surface, but she doesn't let it spill out. I'm almost proud.

'Where do you even spend Christmas, Ivy? Because it's certainly not with your family.' She bites back, something I did not expect at all.

'Are you being serious right now? Whose side are you on, Audrey? You'd think after what happened last year back in Georgia you'd at least know when to step up and when to shut the fuck up. I guess I had you so wrong. You're not who I thought you were – you're just a sheep.'

She gets up off the bench and looks down at me. She throws her arms in the air and exhales sharply. 'You know what? I'm fucking done, Ivy! Screw what I found out.'

I want more than anything to keep shouting at her, to tell her everything Harriet and I discovered in her dad's office. I want to tell her that the Magpie Society doesn't need her anyway and that she's just a spare part. That she has no friends. That she's so desperate for male attention she'll go after her room-mate's ex. But it wouldn't accomplish anything. I've already said enough. There's no coming back from this, for us.

Audrey turns, crosses her arms and walks back towards school. When she thinks she's far enough away that I can't see, she hangs her head and wipes her eyes. Screw this. I'm not sitting here, feeling like a villain for making her cry. She brought this on herself. She could have stuck up for herself and she didn't. She walked away.

With no other plans for the afternoon, and a fire inside me that's burning like a furnace, I get out my phone and send a text to DI Shing asking her if we can meet once again. I know how I can really rock Audrey's world. Her dad needs to be investigated too.

I get up, pull my phone from my pocket and open the Magpie Society WhatsApp group.

> Project poster is a go. Let's release them now.
> Everyone remember where they were assigned to?

I hit send and wait to see who's online and who has read the message. Everyone reads it straight away and they all start typing back.

Harriet:  YES, QUEEN. Let's fucking do this. I'm lockers and pigeonholes. Heading there now.

Yolanda:  I'm common rooms. Got my posters at the ready.

I don't wait for the others to reply. I need to get stationed with my posters before the first bell rings to signal the dining hall's 4 p.m. opening. It might be the weekend, but there are still plenty of students here to get the message. I march through the doors and head up the stairs to Helios House. It's one of the grander staircases in the school, with polished wide oak stairs curving round majestically. It's also pretty high up once you get to the top and you can stand on the landing and look down at the corridor below. Perfect for launching posters into a crowd of students.

I stand at the top of the stairs, my hips leaning into the wooden banister, and wait. The posters are stacked high in my hands and adrenaline kicks in. This had better work. Once the other students know about the redevelopment plan, it'll send Illumen Hall into a complete frenzy.

The silence is slightly unnerving as I wait tensely for the bell to chime. I hear the crack of the double doors below, and students start piling through into the corridor. The bell goes, loud and clear, cutting through the chatter and noise. I extend my arms over the banister, take a deep breath in and let go. The papers spiral, flutter and fly all over the place before softly landing on the ground, where students start scrambling to pick them up and read them. I take a step back so nobody sees me and start walking towards Harriet's room.

It's done.

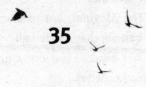

# 35

## AUDREY

It's absolute chaos.

A boy sprints past, almost knocking me over, clutching a bright orange piece of paper. He doesn't stop to apologize when I cry out; it's like he doesn't even notice me. My hands go ice-cold, remembering the last time flyers dropped at school: to promote Clover's podcast. A chill runs down my spine – it's as if Clover's ghost is roaming the halls.

One of the posters has fallen face down on the floor. I pick it up and breathe a sigh of relief. Not Clover after all. But now I know why that boy was racing down the hall in such a hurry.

Ivy's let the cat out of the bag. *SAVE OUR SCHOOL* screams out at me.

I wish I had a window into Ivy's brain so I could find out why she chose that moment to reveal the fate of Illumen Hall to the student body. I don't know what she expected – for everyone to band together, present a united front, stage some kinda sit-in maybe to protest? Instead, it's like the school has a collective freak-out.

It's still the weekend so not everyone is here. Those who are, are in a panic. There's a group of Year Nines crying in the canteen, being comforted by Araminta.

'Do you know who did this?' She lifts up one of the flyers when she sees me.

It's signed *The Magpies*, but of course I know it's Ivy and Araminta can see that written all over my face.

She shakes her head. 'I just don't understand. No one was supposed to know yet.'

My eyes widen. 'You knew about this already?'

Araminta shuts me up with a fierce glare.

'Where will I go to school?' says one of the girls. 'Is my scholarship going to be taken away? My parents can't afford to send me to another boarding school . . .'

'Don't worry,' says Araminta. 'Mrs Abbott has a plan. Let me go and find out more.' She stands up, gesturing at me to follow her. 'Yes, I knew, OK?' she whispers once we are out of earshot. 'But I was sworn to secrecy. It's one of the privileges of being head girl – I get a vote on the school's future. Except it's supposed to be about things like whether to change pastry suppliers in the canteen or if the Tower Wing needs refurbishment. Not something as big as this.' She whistles through her teeth. 'I didn't really have time to prepare myself for this decision. Lola was supposed to be in my position, remember? But, once Mrs Abbott talked me through the specifics, I knew I had to agree. It was the obvious choice.'

My stomach turns. Lola would have had a vote – and, from everything Ivy's said, she definitely would have voted *not* to sell the school. Who stood the most to gain from Lola being 'removed' from the voting?

Mrs Abbott.

And my dad.

The thought makes me sick.

My phone buzzes at the same time as Araminta's. As if I'd summoned her, there's a message from Mrs Abbott.

*Dear students of Illumen Hall,*

*I know you have had a big shock this afternoon, but I want to reassure you that – while I am saddened at the thought of our Illumen story coming to an end – your most exciting chapters lie ahead of you.*

   *Change is always scary, but you will be supported through every step of the journey. I hope that however long you have spent here – whether that's been a few months, or many years – we will have provided you with the tools to handle this change with fearless pride. But, to address your understandable concerns, please click on this link to find your personalized plan for life after Illumen Hall.*

*Sincerely,*
*Mrs Abbott*
*Headmistress*

'Wow, she moves fast,' I say to Araminta. 'Do you think she knew the news was gonna drop today?'

'How could she? I think Mrs Abbott is always just one step ahead, thank God. I hope this calms everyone down. Oh shit – Bonnie is WhatsApping me frantically. I'd better go check on her. Do you mind?'

'You go ahead.'

As Minty hurries away, I watch her back. Knowing now

that she had the ability to veto the sale gives her yet another motive for the murder – if she'd somehow found out last year. I click on the link and it sends me to an acceptance letter from one of the top London drama schools, welcoming me into the sixth form next year.

'Holy shit,' I whisper under my breath. Mrs Abbott *has* got all her ducks in a row. She must have known this reveal was coming. I think back to my conversation with Edison. Did he give my dad a warning?

If it's all my fault, that'll be yet another reason for Ivy to hate me.

Another message pops up, this one from Teddy.

> Did you hear?

> I did – isn't it wild?

> I can't even imagine this place
> not being here. Do you know
> where you'll be next year?

> Looks like in London.

I pause before sending the second half of the message.

> Not too far from you.

Not too far at all. Maybe this news isn't so bad. He adds a winky face emoji. That makes me smile.

Have you heard from Ivy? I dare to ask.

> Nothing. She can't be taking this
> well. I'll go check on her.

An unexpected bolt of jealousy spikes through me, visceral and raw. Despite the fact that I know Teddy and Ivy have a history, that they're friends, and of course it's only natural that he would wanna go to her – in fact, I *want* him to make sure she's OK since I can't. But the emotion still simmers there.

I must really like this guy.

I head to the SCR, hoping maybe to intercept him. Already I can feel that the mood has shifted, the school as fickle as the winter weather. Students are gathered eagerly together in bubbles, sharing their letters and finding out where their futures are taking them next.

Mrs Abbott's message will put a huge dampener on the fire Ivy was trying to ignite.

I just don't think she'll be ready to let it go just yet.

# 36

## AUDREY

It's amazing the difference a week can make. Mrs Abbott has attempted to drown us all in Christmas to make us forget the shock announcement about the school's closure going public.

Ever since I realized the likely motive behind Lola's murder – the fact that she could have stopped the sale of the school with her vote – I've wanted to talk to Ivy. Despite her nasty words. But, even though I'm still willing to give our friendship a shot, she hasn't forgiven me, and every time I spot her she's got a look of thunder on her face. Once, I called her name out in the hallway, and she spun round on her heel to go the other way.

But I also feel a sense of relief sitting alongside the guilt of my suspicions. Life is so much simpler now that I'm not knee-deep in underground passageways and Magpie-related mysteries. I'm back on the surface of things now, skimming along without a care in the world. Yes, part of me can sense the dread of what's in the deep water beneath me, the sharks of truth circling. But ignoring stuff is what I'm good at. Superficial is what's expected of me. I'm gonna lean into that, and hanging out with Araminta, Bonnie, Katie and co. makes that easy. Teddy and I have been speaking non-stop, mapping out our next year together in London. He's laid out our plans already and they sound magical: strolls along the South Bank, cuddling up in a cosy pub in Marylebone, sharing a bubble waffle in Chinatown. It's a pretty awesome daydream.

The school looks beautiful, decked out in decorations for the concert, all in the tasteful colours of purple, silver and green. Huge wreaths hang on the big wooden doors, and all down the banisters are garlands of pine, filling the hallways with a delicious smell. Fairy lights have appeared round the frames of the paintings – you'd never see that in a museum, but this is Illumen Hall. There are no rules. I can imagine why Dad wants to change it. I suddenly think of this as a potential wedding space, a hotel, a spa. I can see the travel bloggers flooding it already. I take a photo for Instagram, posing with the decorations in the background, and the likes swarm in straight away.

The theatre space has had one of the biggest transformations. I know now why Mrs Abbott is pulling out all the stops for the parents (aka investors) who'll be showing up. There's a beautiful star hanging right above the stage, with two big garlands framing it on either side. Bright, sparkling baubles are studded among the fragrant pine needles.

But, in the glare of the house lights, it's hard to appreciate exactly what it would look like. This is a private dress rehearsal for Minty – and it's only Bonnie and me in here watching her.

We have a backing track as she didn't want to embarrass herself in front of Ivy. Her vocal performance is better, but she's having a hard time patching together the dance routine. She'll never be a Broadway – or, I guess, West End – performer if she can't combine these simple moves. Even Bonnie seems a little frustrated, though she wipes her expression whenever Araminta's watching.

Araminta takes it again from the top, but, as she fumbles with the steps, she calls on me to stop the music and stamps her foot in frustration.

'I just can't seem to get this. Should we sub it out for something simpler?' she calls from the stage.

'You looked amazing, Minty,' says Bonnie. 'But honestly you could just stand there and it would sound incredible. You don't need any of this extra stuff. I don't think we should even be onstage with you. Honestly, you can carry this whole number on your own.'

I stand. 'Look – you could just stand there and sing it, but if you nail this you will honestly blow everyone away. That's the difference. So it depends – do you wanna get through the performance, or do you wanna absolutely nail it?'

Araminta pauses – but, to her credit, it's only for a moment. 'I want to nail it.'

'Then let's try it again.'

'Hang on, wait.' Araminta rushes to the edge of the stage, then grabs her cellphone out of her handbag. 'Do you think you can film me while I'm performing? Then I can watch it back later.'

'Good idea.'

She unlocks the phone and hands it over. I point it at the stage and she goes again.

A message flashes up as I'm filming. **HOTTIE** it says, but the content of the message is hidden. I have to confirm if my suspicions are right.

Even straight into the first verse, it's clear Araminta's in trouble. When she fluffs one of the big notes, I put the phone down and clap my hands. 'This isn't quite working . . .' I say. Then a flash of inspiration hits me. 'Do you have your costume nearby? Sometimes it can kinda get you in the mood and help you really feel what your performance is gonna be like.'

'Oh, that's such a good idea. Bonnie, can you give me a hand? It's just behind the curtain.'

'Sure!' Bonnie almost falls over herself in her desperation to get up onstage. I choke back a laugh.

I watch as they disappear into the wings, then I look back down at Araminta's cellphone. It's still unlocked, so I quickly cancel out of the camera function and open her messaging app. I feel a twinge of guilt for snooping – but not for long. Not when I register what I'm seeing.

**Never thought history would be my top subject** Araminta has written.

> With you in class, it's a wonder I get any teaching
> done at all.

**HOTTIE** is Mr Willis. I shudder.

There are photographs being sent back and forth between them, and so much dirty conversation that I shouldn't be reading. It makes me want to vom, thinking of Mr Willis writing this stuff to a vulnerable teenage girl. Sure, Araminta might act tough, but deep down inside I know she's just craving affection and attention – and Mr Willis is taking full advantage. The power dynamic is all screwed up. I scroll back even further, feeling my heart racing in my chest. I know that Araminta and Bonnie could be back at any second, especially as it won't take her that long to change into her costume.

And that's when I see it. A set of photographs that I recognize. Of Araminta sitting in Mr Willis's lap.

Her blond hair hides most of her face in the picture I'm thinking of – the one from Lola's diary. But, in the rest of the series, she's tucked the strands behind her ears. Same pose. Same clothes. Just a much clearer face.

This picture wasn't of Lola after all. It was of Minty.

Goofo/Hottie was two-timing them. No wonder Lola had given him such an unflattering nickname. And no wonder she was so cut up about it. Maybe she went to confront Mr Willis, and he killed her . . .

Or maybe she was so depressed and in shock that she really was driven to the cliffs by herself.

The motives are piling up.

Whatever the answer, I know I can't keep this knowledge to myself. The shark fins have pierced the surface of the water, and I need to sound the alarm.

Working as fast as my fingers can fly, I forward the photographs to my number, as well as screenshots of some of the conversation around the time of Lola's death that I don't have time to read. Then I delete the evidence of the messages I've forwarded. My heart is pounding, my ears on high alert for the slightest sound of Araminta and Bonnie returning.

I place the cellphone down on my seat and I sprint towards the exit. Just at that moment, I hear Araminta and Bonnie come out from backstage. Araminta has on the same costume as Bonnie, a plain white smock with a frilled edge. Is that really what she's planning on wearing? But I can't think about that now.

I hear her call my name, first out of confusion, then a second time – with a tinge of anger.

'Audrey? Audrey!'

But I'm out the door, my heart racing. I need to find Ivy. And she's gonna have to listen to me whether she likes it or not.

# 37

## IVY

I'm back in our bedroom, taking more of my clothes from the wardrobe to bring to Harriet's, and thinking about the message Mrs Abbott sent after we dispersed the posters throughout school. It was as if she was one step ahead of us the whole time, poised to counterstrike with her bullshit, fluffy, positive news. I can't believe the other students have eaten it up.

On the way up to the room, I overheard a couple of girls saying how excited they were about the prospect of going to the school that just opened a little way up the coast. Of course, some students are concerned, but the majority of them have just swallowed Mrs Abbott's shiny alternatives. These kids would be better off staying here at Illumen Hall; they just don't know it yet. Although she has no proof it was me behind the posters, she's already threatened to take me out of the Christmas concert unless I 'stay in line', so there's that too. We need to do something else if we're going to save the school.

I just don't know what.

I scoop up my small jewellery collection and my copy of *American Psycho*, then hear the floorboards creak outside in the corridor. Audrey must have seen me walking up the stairs towards our room, but if she has any sense she'll keep herself away until she knows I've gone. I do miss this room though. It's much bigger than Harriet's and sunlight pours in, casting beautiful shadows through the latticed blinds. The view is pretty epic too, and there's much more space between the beds.

Just as I'm folding a hoodie into my tote bag, Audrey bursts in, making me jump on the spot. She looks like a woman possessed.

'Don't walk out!' she pants, putting her hands up towards me and standing in front of the door to block it. 'You *need* to listen to what I have to say.'

'Fine!' I fold my arms and raise my eyebrows. I'm intrigued, despite myself. Has she discovered something, or is it that she's been stewing over what to reply to me from our argument earlier?

'Sit!' Audrey ushers me backwards on to my bed and she takes up position opposite me on hers, still stabilizing her breathing.

'It's Araminta . . .' she says.

'What about her?'

'She's going out with Mr Willis!'

'You are joking, right?' I want to jump up in horror, but she steadies me.

'No. I saw the messages on her phone. They've been dating for ages. Months, maybe even a year.'

'That absolute CREEP!' I raise my voice.

'That's not all though . . . The photo, the one we found in Lola's diary. It wasn't her, Ivy. It's Minty. They've both got blond hair so it's easy to mix them up. She had the photo on her phone – it was identical. As well as a bunch of others in the same location.'

I sit, open-mouthed, shaking my head. 'How is that possible? Why would Lola have a photo of Araminta in her diary?'

'I don't know. Maybe she discovered their secret and was using it to blackmail him? Maybe the reason she's dead is that she confronted him with this information?'

'Oh my God, you could be right! We don't know whether there was some sort of love triangle going on between the three of them. He also flirted with *me* a lot last year too. Dirty scumbag.'

'God. I wonder if there are any other girls he's currently talking to that Araminta has no idea about? Do you think she knew about him and Lola?'

'I don't know, but it's clear that Lola did!'

'Also, the plot thickens.' Audrey leans forward. 'He *wasn't* in Paris that night.'

'WHAT? But DI Shing says his alibi checked out!'

'I don't know how he's got around it, but Teddy swears that he saw him that night. He has a photograph too.'

'Well, this changes everything!'

'But there's more. I also went on Teddy's boat earlier.'

Oh, here we go. 'Look, Audrey, I don't want to get into that.'

She stops me. 'No . . . you need to know this. Lola had been on the boat. The day she died. I saw her name in Teddy's logbook.'

'Maybe he took a handful of them out that day? I

remember it being nice weather. Who else's name was in for that day?'

Audrey pulls up the photos on her phone, zooms in and holds it out to show me. There it was, clear as day, Lola's name. And nobody else's. Just mine a few days later.

'Only Lola's!'

'I don't know why Teddy would hang out with Lola alone. We were seeing each other then!' My mind starts to whir. Teddy would never hurt anyone. Teddy didn't even really like catching *fish* as he felt bad about it. But this doesn't look good for him.

'I'm not suggesting for a minute that Teddy has anything to do with Lola's death, but it's definitely raised a few questions. Did he tell you about them going sailing together?'

'No. He never mentioned it.'

'And one final, final thing. Sorry to just unload all this information on you, but this is massive. The biggest thing of all.' She takes a deep breath, and I edge forward on the bed in anticipation.

'Spit it out, Audrey!'

She grins. 'Ivy, you won't believe this, but . . . you're a Magpie.'

'What? What do you mean?'

'I saw the picture of your grandparents in your album. The one of them standing in front of a tree. I thought I recognized it as the tree in front of Mr Tavistock's house. But then I decided that couldn't be true. The initials on the back of the photograph, though, read . . .'

'CE,' I whisper.

'CE,' Audrey repeats. 'Clarissa Ellory. I compared her photo to one in a yearbook. She's the same woman, Ivy. You're related all the way back to the school's original Magpies. If you were made head girl for next year, you'd not only have a say in what happens in school, you'd inherit something from Lady Penelope. Her "legacy", whatever that is. It's all in this document I found at Mrs Trawley's house! I wanted to tell you all about it earlier, but our conversations lately have always gone a bit ... sideways.'

My cheeks heat up. She was coming over to try and tell me what she'd discovered, not to rub her morning with Teddy in my face. I think it's time we're both just fully honest with each other.

'This is a *lot* to process, but I have something I need to tell you too,' I say apprehensively. I have absolutely no idea how Audrey will handle the fact I snooped through her dad's house behind her back, but I'm hoping she'll see us as even after she turned up at my mum's flat.

'I went to your family home with Harriet.'

But she seems calm. 'Why?'

'I wanted to find some documentation relating to the school sale. Something that would give me a bit more insight into it.'

Now she starts frowning. 'You snooped through my dad's office? How?' Though she seems mostly intrigued.

'Well ... the office has no door and none of his drawers had locks on them. In fact, most of what we read was just sitting on his desk anyway. We shouldn't have done it; I know that. I think I just wanted to get you back for turning up at my mum's flat. I felt like it was even ground.'

'Shit. Well, did you take anything? Did you leave it as you found it?'

I sense her panic. I get the feeling that Audrey's dad is a pretty powerful man. Only she really knows what the repercussions would be if he found out we'd been through his office.

'We didn't take anything anyway, we only took the photos. And we made sure everything was returned . . .' I think back to the earring in the drawer.

'OK, that's good. I won't lie. It feels weird that you went to my house without me and behind my back, but – like you said – I did the exact same thing so what can I say? I am sorry about that, Ivy. I really am. You have to know I went with every good intention. I wanted to bring back something to make you happy. I was nearby and I just thought I'd say hello, introduce myself, bring back some family photos. It was naive of me to assume that's how it would go. It didn't even cross my mind that it could be far more complex, and I'm really sorry.'

I think this is the most genuine I've ever seen her. I can tell it was hard for her to say; maybe she really did just want the best. She wasn't to know my mother is cold or the history between us.

'Look, I overreacted. You didn't know. Let's just drop it.'

I don't want this to turn into some mushy heart-to-heart where two friends end up sobbing on each other's shoulders, saying how sorry they are. It's easier just to drop it and look past it.

Audrey smiles at me. She gets it.

'I'm pleased I caught you in here and we had this chat.' She gets up to leave.

'Wait, there's one more thing I feel like you need to know.'

She sits back down, her face serious, and I steel myself.

'We found something else in one of your dad's desk drawers. It was at the back. Lola's shell earring. The matching one to the one we found in that cave.'

She sits in silence, her face turning grey. 'Are you sure?'

'Positive.'

Audrey looks as though she might cry. I go and sit next to her on her bed and put my hand on her knee.

'We don't know why he has it . . .' I say gently.

'Ivy, that's so fucked up. Why would he have that? The earring of a dead student!' She buries her face in her hands.

'There could be a reasonable explanation, Audrey. We can't assume anything.'

'Ivy . . . c'mon. It's beyond fucked up. MY DAD!'

She's right. It *is* fucked up. If I was in her position, I don't know what I'd do.

'I think we both need to start looking into this together again. We both want to get to the bottom of this Magpie Society school stuff and everything with Lola, and now your dad's involvement too.'

'Yeah, clearly we work better as a team, right?' A small smile breaks up the sadness on her face and I smile back.

'Ed's gone now, by the way. He moved out with his granddad, but I can still access the society headquarters that we went to: he left me a key. There's also a CCTV room under Mrs Abbott's house. I'll have to take you there to show you. There's a message there we should look into, from Clover. It says what the final piece of evidence was that she would've got had it not been for ... you know. The fire.'

Audrey's jaw drops. 'Seriously? What was it?'

'Lola's phone.'

'*Fuuuck*. Clover thought it was still in the school grounds?'

I shake my head. 'No, but maybe at the abandoned church? I've checked the Magpie Society phone, but there aren't any tunnels out there that I can see .... And there's more. I also found a list at your dad's of all the investors involved in the sale. The teachers are getting a MASSIVE payout. They'll be moved to different schools, but given a year's salary on top of it, so who's going to turn that down? I can almost guarantee the investors are all going to be at the Christmas concert too. If we can get hold of Lola's phone, maybe we can stop it.'

'I've missed you, Ivy. It's been so weird not being able to speak to you, especially about all this stuff!' Audrey puts her hand in mine.

'I'm sorry we fell off the track a bit,' I say. 'I think everything just got on top of me.'

'Same!'

'I've arranged a meeting with DI Shing and I think you should come with me.'

'Deal. Let's get to the bottom of this ginormous mess.'

# 38

## AUDREY

Before our meeting with DI Shing, we walk across the grounds to the abandoned church. It's further than I realized, and a sign on the path shows that we're only metres from the cliffs where Lola died. It's kind of eerie. But I guess if this is the last location her cellphone pinged from that would make sense.

Ivy's got the Magpie Society phone in her hand, and it tracks our location as we make our way. There's nothing out here marked on the map, but it does look like we're in one of the oldest parts of the school, so the pixelation is quite intense and the image not very clear. There could well have been a tunnel out here at one point or another; we wouldn't know.

Unfortunately, our search leads us to a complete dead end. There's nothing in the church building except rubble and old cigarette butts.

To my surprise, Ivy throws down the cellphone in frustration. It smashes against the stone tile floors, breaking into pieces. Gone. She drops to her knees. 'I really thought we'd find it here,' she says through her tears. 'It feels like Clover's death was in vain.'

'It wasn't,' I reassure her. 'Come on. We're gonna lay

everything out for Detective Shing. She'll help us. And then we can relax, as we'll have done everything in our power. You'll feel better once we've gone to the authorities, I promise you. After Alicia, I know I did.'

Ivy stares up at me, her eyes searching my face. Then she nods. I take her hand and help her back to her feet, and we make our way to the bus stop into town.

We pick a corner of the coffee shop that's real secluded, framed by posters of Parisian street scenes. What I wouldn't give to be eating a croissant and gossiping over full shopping bags with Ivy, no cares in the world! Instead, we're waiting to meet a freaking cop. Last time we were here, it was with Patrick – right before the fire.

Sitting with Ivy, I don't feel afraid. We're finally gonna lay everything out on the table for the police, not keeping anything back. This is what we should have done right at the beginning.

And for a detective who really seems to wanna listen to us.

Although we've ordered coffees, we're both allowing them to go cold. There's still tension between us – I feel as if, until this is resolved, we won't be able to get back to the way we were.

Maybe it's just my destiny for all my relationships to be ruined by events out of my control.

I squeeze Ivy's hand. We've both been in a bit of a daze after sharing our respective revelations. Of course, none of those was bigger than the fact Ivy's grandmother was a Magpie. And it turns out it goes even deeper than that. Ivy can now trace her ancestors all the way back to the time of the first female student at the school.

'Do you really think I'm in danger?' Ivy asks me.

'I think whoever killed Lola thought she'd stop the sale of the school. Now *you* have the power to do that – if you're made head girl.'

'Well, there's no chance of that happening. And, besides, if I didn't know this – how could anyone else?'

'Someone put the pieces together. The person who suggested you apply to the school.'

'My old primary-school teacher?'

'Maybe someone encouraged her to point you in the direction of Illumen Hall. The Magpie Society? The *new* Magpie Society? Whoever it is that's arranging for us to discover all these things. They could have planted the idea, but made her think it was hers.'

'Well, as soon as Mr Willis is arrested, I'll feel safe. Then we can think about that part of the mystery.'

'It all makes sense. That's why you've been brought into the Magpie Society. It's because of your legacy.' I bite the edge of my fingernails. 'Do you think we should've taken the photograph from Lola's diary to Shing as soon as we found it?' I ask.

'No. I still stand by that – after all, it wasn't Lola in the photograph, was it? The police would've got the wrong impression.'

'Why would she have the photograph hidden in her diary though?'

'Maybe she was going to expose Araminta and Mr Willis.'

'There are so many suspects, so many motives . . .'

'What motives?'

We both look up as DI Shing arrives at our table. 'May I sit?'

Ivy shuffles down the bench, and DI Shing slides into the booth next to her.

'Um, d'you want a coffee or something?' I ask her.

'I've got one coming. But how are you girls doing? Looking forward to Christmas?'

I exchange a look with Ivy. 'It's been hard to recover since Clover, to be honest. We've both found out a lot. But it's time that we shared it with you. We think some of it has to do with Lola's death. And maybe Clover's too.'

'OK. Getting straight to the point. I like that about you two. So what did you want to tell me?'

'First of all, we have to tell you that we found Lola's old diary last month. We gave it to Patrick and so it probably burned in the fire. But when we read it we realized that one of our teachers – Mr Willis – had been sleeping with a student.'

DI Shing leans back in the booth, her eyebrows shooting up. 'OK. Well, that's serious. Do you know who the student is?'

I nod. 'Here.' I open my cellphone up to the photographs that I forwarded to myself from Araminta's phone. 'We have pictures of them together.'

'This is big. And you think Lola knew about this too?'

'Yeah, and we think she maybe tried to stop them or confront them. Araminta said something similar to me. That all the people trying to stop them were out of the way now.'

'Have you spoken to anyone else about this? Like Mr Willis himself?'

'We tried, at the end of last year. But he denied it.'

'OK. Well, this is very important. You know that he showed us an alibi for where he was that night.'

'The photographs in Paris? Do you know that it's possible to alter time stamps? We have a witness – Theodore Grant – who says that he saw him that night, at the exact same time Mr Willis said he was on the train to Paris.'

'OK. We didn't have any reason to question him further at the time, but now we do. Can I get the contact details for that witness? Thank you, girls.'

'Wait – that's not all.'

DI Shing chuckles. 'It's not?'

'No. We have some other leads. We don't know whether they're relevant or connected, but we thought we'd better let you know everything.'

'OK . . .'

Ivy nods at me. I swallow. 'Speaking of Teddy . . . I mean Theodore. He invited me on his boat recently and I found something there too.'

'You did?'

'Yeah. This is his old logbook from the summer. It shows all the people who've been on his boat, dates and times, etc. Look at this.' I flip to the date of the beach party. There, in her looped handwriting, is Lola's name.

DI Shing frowns. 'Did Teddy and Lola have much of a relationship as far as you know?'

She looks at me, but I just shrug. I wasn't at the school then. All this is new to me – and incredibly uncomfortable.

'No,' says Ivy. 'They weren't even really friends. I had no idea she ever went on his boat.'

'But you've been on it a few times. I see your name here quite a lot.'

'Yeah. He and I were dating that summer. I don't understand why Lola's name is in the log, but –'

I can fill in the end of Ivy's drifting sentence. *But you're the detective.*

'OK,' says DI Shing. 'Can I take this?'

I nod. 'Teddy doesn't know that I have it . . .' I can't help this radical honesty. Once I've started, I seem unable to stop. I'm so tired of lying.

'So you didn't ask him why Lola's name was in the logbook?'

'No, I didn't.'

'Any particular reason?'

'I was . . . scared. Of how he might react while we were out on the water.'

'Do you have any reason to be scared?'

'No! Not really. Teddy's never done anything to make me worried about him. But this is obviously way out of my league.'

'I understand. Thank you for sharing this with me. It's definitely something that I'll pursue. Ivy, was Teddy at the party?'

'I . . . I don't know.'

'You didn't attend with him? Even though you guys were dating?'

Ivy shakes her head. 'We were dating, but not like . . . *dating* dating. We just kind of fooled around for a while.

Nothing serious. But wait, hang on – I did see him at the party. He was one of those who took charge when we found the body.' She closes her eyes. I wonder if she's remembering his arms wrapping around her. I know I'm thinking about it. How Teddy drew me into a kiss. But he seemed so genuinely interested in what happened to Lola. It's hard to imagine that he was keeping such a big secret.

DI Shing slips the logbook into her bag. 'Right. So that's Mr Willis, Theodore, the head girl – anything else?'

'Yeah, actually. There is one more thing – and it's a big one. Did you know that Illumen Hall was being sold?'

'No. I didn't know that. That must be very hard on you girls. Illumen Hall is quite the institution – I'm sure you were looking forward to spending your last year there.'

'No kidding,' mutters Ivy.

'Apparently, that's the whole reason I'm in England,' I say. 'I didn't know, but it was my dad's company that bought Illumen Hall. He arranges big international redevelopments, so it's kinda his thing.'

'I see. And what do you think this has to do with Lola Radcliffe?'

'Well, that's just it. We didn't think it did, not really,' I say. 'But . . .' My voice trails off. Even I find it hard to say the next part out loud. I can't believe it could be true.

But then do I really know my parents? I don't think so.

Ivy takes over. 'When you become a head student at Illumen Hall, you get a vote in the decisions regarding the school. Lola would never have agreed to the sale. We think that might have been enough motive to want her gone. Then I went over to Audrey's house to try to talk to her – we were having a fight – but she wasn't there. Her dad said I could wait for a while and then left. I decided to have a little look round his office . . .'

'Sounds unwise,' says the detective.

'Well, I found this.' Ivy takes her handbag out and slowly unclips the clasp. Then she pulls out the piece of evidence. Lola's earring. The second half of the shell set – the other one lost forever in the cave that has now been completely closed up.

She places it in front of the detective. 'This is Lola's earring,' she said. 'She wore them all the time. Never took them off, to be honest.' Ivy's voice goes all quiet, her eyes misting over. 'She wouldn't have removed them voluntarily so it's a bit concerning that I found this in Audrey's dad's office.'

'Where exactly?'

'In a drawer. It slid forward when Harriet jiggled the drawer.'

'And, Audrey, you're not aware of any reason why Lola would have visited your father?'

'I didn't even know they knew each other. But, let me be honest, I didn't even realize he was in the UK at that time. I was sort of . . . wrapped up in my own drama at that point, and my mom and dad don't exactly go around keeping me up to date with their movements.'

'I see. Well, this is all very serious. Thank you for sharing it with me. But, girls, I have to warn you. While all this investigating has obviously thrown up a lot of new clues, this isn't your responsibility. You have your own lives, exams, schoolwork to deal with. Please promise me something – that you'll concentrate on yourselves from now on.'

'I guess,' Ivy says. 'We won't really have a school to save soon. Let alone any way to investigate.'

'Well, that might not be such a bad thing.'

Finally, DI Shing's coffee arrives at the table, but she asks the waitress, 'Can I take this to go?' and stands up.

'Leaving already?' I ask. I'm kinda surprised. I thought she'd let us know her thoughts at least . . . or give us a bit more of a clue as to what's going on.

Clearly Ivy thinks the same thing. 'Wait, what are you going to do with all of this?' DI Shing now has the photographs, the earring, the logbook. She's got everything.

'Trust me. I'm going to follow up on all these leads. If anything comes of them, you'll be the first to know.'

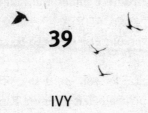

# 39

## IVY

As we walk out of the cafe, we spot the B & B on the corner that Patrick is currently staying in while his flat gets renovated after the fire.

'Should we go and see him?' I ask Audrey, knowing full well this could be a very awkward interaction. She's not been in touch since he was released after his arrest.

'Yeah, I think we should. His parents are on the investor list, and he could be the one hope we have left to change their minds. Lola would never want the school to be sold and turned into a hotel. Maybe her brother feels the same way.'

The sweet old lady at reception calls his room and Patrick gives her the go-ahead to let us up. We knock on his door, stand back and wait.

'Why does this feel dangerous?' Audrey whispers.

He opens the door and I'm shocked by the man standing there. He looks pale and his skin is sallow. His hair hasn't been washed and his usually clean-shaven face is covered in dark stubble. He's wearing stained jogging bottoms and his hoodie is crinkled. He doesn't look well at all.

'Hi. Come in.' He doesn't smile at us. 'I would offer to make you a drink, but I don't have a kitchen in here. There's a communal one downstairs.'

'Uh, that's OK. We just wanted to drop by and check in on you really.' Audrey smiles and takes a seat at a small, round table.

'Thanks. Everyone else seems to be avoiding me like the plague.'

'But the police let you go,' I say, sitting down next to Audrey. With no chairs left to sit on, Patrick perches on the edge of the table.

'I know, but people talk. It doesn't seem to matter that they had no evidence that I kidnapped Clover or started that fucking fire. Who else is there to blame?'

I watch as his face scrunches up. I can already sense the agitation and frustration building.

'There was another reason we wanted to come and see you today actually.' I decide to just dive straight in. 'We found out that they're planning to sell the school and have it turned into some fancy hotel. Your parents are one of the main investors.'

His face looks panicked and he raises his eyebrows.

'D'you know why they'd wanna be so heavily involved in the sale, seeing as your ancestor was one of the founders of Illumen Hall? Seems a bit ... contradictory,' Audrey says softly.

'It makes good business sense. I know that the school has been haemorrhaging money for years and the board shouldn't be the ones responsible for putting scholarship kids through their entire education ... Sorry, Ivy.' He shoots me a pitying look that pisses me off.

'Your family could be the ones to save us, you know,' I say. 'To stop this from happening. They have enough power if they choose to stand with us on this.'

He looks at me questioningly. 'What do you mean "us"? Why would they want to save you? No offence, girls, but this is big numbers, big plans, big money. It's way more important than you and a few friends can stop.' He laughs.

*This guy is a prick.* What kind of friendship did Audrey ever have with him? It pains me that Lola had a brother like this. That these were the people influencing her.

'We're the Magpie Society now – and, before you laugh at us like we're some silly little teenage girls, this is serious stuff. We're going to keep the school running, no matter what anyone else thinks, says or does to get in the way. We won't let Illumen Hall be sold.' I raise my voice slightly and feel the passion rise within me. He doesn't laugh this time.

'Clover mentioned this society to me. She believed that the Magpie Society wanted to protect the school, but then came the night of the party when some arsehole dressed in a magpie costume threatened her so badly she called me to pick her up. If you're the Magpie Society, are you saying *you* threatened her?'

'No, we're saying we're still trying to protect the school. And that means we're still looking for justice for Lola.'

'Well, Clover believed Mr Willis was the killer – I'll tell you that for free. If only she'd found that last piece of evidence, he'd be behind bars right now.'

An idea sparks within me. 'If *we* can find proof that Mr Willis is the one who killed your sister, then will you help us keep the school open?' I look at Patrick, searching for any sign of decency. Lola is the one thing he'll never cast aside. And neither will I.

He pauses, scanning our faces. He must see the

determination there. That or he thinks it's a lost cause. 'Fine. If you can get that creep arrested for what he did to my sister, I will do *everything* in my power to help you keep the school open.'

My shoulders drop with relief.

Audrey jumps up and hugs him. He stands awkwardly, with his arms stiffly by his sides.

'Thank you! Honestly. We won't ever give up on Lola – we're so close to getting the proof we need.'

He raises an eyebrow. 'I hope you're right.'

# 40

## AUDREY

I'm back in with Ivy's crew now, lounging on 'our' sofas in the SCR and, although Araminta shoots me the odd glance every now and then, she doesn't come over to ask what happened. I don't think she knows I've seen or taken the photographs – only that I ditched her mid-practice. Tom and Max are playing video games, and Harriet has gone to grab a hot chocolate from the canteen.

When I'm sure no one is listening, I take a sip of my Coke and turn to Ivy. 'When d'you think we're gonna hear from DI Shing?'

'No idea.'

Ivy's as obsessive as I am, checking her cellphone every ten seconds. But so far there's been complete silence from the detective. It's been a week now, the Christmas concert is tonight, and we're still no closer to a resolution than before. It felt like Ivy and I had gotten so close only for us to have it ripped away.

'Isn't that a bit insane though?' I say. 'We gave her everything . . .'

'I know! But what can we do about it?'

I look over at Tom and Max, but they're still engrossed.

'And what about your bargain with Patrick to get Mr Willis arrested?'

'I'm still working on a plan there,' she says.

'Something other than what we've already been doing, I hope?'

We've been watching Mr Willis on the Magpie Society cameras – probably behaviour that would have us done for stalking, if it wasn't such a good cause. But so far he's been ludicrously squeaky clean, not stepping out of line or spending time alone with any students. Ivy asked him if he'd come to the piano room to listen to her performance, but he wouldn't fall for it.

'I'll figure something out. Any luck with Araminta?' Ivy asks me.

I shake my head. 'But I think she's frustrated. I know she's been trying to see "Hottie" alone for a while now and not getting anywhere. He's avoiding her too.'

'Why is Mr Willis even still here? Surely it'd be better for him just to leave. Especially if the school's going to be closed down soon ... He should have just buggered off after the Samhain party, like he said he would.'

'He must be hanging on for the cash – that big severance package the teachers are gonna get. If he leaves now, he'd be out on his ass and people would want to know *why* he left. Wouldn't exactly be a glowing recommendation from Mrs Abbott if he just disappeared – and that's without the creepy predator behaviour.'

'We just need to catch him in the act. That's the only way we're going to get him arrested.'

I bite my lip. 'I think he's caught on to that. He knows he can't make any mistakes.'

Ivy drums the tabletop with her fingers. 'I wish that detective would make some kind of move. But of course she's not going to. She said that she'd listen to us, and now she's dodging our calls and keeping all our evidence. We shouldn't have just given it to her like that. Now we don't have any of it.'

'I'm sure she will have logged it all. Don't worry, Ivy, it was the right thing to do.'

'I hope so.'

'This isn't like you – I thought you trusted authority!' I nudge her in the ribs and point to her shiny prefect badge.

'Authority? You mean the people in charge who are trying to rip the school away from me? I don't think so . . .' She wrinkles her nose.

'I guess you're right about that. But no. We did the right thing,' I repeat, almost like a mantra. I realize I probably sound as if I'm trying to convince myself – let alone everyone else.

Ivy leans back in her chair, her eyes scanning the room, which is festooned with decorations. It's so impressive, but now we know that it's not for the benefit of the students at all.

'Just think, if this concert happens, then all the investors are gonna see the school and imagine it with all these rich folk swanning around, some Michelin-star chef in the canteen instead of Ms Cranshaw, the swimming pool turned into a cold dip area.'

'Mum says she's going to make a booking as soon as it's open,' says Tom.

'Tell her, if she does, I'll never speak to you again,' says Ivy. Tom laughs, but there's a nervous edge to it. It doesn't sound like Ivy is joking.

The thing is, the concert is only a few hours away. People are gonna be pouring in at any moment. It's too late for us to do anything about the sale now. The only person who looks vaguely happy is Mrs Abbott. She's been walking around, barking orders – her absolute favourite thing to do.

Ivy stands up. 'I'd better go and do a couple of hours' practice before the recital. Guess I have a few people to impress if I'm to have any sort of future after this.'

'Wait.' I grab Ivy's hand. 'You are gonna have a future after this. Trust me. You've done so much practice – you don't need to do any more. Just relax.'

Ivy sighs. 'You've seen how I live. You've seen my home. I've seen your home. You might believe you'll always have a future – because you *will* always have a future. That's really clear. But me? If I don't get into another school on a music scholarship, then I'm royally screwed.'

'I thought they said they'd pay for students to move?'

'See, Audrey? You're so trusting. You actually believe that they'll have my best interests at heart? The school they've chosen for me is Winferne Comprehensive. It's not fee-paying, which means they don't have to cover my scholarship. There's no boarding house, so who knows where I'll live? It has a shit music department so now I won't be able to go on and get the grades I need to get into the uni I want. I was all set to be head girl here next year – that's not going to happen at WC, is it? So I'll be starting from scratch with all my levels of privilege – aka, none at all. This is going to suck. I'm not leaving anything to chance.'

When Ivy's in this mood, I know there's no stopping her. 'OK, go. But let me help you do your hair before the concert?'

'Sure. See you later.' She pauses. 'I really wish Clover was here. I miss her.'

'I know. It's not fair.'

Ivy grabs her bag and leaves.

I sigh, slumping down over the table. Max tries to cheer me up with a joke, but I don't even really hear it. I can't concentrate on anything right now. My social feeds are filled with people at Christmas markets, enjoying the sights. Lydia sends me a picture outside the Savannah Theatre, where they're doing their annual Christmas show. She and I used to go every year.

Somehow I don't think the Illumen Hall Christmas concert is gonna compare, but I don't mind. I feel weirdly detached from that life I used to live. It scares me how fast I can move on.

Alicia can't move on.

Lola can't move on.

Clover can't move on.

Maybe that's why I feel like I *have* to. Because I have the privilege of life.

Speaking of which, I see Araminta stick her head through the door, her eyes darting around the room. She looks officially panicked. Then she ducks back out again.

I jump up. 'Hang on. Minty?' I grab my stuff and chase after her. 'Araminta? Are you OK?'

'What do you care?' she says over her shoulder.

'Look, I'm sorry I had to bail the other day. I had a really important phone call come through, and then I got caught up in some stuff . . .'

'With Ivy. I see you two have made up again.'

'Yeah.'

'Well, I'm happy for you. But I have about a million things to do today and then the concert this evening – I just don't have time to talk right now.'

'Minty, please.'

I can't believe I once suspected her when really she's just another one of Mr Willis's victims. She's got her faults, but she's not a murderer.

'I've been thinking about your performance and I think it's the costume that's wrong. I have one of my old outfits in my closet. I know that sounds weird. But it was one of my favourites. I actually wore it when I was performing in my last show back in the US and couldn't bear to put it in storage somewhere . . . It was made by this incredibly talented costume designer and it's got gorgeous vintage lace. Anyway, it would be perfect on "Christine" and I want you to have it. Why don't you come try it on?'

'Are you serious? I didn't have time to get the costume I want . . .'

'I know.'

She looks down at her cellphone, pauses for a moment, then nods. 'Let's do it.'

'So how are things going?'

'Oh, it's all *super* busy. This has to be just the best Christmas concert ever. Mrs Abbott has made it all my responsibility.' She side-eyes me. 'You know, for it to be amazing. Especially since it's the last one ever.'

'Hopefully, the new costume will help. You should stand out from everyone else. It's your solo really.'

When we get up to the room, I pull the dress out of my closet. It's still wrapped up in its plastic. I pull the sheeting off and Araminta actually gasps. It is a beautiful dress – ivory-white, floor-length, romantic, lacy and hand-beaded – something to really set her apart. It's a huge step up from the crappy costume she'd been planning to wear, the exact same floating white slip as her backup dancers.

'Oh, Audrey, it would honestly be so much better if you were up onstage with me. You already know all the choreography and you can wear my old costume. You'll be perfect next to Bonnie. Please say you'll do it – you'll make it so much better.'

I run the fabric through my fingers, remembering what it was like to be onstage. Maybe this would be something good to do. A little distraction from the Magpie Society drama. Better than sitting in the audience anyway.

'At least that horrible bird flash mob won't be back to ruin this event. I made sure of that.'

'You did?' I ask.

'Yeah. Turned out it was a bunch of students from Winferne Comprehensive. You know, the local school? I'd hate to have to go there – they're all vile. Apparently, someone paid them a ton of money to wear the costumes and crash the party. Someone from a group signed by the Magpies. The same people who did the poster. How ridiculous is that?'

I frown. 'Wild.'

'Oh, Audrey, this dress is just perfect. Thank you so much. You know, when you bailed at rehearsal, I really thought you were going to let me down . . . I'm glad you're still there for me.'

'Of course not. I'll be there. I wouldn't miss it.' I look at Araminta, who's admiring herself in the mirror. 'Are you gonna be performing for someone special tonight?' I ask.

'Maybe . . .'

'You know, I can't shut up about this any longer. Araminta, Mr Willis is a complete creep. You shouldn't be with him. You're so much better than some crappy boarding-school teacher. Even if he was on TV once! They obviously didn't think he was good enough to invite back again. You deserve better.'

Araminta smiles slyly at me. 'Calm your boots!'

'What?'

'I actually told him that. Last night. I ditched him.'

'Oh my God, you did? What did he say?'

She comes and sits beside me on the bed. 'He was pretty pissed off. Asking me why, why, why, saying he was just about to break it off with his fiancée so we could be together after school finishes, blah-blah. That's when I realized how serious he was. I mean, I was into him, but also – he's my secondary-school boyfriend. Did he really think we were going to be together when I go off to Cambridge? Gross. I want to spread my wings.'

'He probably never thought of that.'

'No way.' She rolls her eyes. 'That's why I had to shut it down straight away. He was so angry about it. He flipped out, saying how I could ruin him. How he'd already done so much to make sure our relationship could survive after I graduated.'

'He did?' I arch an eyebrow. 'Did you feel threatened?'

'Oh, not like that. If anyone was doing the threatening, it was me. Seriously, I *could* ruin him. So I told him if he didn't chill out then I'd go to Mrs Abbott and tell her everything. Finally, he let me go. Talk about a terrible break-up. You'd think I'd tried to kill him or something.'

'What a loser,' I say, but my mind is elsewhere. I wonder if Mr Willis really cared for Minty. Or did he just see her as a ticket out of this place?

'Tell me about it. But at least I'm free of it now. And I can spend the rest of the year living my best life.' She tosses her hair – and then glances down at her watch. 'Oh my God. We'd better be getting downstairs. We're going to need at least an hour for hair and make-up.' She gathers up the dress in her arms.

'Come on then, let's go.'

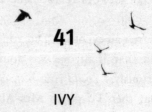

# 41

## IVY

The school auditorium looks absolutely breathtaking. There are long, narrow candles glowing at the sides of the room in clusters of tall, elegant candlesticks, fairy lights draped from every possible angle and huge fresh green foliage garlands framing the windows. There's the usual five-metre Nordmann fir on the right-hand side as you enter, covered in decorations that are older than Mrs Abbott. I feel a sting in my heart thinking this could be the last time I see that tree, those old glass decorations. Where will they end up if the school is sold?

It's stupid to worry, but in that moment I feel just as sad about those decorations being homeless as I am about my own fate.

It's dark outside so early now, and the only light is coming from the hundreds of candles and thousands of tiny bulbs strung across the ceiling. It feels so warm and cosy. The night of the Christmas concert is normally one of my favourites of the season. It's the one festivity every year that truly puts me in the Christmas spirit and fills me with nostalgia.

I'm backstage, watching the seats being filled by families and business folk in suits and floor-length dresses, each taking a flute of champagne as they enter and being guided to their seats by Year Sevens.

The noise of chattering helps drown out the fear of being up first with my composition piece – and the fact that I'm no closer to finding any evidence of Mr Willis's involvement in Lola's death. I've been trying to shove this to the back of my mind all day, but I feel like the clock is ticking. Especially now I'm looking at a room that holds all the investors we found on the list.

There's a horrible feeling creeping over me, like the walls are closing in, like there won't be any oxygen left – as if the lights will all smash and the champagne flutes shatter.

We're really running out of time to get Mr Willis arrested. And the most frustrating part is that it *feels* as though we're so close.

I stand back from the curtain and notice that backstage has got really busy. Students are pacing, some breathing into paper bags or sitting with their heads between their legs – must be their first time performing at the concert. Even now, I'm fighting the same feelings – opening the whole evening is a huge deal and a slot that a lot of students want to fill. I don't know how to give the performance of a lifetime when all I can think is that if I don't get this right I have no idea where I'll be this time next year.

I walk up to one of the mirrors to check my reflection. My hair is in a side parting, pulled back into a sleek bun at the nape of my neck. My dress is floor-length silver silk with a slit up to mid-thigh, it cinches in at the waist and has balloon sleeves. I've had it a while, but never knew what to wear it to – it's very un-me. I slide my hand across my tummy and down my hips, marvelling at how the fabric clings, giving my body some shape. I take my peach lipgloss out of my bra and apply a bit more. I think I'm ready ... am I ready? My hands are trembling.

The room is still filling up, so I take myself off to a quiet corner backstage to gather my thoughts a bit and run through the sheet music. Having gone over it multiple times quickly, I find my mind wandering back to Mr Willis again. There are so many people with question marks over their heads, so many people's actions that don't add up. Teddy and the boat. Araminta and her jealousy. Mr Wagner and the earring. I guess this really is a stark reminder of the fact that Audrey and I aren't detectives. But all I want is for Mr Willis to be behind bars. Then Patrick will convince his parents not to sell the school, and Lola can finally get justice.

I look down and notice my leg shaking uncontrollably so I place my hand firmly on it to stop it. Suddenly I feel very aware that Audrey and I could be sitting ducks. My hands are clammy so I flap them in the air to dry as I don't want to wipe them on my silk dress. Just then, I hear the crackle of the microphone from in front of the curtain and a teacher's voice. Mr Willis should be introducing the concert – and that definitely doesn't sound like him. I mean, I'm happy he isn't the one calling me out on to the stage, but if he's not there ...

*Where is he?*

Mrs Trigg, one of the music teachers, approaches me and taps me on the shoulder. 'Ivy? Are you ready?'

'Of course I'm ready!' I snap.

She flinches.

I step over to the side of the stage and peek out round the curtain as the teacher talks about how important the concert is and how amazing we are as students. I spot Audrey's mum and dad sitting with the Radcliffes, all smiling and lifting their champagne flutes. Patrick isn't here, naturally. I imagine him sitting alone in the B & B, at his little table, with his unwashed hair and face. The other four look far too happy, almost like they're celebrating. What if we've already failed in our goal?

My stomach sinks and I feel my face turn red. If only those champagne flutes would shatter in their hands, the way they're about to shatter my world with their greed. I just want to stay in the one place that truly accepts me for who I am.

No, it's more than that. It's the one place in the whole world that's allowed me to reach my full potential. And it's all about to be ripped away.

# 42

## AUDREY

Backstage is absolutely packed with bodies, crammed around the mirrors, setting powder and hairspray mingling in the atmosphere. Bonnie finishes putting a curl through my hair and it bounces down by my chin. The next step will be to pull it all into a ballet bun, but at the moment it's set in cascading waves down my shoulders.

Araminta has decided to switch up her original hair and make-up plan. Originally, she was supposed to look like I will, with her blond hair in a bun, but now she's wearing it loose down her back. She looks absolutely stunning sitting next to me, wearing my old dress. I'm in her plain costume from before. I feel a pang of sadness at the fact that I'm not the one who's gonna be centre stage. I give myself a shake. No, being in the background is just fine by me.

'Oh my God, I'm so nervous. Can you hear everyone outside?'

The sound of the audience has been building for the past half an hour, and I can hear Mrs Abbott's towering voice over the hum.

'Hey – I better go wish Ivy good luck.'

Araminta clutches my wrist. 'Please, please don't be late.'

'I won't, I promise. I never miss the curtain – don't worry. I'm a professional.'

'Good.'

I push past a bunch of Year Sevens who are dressed up in long white robes, like mini monks going to do a carol showcase. There's someone from each year group about to do something impressive, and a teacher I don't recognize is barking orders. I keep one eye out for Mr Willis, but I can't see him anywhere. I really hope he's not bothering Ivy.

Speaking of which, I can't see her anywhere.

Then I turn a corner and I spot her – peering out at the audience. In her long silver dress, she stands out like a star. She's drumming her fingers against her thigh.

'Hey! There you are,' I say.

She spins around, like I've shocked her out of a trance. 'Oh, hey, Audrey. How's things going?' She checks out my outfit and frowns. 'Are you performing or something? Has something happened to Araminta?'

'Oh no, nothing like that. She asked me to be one of her backup dancers since I know all the choreography and stuff. I'm borrowing her costume because she's wearing one I had from my time performing in Savannah ... Just thought it would be better.'

'Oh, that is nice of you. You still make yours look good.'

'Thanks. You look amazing. Maybe a little nervous ...'

'That obvious, huh?'

'Yeah. But you don't need to be. I heard you – you're brilliant. Any music school would be extremely lucky to have you.'

'Thank you.'

'So what happened to Mr Willis?'

'What do you mean?'

'Well, he's not here. He's been replaced by that angry lady who's always shouting at students in Polaris House. I don't know who she is. She must teach a class I don't take.'

'Miss Chigwell? That is weird. This has been Mr Willis's pet project. I wonder where he is. Oh my God, maybe he's been arrested! Should we call DI Shing?'

'No,' I say firmly, taking her by the shoulders. 'You have your piece to concentrate on. Do that. Blow everyone away. He's probably just sore that Minty dumped him.'

'She did?' Ivy gasps. 'Bet he's not happy about that. OK, I will. But after the concert . . . we'll go and find out what happened?'

'Definitely.'

'OK, thanks, Audrey. I should go. I'm on soon. They better have tuned the piano again – it was in terrible shape yesterday.'

'Sounded pretty good to me. Break a leg. But not, you know . . .'

'I know. You too.'

I dart back into the crowd. Actually, I'm running a little bit behind now – I still have to finish off my hair and change shoes. It's so crowded with people rushing around that I can't get back to the other side of the stage. Screw it, I'm gonna find a way around.

I change direction, heading out into the hallway, where it's blissfully empty. I feel so much more comfortable around Illumen Hall now; it's like my second home. I know all the hallways. The shortcuts. Heck, I even know the secret passageways! I know the views out of the windows, and I'm looking forward to seeing the change of seasons. To watch spring bloom outside of our bedroom window, to see the new baby magpies hatch and maybe get to look at the ocean when it's not under such a grey pall. I can imagine me and Ivy going for walks on the beach in the summer, maybe searching for shells to add to the grotto. I stop by a window and stare out. I almost don't understand what I'm looking at. And that's when I realize.

It's snowing. Soft flakes falling from the sky.

It's so beautiful. Peaceful. The grounds have never looked so serene.

I grab my cellphone to take a photo. No, maybe a selfie would be better. I turn the camera around.

And that's when I see him coming towards me.

My world goes black.

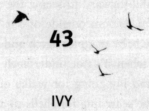

# 43

## IVY

Mrs Abbott has almost finished her Christmas concert opening spiel and it's nearly time for me to perform.

'With the exciting new expansion plans on the horizon, it's truly an honour to be taking you all on this next adventure for Illumen.' I almost retch at her glee.

'These walls have served students very well over many centuries, but I think we can all agree that it's time for a rebirth. Just before tonight's entertainment begins, I'd like us all to give a very warm and gracious welcome to the investors here tonight.'

The room erupts into cheers, the clinking of glasses and some whooping from a couple of red-faced, sweaty men in suits towards the back.

I take a few deep breaths and try to compose myself. Audrey's right: I can't think about the future and everything that's out of my control. I need to close my eyes and imagine the notes and the keys I'm about to play.

I've worked so hard on this piece – I've never composed anything so intricate – and I want it to blow the audience away. If this goes well, and there's someone here from any prospective music colleges, universities or music studios, I need to make an impact. I'm going to play my heart out, attacking the keys with everything I have in me, imagine they're Mr Willis, the Wagners, Mrs Abbott and the Radcliffes.

In this moment, I feel very grateful for everything Illumen Hall has given me. It's housed me; it's taught me; it's literally grown me from the ground up. I look round the hall one more time and try and take in every ounce of its beauty.

But, just as I sense Mrs Abbott is about to introduce me, my phone starts ringing, the vibration travelling up my legs. I ignore it. It rings again. Who could be calling me right now? Everyone I know is here. Maybe it's DI Shing? I reach down and check quickly. It's Ed. I have five missed calls and six text messages. Something about this screams emergency. Ed never calls me. I open the newest text message.

**IVY. CALL ME RIGHT NOW.**

I quickly tap back.

**Ed, I can't. Going onstage.**

Instantly, he replies, just as I hear Mrs Abbott call my name.

'With her exceptional composed piano piece – "My Home is my Heart" – Ivy Moore-Zhang, ladies and gentlemen!'

The audience starts clapping, waiting for me to step on to the stage.

IT'S AUDREY. SHE'S IN
DANGER. YOU NEED TO CALL
NOW. THIS IS SERIOUS.

My stomach sinks and I instantly want to drop my phone like it's a hot coal. I listen as the audience continues to clap for me. What do I do? I have seconds to make a decision. Do I go on and perform for my future, or do I leave to find Ed and Audrey?

She was literally here MOMENTS ago. What could have happened in those last few minutes? I look at the audience through the gap in the curtain, then back down at Ed's messages.

I hear Mrs Abbott crack a joke about first-performance nerves and introduce me again.

'Ivy Moore-Zhang, ladies and gentlemen . . .'

The clapping starts again, this time tinged with a few laughs.

It's obvious what I have to do here. I have no other choice than to leave and find out what's going on with Audrey. I grab my bag and run backstage past Miss Chigwell, who is shouting at me, and other students, who are gasping and hollering after me. I don't even look back.

'IVY! WHAT ARE YOU DOING? What's wrong?' she shouts. I don't want her to follow me so I lie.

'I'm going to throw up, Miss Chigwell.' Her hand flies to her mouth and she rushes over to the main stage to update Mrs Abbott.

As I run out into the empty hallway, I hear the choir start singing in the auditorium behind me through the closed doors. It's dark but I notice, on the floor by my feet, a piece of Audrey's costume, torn and frayed. What the hell has happened? I hold the scrap of fabric in my hand and close my eyes. *Where are you, Audrey?*

I call Ed. He answers instantly.

'Ivy?'

'Ed?'

'It's Audrey. I saw Mr Willis take her in his car!'

'OH MY GOD. Where did he go?'

'I don't know – he drove off school grounds.'

'Let me check my app and see if it tells me her live location.'

I end the call and immediately check if my friend-finding app can show me where Audrey is. I had blocked her, but as soon as I unblock she becomes visible again.

I open the app and wait for it to load. The internet signal is shocking down here as the walls are so thick. The wheel on my phone is spinning and every second feels like a minute. My breathing is sharp and my face feels fuzzy. How have I let this happen? How was Audrey taken from backstage? I knew the school was dangerous with Lola's killer on the loose, but this has happened at the busiest event of the year. There are people everywhere! Finally, the app loads and I can see Audrey's phone location. It's moving, but I know exactly where he's taking Audrey.

I throw my phone in my bag and run.

# 44

## AUDREY

When I come to, my head is throbbing and the world is still dark. I thrash my legs out and my shins bash against what feels like a car dashboard.

'Stop it, Minty – be quiet!'

I scream and thrash again, and I feel a hand clamp down around my mouth. 'Shh, please. Just let me drive.'

As soon as the arm is gone, I scream.

'What the fuck is your problem?' says the man's voice. 'It's just me. We need to talk.'

I finally manage to speak. 'Let me go! What the fuck is going on!'

He sounds panicked. '*Shit!* You're not Araminta . . .'

'No!' I shriek. 'No, I'm not fucking Araminta. What the hell?' I try to pull the cloth from my head – I think it's a bag of some kind – but my hands are bound. There's a strap across my body – I'm guessing that's a seat belt.

'Shit. Shit, shit, shit,' he says.

My head begins to clear, and my brain starts putting the pieces together. I'd been standing by the window. On my way to the other side of the stage. When I'd seen Mr Willis in my phone camera screen.

He'd grabbed me, throwing something over my head,

and then, in my effort to push him off, I'd bashed my head against the stone window sill.

That was the last thing I remember.

'Mr Willis? I know it's you. Please get this thing off my head. Let's talk. Come on.'

I'm thrust up against the door as Mr Willis jerks the wheel of the car. He's panicking. There's a screech of wheels against tarmac and I can feel the car pick up speed. He's losing control.

*I'm* losing control. Panic rises in my throat. I take a deep breath. I have to do something – or else we're both gonna end up dead.

'Please, Mr Willis,' I say, trying to control the tremor in my voice. 'Harry, it is Harry, isn't it? Come on. Just turn around and drive back to the school. I know what happened with you and Araminta. She dumped you, right? I'm real sorry about that. But you don't have to put me in the middle of it.'

'You're already in the middle of it,' he mutters. 'You're in my bloody car!'

I try to speak again, but he continues talking.

'No, don't. We're almost there. I'll figure this out.'

He's not gonna listen to me; I realize that now. I try to rub the bag off my head. I manage to get it hooked on the edge of the headrest, and I work my chin until finally the end of it reaches above my bottom lip.

'Hey, hey, what are you doing?' he asks me, but, because I'm turned away from him, he can't do anything about it. I twist my body as much as I can, even though my hands are crushed beneath my hip.

Finally, with the fabric over my lip, I'm able to use my mouth to push the bag higher. I'm able to get it up over my nose and then it's not too difficult to drag it over my head. My face finally clear, I take a huge breath and blink rapidly to get used to the lights.

Then I flip my body back around under the seat belt so that I can stare him in the face.

'Look at me,' I say, trying to keep my voice as calm as possible. 'Let's go back to school. I'm supposed to be onstage . . . I mean, God.'

I'm still in my costume, the hem of my dress spilling across the seat. That's also when I spot flecks of blood on the edge of the torn fabric. My blood. I feel like I'm gonna throw up. Pain hits me like a truck. It's as if I'd been in such fight-or-flight mode that I hadn't realized I have a massive bump on my skull.

Tears spring to my eyes. I'm not a strong person, and this is too much for me. I have no idea what Mr Willis is gonna do. I've seen him now. I know about his relationship with Araminta.

*Oh my God, I'm Lola.*

'Please, please let me go. I won't tell anyone, I promise. I just wanna be back to school. With my friends.'

The car turns into a darkened lane, with no street lamps, so it's hard to see where we're headed. But I spot a sign in the reflection of the headlights before he speeds past it: WINFERNE COASTAL WALK.

Shit. He's taking me to the cliffs.

'Where are we going?' I say, to try and get him talking.

'I'm going to lose my job – I'm going to lose everything.

All I wanted to do was talk to Araminta. Make her see sense. Now I've got *you* to deal with.'

His eyes are darting around the road, as if he's on the lookout for something about to jump on to the road. But there are no deer or anything here. He's trying to think through his plan.

Think what he's gonna do with me.

'Just like you did with Lola, right?'

'What? What are you talking about?'

'You brought Lola here, didn't you? You drove her to the cliffs.'

'She *asked* me to bring her here that night. She was so angry with me after she found out about Araminta. I think Minty left the photograph to deliberately rile her or something. I don't know what you kids do to each other.'

'Kids? Excuse me, you're the one who can't seem to keep your hands off us.'

'I know, all right! It's not my fault. You can't help who you fall in love with.'

He pulls up in a grass-covered parking lot. The snow is still falling, settling on the ground. He unclips his seat belt and gets out of the car.

'Wait! Where are you going?' I shout.

He storms around to my side and flings open the door. He reaches over me to undo my seat belt and I scream, trying to get out from under him. But my hands are still tied with a belt or something. It's thick leather and impossible to break out of. I still struggle, thrashing my body, trying to move away, to get some purchase with my fingers. But he grabs my shoulders and drags me out.

The air is frigid, and in my thin costume dress I'm freezing. I start to shiver, as much from fear as anything else. Mr Willis's eyes are wild. This isn't what he planned for. I'm not who he intended to kidnap.

And no one knows I'm here.

My mind instantly flies to my cellphone – he must have stashed it somewhere, as it's nowhere on my body. I can't call for help. I'm utterly at his mercy.

The wind picks up, swirling my dress around my legs. I think about running, but he sees that in my eyes and grabs me by the arm. Where would I run to anyway? I could stumble my way along the clifftop, but I'm just as likely to slip and die as I am to find help. I can't imagine anyone's up here at this time of night.

We didn't drive for very long, so I guess we're still near the school. But everyone there will be listening to Ivy perform right about now. They won't know I'm gone for hours. There's no one looking for me.

*There's no one looking for me.*

If I'm gonna get out of this situation, I'll have to do it by myself.

In my thin ballet flats, I slip in the snow. It hasn't fallen thickly enough to be deep, but it's disguising where puddles of water have turned to ice. I fall to my knees, my arm wrenched back by the force of Mr Willis attempting to keep me upright. He lets go as I struggle to pick myself up.

'What's your plan?' I cry out at him. 'Are you just gonna kill me, like you killed Lola?'

His face looks stricken. 'I told you! I didn't kill her. I couldn't. I loved her.'

'Then what happened that night? And don't spin me some bullshit about being in Paris because we know you weren't there. You were seen in Winferne Bay when you said you were already travelling.'

I try to stand as I speak, although it's a struggle with my hands tied behind my back. I slip and he leans down to help me, but I yank out of his grasp. My mind is racing. I'm thinking that maybe, if I can reach the car, I might be able to get away from him. But not unless I can untie these hand restraints. The slip had the added benefit of moving the buckle of the belt around so that it's just within reach of my fingertips. If I can keep him talking long enough, I might be able to loosen it and break free of my bonds. It's not like Mr Willis is some criminal mastermind.

At least I really hope he isn't.

As I struggle to my feet, he talks. 'We did go to Paris. Just . . . not until the next morning.'

'So what happened that night?'

He pushes me forward, so that I'm forced to walk along the path. He seems to have some sort of destination in mind. I look up and think I see the dark silhouette of a building against the night sky. Thankfully, it's not pitch-black quite yet. I rack my brains for what kind of building there could be along the cliffs. I have no idea. I keep walking. My toes are freezing, goosebumps rising up and down my arms. I almost wanna ask him for his jacket – how dumb is that? Asking your kidnapper for help.

I also daren't look at quite how perilously close to the edge we are. How, with one great big shove, Mr Willis could send me to the same watery grave that Lola had.

'She called me. Asked me to go for a drive. We came to the cliffs. We had a conversation in the car park and she told me it was over. I agreed that was for the best. I dropped her back off at school and I left for Paris. Next thing I heard, she was dead!'

'She ended it and you were OK with that? You expect me to believe you?'

'Look, you didn't know Lola! When she said it was done, I knew I had to accept it. But I've never come back to the cliffs. Until now.'

He pushes me again, and I stumble forward. Tears stream down my face.

He's gonna kill me. Maybe he's telling the truth about Lola; maybe he's not. But, regardless of whether he's killed before, he's gonna do it now.

We get closer and closer to the edge, moving away from the building I thought I'd seen before. I realize it's the old church ruins – I see the outline of a broken cross. If I'd been a religious person, I might have sent out a prayer.

The bonds still aren't moving. The cold saps my strength and, with every step we move closer to the edge, my fear increases. My pulse is racing, and I'm becoming more and more clumsy, my feet tripping over each other. I don't even need Mr Willis to push me – at this rate, I'm gonna fall off on my own.

'Audrey, I never meant for this to happen.' Mr Willis's voice has softened again.

We should have had him locked up when we had the chance. *Ivy, why didn't we do the right thing?*

Ivy's reply rings in my ears. *Because we didn't know for sure.*

Well, now I am sure. And I also know what I have to do: it's either gonna be him or me. I just have to make sure that it's him. I'm not ready to die.

'You know too much now. There's no way for us to turn this around. Even if I could just disappear . . . I'll never be able to resurface. I can't live a life on the run. I just . . . can't. Mrs Abbott promised me everything would be OK if I just did what she asked. But she won't have any control over this.'

His grip tightens on my biceps and he thrusts me forward again. My knees buckle, the instinct to become like a deadweight, a rag doll, the only defence I can think of right now.

And it's a good thing too, because a shadow flies over my head and collides with Mr Willis, sending him stumbling backwards.

'Stay back!' cries a voice.

I start to sob because I recognize it.

It's Ivy. She's come to rescue me.

# 45

## IVY

My feet pound the ground so hard I'm almost bouncing as I go, and the fact I'm wearing heels in this scenario doesn't seem to have fazed me, even though I never wear heels and look like Bambi on ice when walking in them. I do know how to run, though, and it's like my feet are taking over.

It's absolutely freezing, but adrenaline is pumping through my body, keeping the sting of the snow hitting my bare skin at bay. It's really dark and quiet along the path, but I've taken this track so many times I know where to jump, where to avoid bumps and where to bend down to avoid branches. I quickly check the app again, and Audrey is exactly where I thought she'd be, near the abandoned church up on the cliffs. She's stopped moving now. Is she on the cliff edge?

I try not to think about it, or who has taken her there. The wind is so strong near the cliffs and, with this snow, there's less visibility. It's a dangerous night to be anywhere near such a spot. I arrive just in time to see two people wrestling at the edge of the cliff. I can hear the muffled whimpers and notice Audrey's hands are tied behind her. I know the back of his head, his clothing, his car parked up with the headlights still illuminating the two of them. It really is Mr Willis.

Before setting off to track Audrey down, as I was leaving the school, Teddy ran up to me in a panic. Although I told him I had no time to talk, he followed me out and told me how fuming Mrs Abbott was about the fact I'm not performing.

'I'm sorry, Teddy, I can't have this conversation right now. I couldn't give any less of a shit. Audrey's in trouble.' I carried on jogging through the courtyard.

He jogged alongside me, panic on his face. 'What do you mean she's in trouble?'

'Look, I need to go. Call the police, OK? Tell them to get here as soon as they can.'

'What are you going to do, Ivy? Where are you going?'

I picked up my pace to get away from Teddy and closer to Audrey.

'I think I know where she's being taken. I need to get there now or I'm worried she'll die. I've sent you my live location – meet me there with the police, OK?'

Teddy stared back in absolute disbelief, but got out his phone to check.

I started running faster and faster until eventually I was sprinting. I could just hear Teddy's voice in the distance as he dialled for the police and they answered.

'Let Audrey go, Harry.'

He's spooked by my voice and trembles on the cliff edge, his unstable feet sending stones and rubble tumbling over into the sea. Audrey screams and he puts his hand over her mouth to muffle the noise. He looks at me, then takes another step forward.

'Fuck off, Ivy. Leave me alone,' he says savagely.

'If you take one more step, you'll fall off that cliff with Audrey too. Step back NOW! You can't kill us both! So how about you leave Audrey alone.'

I shout and jump forward just as it looks like he's about to take a step. I yank them both backwards with my full body weight and the three of us land on the ground. My heart is in my mouth and my ribcage vibrates with palpitations.

Audrey is lying on the ground on her side, her entire body shaking and her skin an unnatural blue. She's sobbing and saying sorry over and over again. I quickly kneel down next to her and start to untie her wrists. They're bruised and bleeding from the leather strap being too tight. She rubs them and draws her knees into her chest. I pull her into me and look around to see where Mr Willis has gone.

He's crawling over to his car on all fours, rubbing his head. Audrey jumps up, and instinctively we both charge towards him.

In the distance, I can hear the faint sound of sirens. Mr Willis scrambles to his feet and runs. He goes over to the driver's side of his car and fumbles with the door handle. The blue lights get brighter, and the sirens are loud now as three police cars swerve into view – Mr Willis gets in, locks his car doors and starts the engine, while Audrey and I tug on the handle. But he begins to drive away, dragging us a few steps, forcing us to let go – just as the police cars pull in.

One of them cuts in front of Mr Willis as he accelerates, and the front of his car smashes into the side of the police vehicle's passenger door. Audrey and I grip each other tightly, watching it all unfold as if in slow motion.

The other police cars come to a stop, and a half-dozen police officers swarm his car. One officer comes straight over to us with blankets and places them round our shoulders. The snow is still falling, even heavier now than it was before, and Audrey's knees are knocking together. I'm holding her up as her whole body starts to tremble again. Two of the officers have guns pointed at Mr Willis as he sits behind his steering wheel, his face like a rabbit in the headlights.

'GET OUT OF THE VEHICLE!'

'PUT BOTH HANDS ON YOUR HEAD AND EXIT YOUR VEHICLE, SIR.'

He slowly opens his car door and places both his hands on his head as he steps out. He's crying.

I feel a huge sense of relief wash over me as I watch the officers handcuff him.

Finally. It's all over.

# 46

## AUDREY

I bury my face in Ivy's chest. She pulls me in tight. I'm shaking so bad from the cold and fear, I can barely feel my body any more.

Someone runs up to the two of us and throws blankets over our shoulders – one for me, one for Ivy. I wrap myself in it.

'Are you girls OK? Are you hurt?'

My eyes are squeezed tightly shut – I don't wanna open them. I want this all to be a dream.

Ivy whispers into my hair. 'Are you OK?'

'He . . . he hit me over the head. I think I'm bleeding.'

'Come on, we have to get you checked out.' Ivy helps me to my feet, and DI Shing appears on the other side of me. My legs are weak. But then I see something that gives me strength: Mr Willis up against his vehicle, a police officer holding him down.

'How did you find me?' I ask Ivy.

'Ed saw you get taken. He was keeping an eye on the cameras for me tonight. I had a hunch something might happen, like during Samhain. Good thing too. I went looking for you and found a bit of your dress; it was torn . . . I checked your location and, as soon as I saw where you were, I knew he was bringing you to the place he killed Lola. And I realized I could get here quicker by running than by car, with all those winding roads. This is my normal route.'

'Thank God you did. I think another few moments . . .'

Ivy squeezes my arm. 'It doesn't bear thinking about.'

'An ambulance is on its way. Come and warm up in my car until it gets here,' DI Shing says.

'Is he going to be arrested?'

'Yes,' she said. 'For the assault on you, yes. I'm only sorry that we weren't able to take him into custody until he struck again. His alibi for Lola's murder was strong and we just didn't have enough physical evidence to convict . . .'

'Shing! Over here!' one of the other police officers shouts from beside Mr Willis's car. He's bent over the passenger-side seat.

'Excuse me, girls.' She leaves me shivering in the back seat, Ivy looming over me.

'What's happening?' I ask Ivy. I still have this fear that Mr Willis is gonna get away. Because he didn't actually manage to kill me . . . maybe he'll find some way to worm out of the situation.

'I think they've found something.' She stands up on her tiptoes, craning her neck to see what's going on. Her face is illuminated by the car headlights, her cheeks still flushed from the sprint to get to me. I'm so grateful that she managed to find me.

'Go look,' I say. 'Find out what's happening.'

'Are you sure? I don't want to leave you.'

'I'd rather know. I wanna know everything.'

'OK. I'll be back.'

Ivy sneaks away. I pull the blanket tightly around my shoulders and huddle into the back seat of the car. I can imagine the fear that Lola must have felt when she was up here so easily now.

I managed to get away. She hadn't been so lucky.

There are more sirens, and an ambulance drives up to the car park. Someone must point the paramedics in my direction because soon a young man and a woman in dark green uniforms approach me, leading me into the back of the ambulance.

They check my head, asking me a flurry of questions: do I remember my name, what day it is, what happened to me? I seem to be able to answer them all, which satisfies them that I don't have terrible concussion.

'We'll take you to the hospital to be sure,' says one, while applying a butterfly plaster to the place on my forehead where I've been bleeding. I must look an absolute state.

'No!' I cry out. 'Not yet. I need to wait for Ivy. I need to know what they've found. I need to make sure he's arrested.'

'What you *need* is rest, assessment by a doctor, and possibly a head scan to make sure there aren't any internal injuries.'

I push the paramedic aside, trying to get out of the back of the ambulance.

More cars seem to be arriving all the time, including some press. I'm wondering how they got wind of it so quickly when Teddy appears, climbing out of one of the cars and making a beeline for the ambulance – and me.

He hugs me tight. 'I'm so glad you're OK!'

'How are you here? I thought you'd be at the concert.'

'I left when Ivy didn't perform. I knew something was up. She told me to call the police and send them to the cliffs. As soon as I could, I jumped in my car and came too.'

'Oh my God! Audrey!' Ivy's voice carries over the crowd.

I slide forward in the ambulance, standing up. My head is still a bit woozy, and the paramedics tell me to stay still, but I can hear the urgency in Ivy's voice and I wanna be with her.

Teddy takes my hand and we go over to Ivy together.

'Look,' she says. One of the police officers is bagging a piece of evidence from Mr Willis's car. 'It's Lola's phone. They've found it.'

'Are you sure that's hers?'

The police officer holds the clear plastic bag up. He turns the cellphone around, and the back of phone case is clearly visible: Lola's name is printed in curly rose-gold handwriting, surrounded by glitter. It's definitely hers.

Her cellphone had been the missing piece of the puzzle. Now that it's been found, there's no doubt that Mr Willis is the perpetrator.

'You're sick,' Ivy says in his face as he's pushed into the back of the police car.

'I didn't do this, Ivy. I would never have hurt her. I wouldn't have . . .'

DI Shing shuts the door on him, cutting off the end of his sentence. 'Well done, girls,' she said. 'If you hadn't kept up the pressure, maybe we wouldn't have him in custody.'

'One of us just had to get hurt in order for that to

happen,' snaps back Ivy. But I can tell she's happy that he's finally been arrested. She's just feeling defensive of me.

'I am truly sorry about that. Now, Audrey, I've been told to get you back to the ambulance at once.'

'I'm going with you,' says Ivy.

'Me too,' says Teddy.

'Only one of you,' says the paramedic.

'Ivy,' I say without a moment's hesitation.

We clamber into the back of ambulance, and the paramedics make sure we're secure before closing the doors and driving away.

## 47

### IVY

The next morning, I sit in the dining hall having breakfast with Harriet, Tom, Teddy and Max. It feels like the entire school crowds round us, asking me questions about what happened last night. Harriet and Tom are batting them all away like my personal security guards.

'No questions, please. Move on. No photographs. No autographs.'

Yolanda and Lyra walk over to our table together, arms linked.

'Ivy, what a badass bitch you are!' Yolanda exclaims.

'Yeah, seriously, we're in absolute awe of you!' Lyra adds.

'Honestly, right place, right time. Anyone would have done the same!' I smile meekly through mouthfuls of food as they head on past, towards the buffet queue.

Audrey didn't stay at Illumen last night; after the paramedics checked her over, she had to be interviewed by the police and then stayed with her parents. I gave a statement to the police too, then came back and lay awake most of the night with Harriet next to me, reliving each moment over and over. What would have happened to

Audrey had I not arrived when I did? If I'd chosen my performance over going to find her? I dread to think.

Mrs Abbott has already spoken to me this morning about my bravery and courage, and what a credit I am to the school and my friends.

Just then, the dining hall erupts into a mass of applause and whooping. I stand on the bench and see Audrey walking in, smiling through her embarrassment and clearly looking for us. I wave at her and she runs over.

'Oh my God!' She laughs as she climbs on to the bench and throws her bag down on the table. 'What a welcome! I didn't do anything besides tremble and weep at the edge of a cliff.'

'You went *THROUGH IT*!' Harriet says and she hugs her tightly.

Teddy slides along the bench and wraps his arm round her waist. She smiles at him warmly and holds his hand, giving it a reassuring squeeze.

'It was Ivy that saved the day. Honestly, I'd be lying in a morgue if it wasn't for her arriving when she did. Thank God for that app! And to think . . . I almost blocked you on it when we weren't speaking!'

We both laugh.

She seems in fairly good spirits considering she was inches away from death a mere nineteen hours ago. Slightly off balance maybe. I can tell she's not had much sleep either.

'What happened after I left?' I ask her.

'I was taken to A & E and checked over. Only a few cuts and bruises and a bit of shock, but apart from that unscathed.

Then I was interviewed by a couple of the city police force and eventually sent home with Mom and Dad around midnight. I just wanted a deep, hot bath and a massive cry, to be honest.'

She pulls her school jumper sleeves down over her wrists when she realizes you can clearly see the markings of the leather strap Mr Willis bound her hands together with.

'So was Mr Willis arrested?' Tom asks eagerly while biting into his sausage sandwich and spilling brown sauce all over the table, then promptly wiping it up with his finger and licking it off.

'Yep. Last we saw of him he was being driven off in handcuffs in the back of a police car. Apparently, his car was towed away this morning too.'

'Has anyone seen Araminta today?' I ask. This will have shaken her to her core.

'No, I've not actually, and she's usually pretty punctual for breakfast,' Harriet says through a mouthful of croissant.

Audrey shoots me a look.

Her phone buzzes in her hand.

'I bet that's been going off like crazy!' I laugh.

'It's Patrick! He says he's outside and can we pop out and meet him?'

Audrey and I jump up from the table and walk quickly from the canteen.

'Ivy, Audrey! Are you both OK?' He stretches his arms out round us both.

'Fine, all things considered,' Audrey says, smiling.

'I heard Mr Willis was arrested.'

'He was,' I say. 'Does this mean that you'll keep your

side of the bargain? We risked our lives for you. Can you convince your parents to keep the school open and stop the sale?'

'Yes, well, that's why I'm here really. I've already spoken to them. Explained everything. Mr Willis's connection with Lola, what happened last night, the school and its history . . . the lot. They're eternally grateful that you both invested so much time in seeking justice for Lola and seeing that Mr Willis was put behind bars.'

'So does that mean . . .'

'Well, without my parents' investment, the sale and development won't be able to go ahead. The school will almost certainly remain open.'

My entire body turns to jelly and I feel an overwhelming sense of relief. Tears start streaming down my face and I try and find the words to reply to Patrick, but nothing comes out. I can hear great heaving sobs coming from someone and realize numbly that it's me. I feel Audrey's hand slip into mine and squeeze it. This is everything I wanted. It's all working out.

'Thank you, Patrick!' I manage.

'Thank YOU both. Even after losing two of your friends, you've both done so much to try and resolve this. You should really consider careers in solving crime! Anyway, I must dash. Keep in touch! I'll be back at uni in a few weeks, but you have my number.'

We say our goodbyes as Patrick heads out of the school grounds and we make our way back into the dining hall. Araminta is now at our table with the rest of the gang. She's wiping her eyes.

'IVY! AUDREY! Oh my God. I honestly don't even know where to start. Audrey, I've been trying to call and text you all night. I KNOW for a fact that it should have been me up there on that cliff edge, not you. I feel like this is all my fault. I knew he'd be so angry ... I should have handled this whole thing much more sensitively.'

'Minty ... stop. This isn't your fault. How were you to know he'd be so unhinged and react in that way? Don't blame yourself. Just be glad you have nothing to do with him any more and that he can't touch any of us ever again.' Audrey places an arm round Araminta and gives her a reassuring nudge.

'Well, just know I'm sorry you had to go through that and I'm so pleased you're OK! And, Ivy, you're a real-life hero!' She looks up at me from the bench. 'I know how much it would mean to you to be head girl. I'm aware it's probably what has caused so much tension between the two of us this year, and I want to surrender my position to you. You deserve it far more than I do, and deep down I've always known you'd make a far better head girl than me when the time came. Maybe that's why you've always rubbed me the wrong way. You've given so much to finding justice for both Clover and Lola and you're honestly the strongest woman I know.'

'OH MY GOD!' Harriet claps her hands together.

'Ivy, this is what you've always wanted!' shrieks Max.

'But Mrs Abbott is in charge of these decisions. You can't just hand over your head girl status to me a year early, Minty ...'

'I've already spoken to her and she's agreed. It's done!

You'll be the first head student in history to wear the badge for a year and a half!'

The whole table starts clapping and my cheeks go pink. Audrey grips my hand. I feel like it's her way of saying, *See, everything works out well in the end. You deserve this.* Maybe there is no need for the Magpie Society now justice has been served. The school's been saved. We've done what we needed to do. The relief pours over me like a deep, warm bath and tingles shoot up my spine and spread through my whole body.

This must be what pure joy feels like.

# 48

## AUDREY

'Come with me,' I say to Ivy.

The driver beeps his horn at me, the car loaded up with my things. 'Spend Christmas with me. Come on ... the atmosphere will be horrible, but way better with you there. At least you know my mom will hire some amazing chef for Christmas dinner, and Dad will be fuming because his contract's fallen through, so that will basically mean we won't have to deal with him at all. Look, he even sent a driver to meet me – couldn't be bothered to come himself. We'll have a great time.'

Ivy shakes her head. 'No. We talked about this. I'm going to get the train home later. Now that everything is sorted here, it's time I figured things out with my mum.'

The shiny HS pin glints on her lapel. It suits her. And, as the first Magpie to make it as head student, she'll have access to Lady Penelope's legacy. In the New Year, I'm going with her to Coutts bank to find out just what that is.

'OK. If you promise that you'll stay in touch with me every day and, if anything happens with your mom, you'll come stay with me straight away.'

'You got it. Of course.'

I pause, staring at Ivy. 'I don't wanna leave you ...'

'You have to. Go on. You need all the rest you can get.'

'OK.' Reluctantly, I get into the back of the car. The driver pulls away, and I turn around, watching Ivy and Illumen Hall become smaller in the rear window. Eventually, Ivy turns away and walks inside. I close my eyes, tilting my head against the headrest. It's gonna be a long Christmas. I have a ton of schoolwork to catch up on too. Now that I know I'm gonna be at Illumen for the next year and a half, I can't slack off any longer.

No more mysteries. No more deaths. No more distractions – except the good kind, like Teddy. That's what I'm hoping for. It's not too much to ask now. Mr Willis is behind bars. We assume he's been acting as Mrs Abbott's lackey all along. She must have used him to clear up the scene in Clover's room, to remove the green ribbon on the tree to get rid of the Tavistocks, to keep Ivy too busy to investigate ... and, of course, to eliminate Lola – the obstacle in her plan to sell the school.

Ivy and I had wondered if Clover's death wasn't an accident either. The thought was almost too awful to bear.

It's in the past now. Mrs Abbott is resigning. My dad is fuming that his deal's fallen through. But the Radcliffes are interviewing replacement heads, and there's gonna be a spring concert instead, to fire up those investors and increase the school's profitability again. Illumen Hall has been in the news so much that there's a lot of interest. Ivy had a full-page spread in one of the big Sunday papers about how she saved me by not giving up on the mystery of Lola's death. There won't be any problem keeping the school afloat now. Even Mr Tavistock's been hired back, and I wave to him as I drive past the hedges he's already back to trimming.

And my family will be fine. If Dad cuts me off over this? I'm sure there'll be a place for me at Illumen. Maybe I can come back as a teacher. Ivy and I could work together. Live together, like old times.

But I'll have to study first and that's when I realize I've forgotten my laptop bag. This driver is gonna kill me.

I lean forward and tap him on the shoulder. 'Hi, sorry, I forgot something in my room. Can we turn around?'

He stares at me in the rear-view mirror. 'Seriously?'

'Yeah. We *have* to. Now.'

Reluctantly, the driver obeys, spinning the car around on the big driveway and bringing me back to school.

'I'll be two seconds,' I say, before jumping out and running up the front steps. He grunts in response.

I must have left the bag up in our room, so I head straight there, passing beneath the portrait of Lola – far less sinister now. The door is partially open when I arrive. 'Ivy?' I call as I go in.

But she's not there. The room is deserted. My laptop bag is leaning against the leg of my bed – I must have overlooked it when gathering the last of my belongings. I pick up the satchel and swing it over my shoulder. I take one last glance around the room, making sure I haven't forgotten anything else.

A gust of wind tickles my cheek, lifting strands of hair. I turn, frowning, and see that the window is open just a crack. I walk over and push it shut, locking the mechanism.

When I look back, I see something odd about the wall

on Ivy's side of the room. It's partially ajar, as if one of the wooden panels has fallen off its hinges. I already know that there are secret cavities behind the wall; that's where we found Lola's journal, of course. And, with the number of servant hallways and secret passageways in the building, nothing surprises me any more.

I pry the panel open with my fingers and, sure enough, there's a small doorway, a little shorter than my height. I duck under and see a hatch in the ground. Frowning, I lift it to reveal a set of stairs leading down.

I text Ivy, telling her what I've found. But curiosity has got the better of me. Surely there's no more danger now that Mr Willis has been arrested, and now the school has been saved there's no more need for the Magpie Society. I go down without waiting for her.

This passage is actually surprisingly clean – and no spiderwebs. In fact, it seems like it's been used recently – and frequently. I frown. This is really weird. I definitely don't remember seeing this on the Magpie phone map. Ivy would have definitely noticed if there was a passageway coming off our bedroom. It's quite creepy to know that there's been secret access to our room all this time.

I wonder if Lola knew about it?

The tunnel seems to go on for miles, and I'm sure I must have left the foundations of the school building by now. I don't wanna follow it any further. I wish Ivy was with me. But I keep heading on. I need to know where this leads.

Finally, I see a door at the end of the tunnel. It's got a heavy padlock on it, but fortunately it's unlocked. I push through and emerge into a stone-walled room filled with plush cushions and candles half burned down to stumps. It looks . . . cosy?

'What is this place?' I ask the darkness.

I fumble over towards the wall, where I find a light switch. The first things I see when the light goes on are the broken remnants of a stone cross.

I suddenly get a sense of where I am. It must be a room underneath the abandoned church – close to where Mr Willis took me on the cliffs.

I don't wanna be here.

Then I look around the rest of the room and I gasp. All across the wall, there are portraits of Lola – photographs, paintings and sketches. I walk over to the kaleidoscope of images and run my fingers along the edges. OK. This is majorly creepy. Is this Mr Willis's lair? That's not all. There are sketches of magpies – drawn in Sharpie – that look suspiciously like the one that was on Lola's back. One of them is identical. It's signed: *Harriet*. A shiver creeps its way down my spine.

I look at the desk. There's a neat little collection of things that reminds me of what we found in the cave. I wonder if it's the same person. There's a set of car keys in there, for a Mini. I frown. Didn't Mr Willis drive one of those? There are other things too: blueprints of the school; a vivid green ribbon like the ones marking the trees Ed Tavistock was gonna cut down; and letters that look a lot like those we received earlier in the year, inviting us to join the Magpie Society. These are practice versions, with bits crossed out, the wording revised and perfected.

There's a bundle of tech equipment too – a laptop stand

(but no laptop) and several broken iPhones, similar to the Magpie phone I received. This must be where ours was programmed.

Last thing I spot is a spiral-edged notebook, open to a page of handwritten poetry, twists on the magpie rhyme Ivy recited to me in the library. I think of Clover's voice all those weeks ago, disguised in the podcast: '*As we all know, Lola's full name was Dolores. Dolores in Spanish means sorrow.*' And wasn't Clover's last name Mirth?

It all fits with the poem I'm reading now.

> *One for sorrow,*
> *That much you've learned,*
> *Two for joy,*
> *Who had to burn . . .*

But I bite my lip. I don't think whoever did this had anything to do with the *real* Magpie Society. Ed was right about that. I take out my phone and text him that there's another secret room he needs to close off. There's only one bar of signal so he might not get it until I go back outside.

'Shit . . .' I say out loud. I have to tell Ivy about this.

But then I see something that makes my blood run cold. It's a stylized version of two names looped together – and I recognize the handwriting. I drop the paper like it's on fire.

I know who's been hiding out here. And it's not the man behind bars.

There's a noise from behind me.

And the last thing I want to do is turn around.

# EPILOGUE

She found it. The place that was all mine. This abandoned church on the edge of the grounds has been my sanctuary. When the text came through that she'd found the tunnel, I'd had to run, faster than I've ever run in my life. But I caught her just in time.

'It was you?' she whimpers as she inches round to face me.

'Yes.'

'But why, Ivy? I don't understand. Why would you do this?'

I drag my fingertips along the wall, over photographs of Lola, over everything I've assembled and accumulated. When I discovered who I was, what my legacy should be, I knew I had no choice but to sacrifice everything to keep that legacy alive. Even my friendships.

Audrey looks at me with her big, pathetic blue eyes. It actually feels good to share with someone what I've done. It's just been me for so long.

'Illumen Hall means everything to me. I first found out about it from that photograph of my grandparents. My primary-school teacher set a family-tree project for me. I traced my dad's ancestors all the way back here. When I researched the school and found out they did scholarships for students, I wrote a fake letter to my primary-school teacher, encouraging her to nominate me. That was the easy part.

'Then, when I got here, I went to the old stables. I wanted to see if there was any connection to my family. What I found instead was my first tunnel underneath the school. That's when I realized who my grandmother was. That she was a part of the Magpie Society.

'I devoted so much time to exploring it all. The school was once great, you know. A pioneering place where people who weren't welcome elsewhere could find safety. But it's changed. I knew I could restore it to its former glory. I realized that by being a descendant of an original Magpie Society member, if I could get to become head girl, then I'd be able to protect its legacy.

'I only told one person what I'd found. My mentor, my best friend in the school.'

'Lola?'

'Lola,' I confirm. 'The hidden tunnels became our secret kingdom. She fell in love with the idea of a secret society running the school, of magpies and feathers. It was her idea initially to make this crypt our secret place, since the passageway ran from her room. I wouldn't come here without her. When she went home over the summer, I stayed at school, making my home in the cave. You know. You've been there.'

I think about the home I made, falling asleep to the sound of waves crashing against the cliffs. Anything was better than going back to my mum's. Illumen Hall was my home.

'Lola was incredible – but she had a hold over me, and she knew it.

'We found out Mrs Abbott was putting the school up for sale last year. We think she'd figured out my connection to the Magpie Society and knew that if she waited until I became head girl I'd have the power to stop it. She had to make sure it happened this year.'

'But Lola could have stopped it too . . .'

'Exactly. Lola had all the power. She was to be the next head girl; she had a vote. I thought she was going to! That was the plan.'

'So what happened?'

I can tell Audrey's trying to keep me talking, her mind working in overdrive to figure out a way to escape. I'll let her think that. It suits me. I have to come up with a plan of my own.

'The night of the beach party Lola asked me to take her on an adventure. "Take me somewhere," she'd said. She wanted to celebrate. She'd finally dumped disgusting Mr Willis. I hated that they'd been together. What a sicko. Anyway, he dropped her off back at school and we could begin. I planned this whole incredible evening. I'd taken Harriet's drawings of magpies and I traced one on her back – and she drew one on mine too, except nobody ever knew that.

'The images were perfect. They bound us together. Magpies.

'But that's when she laughed at me. This was all just a joke to her. She told me her family were going to make so much money off the sale that she'd never try to stop it. Her ancestor might have been one of the founders of Illumen Hall, but the rest of them didn't care about it the way I do – the way the Magpie Society, the caretakers of the school, care. The Radcliffes love it for the prestige, the kudos, the elitism it brings. But I know that a school is more than that. It's my home.

'I couldn't believe what she was saying. She said I was a child, that all the stuff we'd shared and learned together – about the Magpie Society and how important it was – was silly. A laugh! Not something real, as it was to me.

'She had no idea what it's like not to be understood. It's been that way my entire life. My mum couldn't understand my obsession with coming here. She didn't think my love for the school was very healthy. She tried to get me help – but I didn't need help from her. When that didn't work, she told me to leave. So I stayed away from her. Instead, I focused on Lola. I bent over backwards for that girl. But, when she wouldn't help me, I had to make sure she couldn't stand in my way.'

'So you killed her.'

I roll my eyes at Audrey. Always so impatient to jump to the end of the story. There was more to it still.

'She ordered me to drive her to the beach, but I wasn't done with our adventure yet. I drove us to the cliffs. She loved it up there. We walked to the edge because she wanted a dramatic photograph to post on Instagram before the party. That's when I gave her one more chance. I asked her if she was serious about what she'd said. And she confirmed it. That it was all one big joke to her. A total betrayal of me, of our friendship.

'I was so angry. So when she stepped too close to the edge . . . I couldn't help it. And I didn't feel sorry about it. Not once.

'After her body showed up on the beach, I covered my tracks well. The police had no idea I was involved. It was only when Clover started raising questions again with that podcast that I had to do everything in my power to throw her off the scent. And I succeeded, didn't I? I faked evidence wherever I could, found a way to make everyone else a suspect but me.'

'My God. You're a great actress. You're wasted doing music.' Then Audrey blinks. 'Wait . . . You planted all that evidence? Teddy's boat, my dad's office, even Mr Willis?'

'It was a lot of work. The earrings, the logbook . . . all so easy to manufacture. Still, Clover was smart. She pieced everything together. I bribed one of the Winferne Comp kids to dress up as a magpie and scare her on the night of the Samhain party. Tell her to back off her investigation. But she went to that idiot Patrick. Kept searching for that final bit of proof: Lola's phone. She had the location and everything. I'd kept it here all that time. When I realized she was that close to finding my secret lair, I knew I had to act.

'So, when you went to Mrs Trawley's house, I went over to Patrick's apartment to stop her. You'd already told me about the fireplace. It was magnificent. All it needed was a tiny bit of extra accelerant . . .'

Audrey looks like she's about to vomit, but I can't stop.

'Bringing you into the Magpie Society made it feel like it was the two of us against the world – it was the perfect alibi, the way to keep control of the investigation. That poor detective trusted us so much, didn't she? Always willing to listen to teenage girls, sure. But she never took us seriously enough to believe one of us could be capable enough – smart enough – to pull this off. Planting the phone in Harry's car was a stroke of genius, wasn't it?'

'This isn't smart,' Audrey says. 'It's sick.'

'Get off your high horse, Audrey. I know you're a killer too. When you told me about Alicia, I felt safe bringing you in. You've done bad things.'

She shakes her head. In fact, her whole body is shaking. 'Not like this . . .'

'Anyway, it doesn't matter now. Clover's gone. Mr Willis has been arrested. The evidence on that phone is bulletproof. He'll go to prison. The school will be saved. Honestly – nothing was ever going to stop me from achieving my goal.' I pause. 'Nothing is . . .' I correct myself.

She notices. It's a shame. The school could have been ours to rule. But now there's one more end to tie up. But this one's going to be easy. Because, thanks to Ed, all the entrances to the Magpie Society tunnels have been sealed. The only way out is the way I came.

I reach out, grabbing the notebook with my unfinished poem. I step back through the doorway. Realization dawns on Audrey's face at the final moment. She runs towards the door as I slam it shut, bolting the lock.

*One for sorrow,*
*That much you've learned,*
*Two for joy,*
*Who had to burn.*
*The time has come,*

*I'm the last magpie.*
*Three for a girl,*
*Who now must die.*

# ACKNOWLEDGEMENTS

We would first of all like to send love and gratitude to everyone who has sent us messages and photos while reading *The Magpie Society*. Hearing the love is what makes this whole writing journey so worthwhile.

As ever, there's a big publishing team for us to thank. First of all, thank you to everyone at Penguin Random House Children's Books and especially Emma Jones, Wendy Shakespeare, Pippa Shaw, Simon Armstrong, Alesha Bonser, Tania Vian-Smith, Gemma Rostill, Andrea Kearney and Anne Bowman, for all your support and hard work on this series. Thank you to all our publishers around the world for your brilliant translations and lovely covers.

To our agents, Zara Murdoch at Gleam Features and Juliet Mushens of Mushens Entertainment – you are both superstars.

Also, we are both indebted to our friends and families for being so supportive. Writing this book in the most difficult of times (a pandemic!), with so many additional challenges being thrown our way, has been tough and we couldn't have done it without them. You know who you are <3